FOUR COLD MONTHS

A DETECTIVE MAX GRADY THRILLER

KJ KALIS

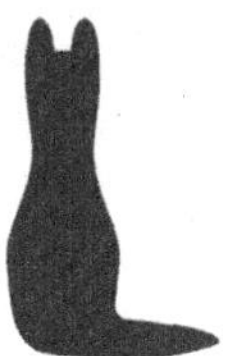

eISBN 978-1-955990-26-4

ISBN 978-1-955990-27-1

Published by:

BDM, LLC

ALSO BY K.J. KALIS:

New titles released regularly!

If you'd like to join my mailing list and be the first to get updates on new books and exclusive sales, giveaways and releases, click here!

I'll send you a prequel to the next series FREE!

OR

Visit my Amazon page to see a full list of current titles.

OR

Take a peek at my website to see a full list of available books.

www.kjkalis.com

PROLOGUE

The screaming never stopped. Never.

Max pressed his hands over his ears as hard as he could as he sat on the edge of the bed. It only muffled the sound a little, the ear-piercing screams from his terrified mother and the low guttural yells from his brother only seeming slightly farther away, punctuated by intermittent growls and shouts from their father.

Dad was on another one of his rants.

Max squeezed his eyes as tightly together as he could, wishing he was somewhere, anywhere, else. He sat down on the side of his bed, trying to chase the echoes of the screaming out of his mind, grabbing a stained pillow and wrapping it tightly around the back of his head, closing his eyes again.

It didn't help. The screams cut right through the thick batting. "No!" Max heard his mom scream, her voice panic-stricken, the high pitch echoing off the thin walls of their small house.

Things weren't calming down, they were only getting worse.

Another round of shouts erupted from the bedroom, words that Max couldn't make out through the pillow pressed to his ears. He pulled the pillow tighter down on his head, wanting nothing more than to become part of the thin mattress he slept on every night. At least then he'd be invisible. He knew if he left the safety of his tiny bedroom, he'd find his brother Ben, two years older than Max, cowering in the corner of his room, curled in a ball on the floor, rocking back and forth, singing a song he'd made up to drown out the horrific noises from his parents. Down the hall, if Max dared to open the door, he'd find his father, with his boozy bourbon breath towering over their mother, her face pale, her hands shaking, and her eyes rimmed red from tears, cowering against the wall in their bedroom.

Max sat up on the edge of the bed, blinking, dropping the pillow to the side. He'd give it until the count of ten.

He closed his eyes, feeling the flutter of his heart in his chest.

One... Two...

Max stared at the floor, his breathing shallow, the blood rushing to his face.

Three... Four... Five... Six.

When he reached seven, there was a single ear-piercing scream from his mother, the likes of which Max had never heard before. It curdled his stomach, a veil of perspiration collecting on his forehead under his dark hair. He shot up from the edge of the bed and opened the thin wooden door that separated him from the chaos. He charged down the hallway, his hands balled into fists. As he passed Ben's room, the door to his bedroom open, he saw his older brother curled up in the corner, just as he'd imagined, his eyes squeezed shut so tightly that wrinkles had formed at the corners of his eyes. Ben was moaning and rocking, far off in some other world he'd created to protect himself from the nightly chaos. Ben couldn't understand the fights. He didn't have the capacity for that. His dad knew that. The fact that his dad didn't care only infuriated Max even more.

Another ear-piercing scream jolted Max as he watched Ben. It came from inside his parents' bedroom, "Please..." his mother was whimpering.

As Max reached for the brass doorknob on his parent's bedroom door, he realized his hand was shaking. Without thinking, he shoved the door open and stared into the bedroom. It had become a war zone. His mom was pinned up against the wall, the thick dirty hands of his father wrapped around her neck. Her face was more pale than Max had ever seen, as if the very lifeblood had been drained from her face. There was an angry red cut on her left cheek, blood dripping down the side of her face. Her eyes were half opened, one of them swollen almost closed, "Max, no, honey..."

At the mention of his name, Max's dad glared over his shoulder. He growled, "Stay out of our business, boy! I told you that more than once. Get out of here."

A chill ran down Max's spine and then subsided. He narrowed his eyes and straightened his back as far as his fourteen-year-old body would go. "It is my business. That's my mother you're beating up on!"

Max's dad let out a grunt, turned and started to lunge for Max, his hands still on Max's mom, dragging her with him. Max darted to the side and got out of the way as he heard a noise behind him.

Out of the corner of his eye, he saw Ben. His brother's eyes were wild, his mouth hanging open, a drip of saliva running down the side of his face. Max's heart clenched as his stomach burned with fury. Ben couldn't understand what was going on. His intellectual delay had left him operating at the level of a five-year-old, not his actual age of sixteen. Ben's face was red, a low moan coming out from inside of him, the veins on either side of his neck sticking out.

Before Max could do anything about it, his father dropped his hands off of his mother's neck, her body sliding down the wall, her flimsy torn clothes rumpled around her. He took his eyes off Max and lunged for Ben, "Don't you start, you stupid moron!"

Fury raced through Max's body. He jumped on his father's back, pummeling him with fists that were half the size of his father's, not thinking about the consequences. His father turned around, his mouth open, the rot of his stinking breath blowing in Max's face. He grabbed Max's left arm and twisted it. Max screamed as he felt the bones in his arm pop. "I told you not to get involved, boy! Mind your own business!"

Max crumbled to the ground cradling his left arm, hot tears stinging his eyes, pain surging through his body. He crawled toward the far side of the bed, looking for a place to hide, the side where his father slept when he wasn't drunk and passed out on the couch in the family room, beer cans littering the floor as the sports scores from the night before droned on in the background.

As he tried to catch his breath, the screaming only intensified. From the other side of the room, Max could hear Ben grunting as his father punched him over and over again, his mother screaming, trying to pull his father off of her older son. Max looked up in time to see his father backhand his mom so hard that she fell backward, hitting her head on the nightstand, her eyes closing...

Without thinking, Max stood up, still cradling his left arm against his body, the pain rippling through every nerve. He pulled open the drawer in his father's nightstand and grabbed the pistol his father kept in case of intruders.

Whirling around, he lifted the gun in front of his face with his right hand. He stared at his father and yelled. "Stop it! Leave us alone!"

Then he pulled the trigger.

1

Noah Chandler brushed the brown hair away from his forehead, scratched at his chin, and then replaced his glasses. As his eyes traveled back to the brand development report he was creating for one of his newest marketing clients, Grinders Custom Coffee — his eyes settled on the picture of his wife, Macy. He ran his finger along the bottom edge of the frame, dust collecting on his fingertip. He wiped it on his jeans. If Macy was there, she'd yell at him and tell him it was about time for him to dust his office.

Noah drew in a deep breath and glanced out the window as a thick blanket of heavy dark clouds gathered on the horizon. The temperature had plummeted for the first time that season. Even though it was early, snow was in the forecast. Based on the way the air felt and how long he'd lived in Pittsburgh, he knew they were about to get walloped by the first winter storm. Glancing back at the picture of Macy, his heart tightened into a small knot in the center of his chest. It had been so long. Where was she? Was she okay? Would she make it home in time for Christmas?

Noah got up from his desk and crossed his arms in front of his chest, wandering to the window, staring out at the yard behind the farmhouse he and Macy had bought when they first got married. It was on the edge of Pittsburgh. At that time, she was a graduate student at Bedford College and he'd just started his own marketing company. Now, more than two decades later, she was a literature professor at Bedford and he had a stable of global clients that he could service right from the comfort of their home, allowing him plenty of time with their two kids — Kate, who was a junior at Bedford and Gabe, who'd come almost a decade later, a gangly twelve-year-old who liked nothing more than sports and video games.

As he saw the clouds hover overhead, Noah's mind played back memories of seeing Macy walk back toward their house from the garden, the hem of her shirt flipped up as an impromptu basket for tomatoes, cucumbers, peppers in all shapes and sizes, and ears of sweet corn, or at least as many as she could salvage from the squirrels and the deer that lived at the back of the property. He remembered the smile on her face as if bringing in the produce she'd grown was equivalent to winning the lottery. "Look, Noah!" she'd exclaim after every trip to the garden, a wide smile pulling across her fair skin, her thin, blonde bobbed hair looking like cornsilk against the light streaming into the kitchen windows. "Look at all this beautiful produce. Isn't it amazing? It's such a miracle!"

Looking out of the window now, Noah could see the garden off in the distance, the fallen leaves from the maple and oak trees nearby tangled in the chicken wire fence they'd built one weekend, the vines from the tomatoes and cucumbers yellowed and bare. For the first few weeks after Macy had left, he'd tried to go out to the garden to bring in the produce that had been so happily growing, but he couldn't bring himself to do it. It was Macy's garden. She should have been there to take care of it.

And she wasn't...

Noah ran his hand through his hair again, brushing it away from his face. He needed a haircut. Usually, Macy was the one that would say something. Her voice echoed in his mind, "Noah, you look scruffier than a grizzly bear. You need to stop in town and go get your hair cut."

Everything reminded him of her.

Staring at the back of their property, he saw the first flakes of heavy wet snow float from the dark clouds above. He looked down at the ground outside of the window to his office, seeing a single flake land on the grass, quickly melting into the greenery. His heart sank. With every day Macy was gone, he felt like that was what was happening to his soul. He was melting away.

Noah sighed again, scratching the stubble on his chin. He blinked at the time on his watch. He only had a few minutes left to work before he had to wake up Gabe for school and send Kate a good morning text. She was living on campus, but he still liked to text her every morning. And as much as Noah wanted to stand and stare at the first wash of snow floating out of the sky, drink his coffee and forget everything, he knew that wasn't his reality, at least not at the moment. He sat down at his desk, his chair giving a squeak, determined to get another page of the report done, just as his phone rang.

Pushing his glasses up a little farther on his nose, he frowned. His clients never called this early, or if they did it was because they were across the world in some other time zone, but most of them were very respectful of his working hours and his family. He glanced down at his phone. The display read, "Unknown number." For some reason he couldn't identify, his stomach sank as he reached for it.

"Hello?" Noah answered, his voice tentative.

An automated voice responded. Noah fumbled with his phone, his hands shaking, trying to turn on the recording app he'd added to his phone for client calls. "Is this Noah Chandler?"

"Yes..." Noah whispered.

"We have your wife."

2

Noah's heart pounded in his chest. His hands were so slick with sweat he nearly dropped the phone. He put it on speaker, glancing toward the office door. This wasn't the time for Gabe to walk in. "What? What do you want?" he whispered. The thumping of Noah's heart in his chest only increased in speed and force as he waited for a reply. It felt like a percussion section had taken up residence in his body. He looked down to see his hands shaking. It was a good thing the phone was on speaker, otherwise he probably would have dropped it. "My wife? Macy, is she okay?"

"She is — for now. We want the key."

Noah frowned, his mouth dropping open, "The key? What key?"

"Don't play dumb with us, Noah. We know she has the key. She stole it. It doesn't belong to her. And now, we want it back."

"I'm sorry," Noah stammered. "I have no idea what you're talking about. What key?"

The tinny voice at the other end of the line grunted, "Well, you'd better figure it out if you want to see her alive again. We'll be in touch."

Noah ended the call. He could hardly line up his finger to touch the red dot on his phone. He stared at it for a second, trying to catch his breath. Blinking. The doorbell rang. He sucked in a sharp breath, nearly jumping out of his skin. Using the armrests of his chair, he pushed himself to a standing position, his legs feeling weak. His mind was racing. Someone had Macy, his precious wife.

Moving like a robot, the words from the mysterious caller rolling through his mind, Noah walked to the front door and unlocked it, expecting to receive a package for work or a delivery of something Gabe had bought. Without thinking, he opened the door, feeling the whip of the cold wind cut across his face and stared at the ground. A key? The caller had asked for a key. Noah's heart pounded in his chest. Where was Macy? A single brown cardboard box sat on the rough coir mat in front of the door. He bent over and picked it up, closing the heavy wood door against the snow that was floating from the sky outside. He stared at it for a second, realizing there was no label on it. Rolling it in his hands, he turned and twisted it, trying to see if it was for him, Gabe or Kate.

He had a sinking feeling in his gut that he wasn't going to like what was inside. As Noah held the box in his hands, part of him wanted to go right back outside and set it on the mat, pretending it hadn't been delivered. Instead, he carried it to the kitchen, the wood floor squeaking under his sock-covered feet, setting the box on the corner of the kitchen table. He stared at it for a moment, a wave of nausea covering him. From out of his pocket, he pulled out a pen knife, quickly slicing the tape and opening the lid.

As he looked inside, he sucked in a breath. He stared down at the contents for a minute, almost afraid to touch them. His hands still shaking, he finally reached down into the dark box. From inside, he drew a folded scarf, pale green, with peach, yellow and pink flowers woven into the filmy fabric. It was one of Macy's favorites. Next to it was a watch with a gold face and a matching narrow band. Noah had given it to Macy on their first anniversary. It wasn't anything fancy. His business was new and it was the best he could do on his meager income, but Macy had insisted on wearing it ever since, except for the times it had broken. She had begged and pleaded with the jeweler in town to fix it and get it running again. Noah reached down into the box and pulled it out, rubbing his thumb over the smooth crystal of the face. But it wasn't smooth anymore. It was cracked, the hands of the watch stopped at ten after eleven...

...the moment Macy had been taken.

3

"You've got to be kidding me!" Max Grady slammed his fist against the steering wheel of the black SUV he was driving. He caught a glimpse of himself in the rearview mirror, a grimace on his face, the temples of his dark hair graying ever so slightly, the faint hint of stubble on his chin. The freeway was backed up with the sudden snowfall, the wide lanes of the I-279 highway covered over with a combination of freezing rain and thick snowflakes. The red taillights extended in front of him as far as he could see.

Twenty minutes later, Max finally pulled his SUV onto an offramp, only driving a little slower than he normally did, which was always at least fifteen miles above the speed limit. He considered it one of the unsung benefits of being a detective. If he got pulled over — and he had, dozens of times — he'd simply hold out his badge, have a good chuckle with the officer who'd pulled him over and be on his way. At least, most of the time. Only one time did he actually get a written warning. That was when he was driving ninety down the freeway in a work zone that was limited to an achingly slow fifty-five miles per hour. Even his badge couldn't save him then. But at least it was a warning and not a ticket.

The twenty minutes of extended travel time put him thirty minutes behind in getting to the headquarters of the Pittsburgh police department on Western Avenue, where Max was a detective and had been for the last ten years. One of the youngest officers to be promoted to the detective unit, the police brass had quickly learned two things about Max when he'd finished the Academy. Number one, he was a quick study, wickedly smart with a nearly photographic memory. Number two, he was better off not dealing with people. Managing people's emotions, not to mention his own, wasn't exactly his strong suit.

Max Grady was one of the most intelligent officers they'd ever run across in the Pittsburgh Bureau of Police. Knowing that, the department brass decided they couldn't exactly afford to cut him loose, despite the fact that his approach to most things was unorthodox. Putting him in the detective bureau gave him a chance to do what he did best — solve problems, and to do so mostly without having to deal with too many people. That allowed the department to get what they wanted — cases cleared without an onslaught of lawsuits brought on by Max's challenging personality.

After finding a spot in the parking lot across the street for his black SUV, Grady made his way upstairs to the seventh floor, hearing the elevators beep and then chime as the doors slid open. He checked the time on his cell phone. Precisely thirty-two minutes late for his shift. The thought crossed his mind with no more weight than the fact that there was snow outside. It was a fact, nothing more. The ability to feel guilt or shame or anger was buried deep inside of him. Even if he had wanted to feel upset at himself, he would have been hard-pressed to do it.

As he entered the pit, what the detectives affectionately

called their offices, Max noticed Cassie Reynolds, his partner for the last three years, was sitting in his desk chair. He shook his head. She knew he hated that. Striding toward her, he was so busy looking at Cassie that he bumped into the edge of a desk nearly spilling his coffee. Trying not to curse, Grady kept moving. The day wasn't off to a good start.

When Grady had arrived on his first day after being assigned to the detective unit, he thought it looked more like a misfit furniture store — a place where mismatched chairs and desks went to try to find some semblance of usefulness. In the ten years he'd been a detective, nothing had changed. The same mismatched desks and chairs, some of them brown, some of them black, some of them fabric covered, and some covered with fake leather, only looked more worn and dinged up than they did on the day he'd arrived.

Narrowing his eyes at Cassie, he said, "You mind?"

Cassie sprung up from his chair, a grin pulling at her cheek. "I can see you're in a good mood again today."

"Very funny." Grady set his coffee cup and his cell phone down at his desk and went through his morning ritual. He'd log into his computer, letting emails load, carefully putting his cell phone at right angles to the desk calendar that was provided to him by the department. Not that he had any use for it. Grady's days weren't scheduled like a normal person's. He went with the flow of the cases that were in front of him. He didn't do meetings unless he was forced to and even then, he'd only show up if someone came to find him to make him attend.

Grady took two sips of his coffee and then set it next to his phone, making sure the seam from the sleeve was facing toward the back, the small hole cut into the lid facing toward him. He was beginning to check his email when he heard a voice yell his name from the other side of the pit. "Grady?"

Looking up, Grady stopped what he was doing, staring dead

ahead and blinking only once before turning his chair to face the other direction.

Williams.

In typical fashion, Williams hobbled over toward Grady's desk, a grim look on his face. Lieutenant Jerry Williams, Grady's boss, was well ready to retire but hadn't pulled the trigger yet. No one in the department knew why. He walked with a distinct limp, a painful bone-on-bone hip joint constantly reminding him that he was due to see his orthopedic surgeon for a hip replacement, an appointment that had come and gone at least a half dozen times. The rumor flying around in the pit was Williams was relatively sure he'd be forced to retire once he had his new hip.

Clearly, Williams wasn't ready to give up.

Lieutenant Williams stopped behind Max. "Where have you been?"

Grady spun his chair slowly, his lip curling. "Have you seen the weather outside, Lieutenant?" The expression on his face was stony, the tone of his words cutting. "I mean, seriously. It's snowing to beat the band out there. And you know how people are. The first couple of snows around here and they act like we're in the middle of the apocalypse. I got backed up on the freeway, nearly got sideswiped by a minivan with a bumper sticker on the back that said, 'Cowboy Butts Make Me Nuts,' and yet, I still managed to get here in one piece. Aren't you at least happy about that?"

Williams grunted, "Yeah, but you're late."

Grady turned back to his desk, staring at his emails. Jerry needed to go away.

Williams wasn't giving up that easily. "Grady, look at me when I speak to you."

Grady's stomach tightened into a small knot. He pressed his lips together, spinning on his chair and staring at Williams, not saying anything. The heat rose in his face, the tension in his hands as his fingers balled themselves into fists.

"Easy, tiger," Cassie whispered under her breath.

"Listen, I'm a nice guy," Williams began. It was the same way that all of his chastising started. "But you gotta throw me a bone here. If you're gonna be late, give me a call. Better yet, check the weather forecast, for God's sake, and leave a little earlier. You should know better by now. Now," he said, spinning on his heel and limping away, "get to work. We're buried in cases, and with the weather changing, it's only gonna get worse."

A moment later, Grady heard the Lieutenant's office door slam closed. Grady had once read that people who were in physical pain had terrible personal skills, the condition of their physical body causing them to lose any semblance of nicety or manners. Not that Grady's were up to snuff if he were invited to a formal dinner. That was something Grady didn't worry about. Not only would he never be invited, but he would never accept the invitation in the first place, preferring to stay home and eat his nightly baloney and American cheese sandwich on white bread. Maybe Williams should do the same.

As Grady looked up, he saw Cassie staring at him, her arms crossed in front of her chest. "You couldn't have jumped in there?" he mumbled.

She grinned. "And miss the fun? Watching the two of you is like watching two little rams butt at each other. It's kinda cute."

"Not funny."

Cassie plopped down in the chair next to Grady's desk. He felt the muscles in his back tighten up a little. What did she want?

"So..." she started.

Grady stared at his computer, not looking at her, wishing she would go away. "So?"

Making Cassie Reynolds his partner from her first day as a

detective was one of their lieutenant's more solid ideas during his tenure. That wasn't to say she didn't grate on Grady's nerves at least six or seven times a day, but then again, pretty much everyone did.

Cassie had been with the department only seven years, spending five on the road and another three in the detective bureau. Cassie was someone whose life seemed to be dipped in sunshine — she was always upbeat and always cheerful, no matter the situation. She even had a dog she'd rescued from the pound, a shepherd-Labrador mix who she'd named "Happy." Grady had met him one time when Cassie's car was in the shop and she needed a ride home after work. He'd wagged and drooled all over Grady's shoes. The dog fit Cassie perfectly.

When he looked up, Cassie was staring at him, a glint in her eyes. "What's on the agenda today?"

Grady stared at his computer again, ignoring her question and not looking at her. He knew what he'd see if he did. She'd be sitting in the chair next to his desk, her legs crossed, her long strawberry blonde hair caught in a ponytail that extended down her back, a few freckles collected under her green eyes, the gray suit and blush-colored blouse bringing out the pink in her cheeks. In a moment, she would start tapping her fingers on the edge of his desk, a scar on top of her hand from sliding into a base during a college softball championship where she was a shortstop at the University of Pennsylvania bright white against her skin.

Grady had a memory for details. That's what made him so good at his job.

Grady sighed. "I don't know." He glanced at the inbox positioned on the corner of his desk. It was filled with a stack of manila file folders, all of the tabs turned to the right, the fronts of the cases facing upward. "If I don't get some of these cases closed and the reports done, Williams is gonna start bellowing like a wildebeest in heat again."

Cassie chuckled. "A wildebeest? What? You been spending your evenings watching 'Wild Kingdom' or something? I wouldn't know a wildebeest if it came up and kicked me in the shins."

"I bet you would."

"Maybe..." Cassie picked at a cuticle. "Listen, about Williams..."

Grady shot Cassie a look. "You know how I feel about him."

She cocked her head to the side. "You don't actually hate him," she said, leaning into the word "hate."

"Yes, I do."

"No, I know you don't."

Grady gritted his teeth together. One of his many pet peeves was when people told him what he thought or what he felt. He'd had more than one therapist try to explain to him how he'd felt after he'd killed his father. The therapists were so sure that he felt guilty or angry or sad or conflicted.

In fact, he'd felt none of those emotions.

More precisely, Max felt nothing at all when it came to seeing his father's dead body on the floor after he'd shot him. And mostly now, he either felt numb or angry. There wasn't much in the middle.

But on that snowy morning, he didn't feel like arguing with Cassie. It wasn't an argument he could win. He shrugged. It wasn't as if he'd lose either. It was more of a stalemate. Cassie had become more like a younger sister than a partner to him. They'd bicker and argue and go right back to work. And as much as she annoyed him on virtually a daily basis, his other alternatives for partners, should he request one, were grim. There was another detective, Roger Blank, who had been with the department nearly as long as Williams. He was just as cranky too. There were two other female detectives, neither of which he wanted to even talk to. They were alternately as chirpy as a couple of cheerleaders at the halftime of a game and cranky. Moody wasn't his thing. The remainder of the detectives who were assigned to the pit Grady didn't spend a moment thinking about.

He glanced at Cassie. Even as overly optimistic and cheerful as Cassie was, at least he knew what he was dealing with. And for him, predictability was like gold.

He was about to suck in a breath and explain to Cassie the pile of paperwork that he had in front of him, telling her to go work on reports, when he saw a man and what Grady immediately assumed to be his son walk into the office, the man carrying a cardboard box under his arm.

Williams came out of his office, shot a look at Grady and Cassie and bellowed, "Grady! You're up!"

4

In Grady's eyes, the appearance of the disheveled man and his son was a welcome interruption. It stopped his conversation with Cassie dead in its tracks. Cassie took their arrival as her cue to go introduce herself to the visitors who had dragged themselves into the detective unit of the Pittsburgh Bureau of Police, playing part tour guide and part hostess as Grady trailed along.

"Can I help you?" she asked. From where Grady was standing behind her, he saw the strawberry blonde ponytail hanging halfway down her back swing to the side as she tilted her head.

Grady narrowed his eyes at the two people in front of him. His mind was already clattering in the background, concocting a story about who they were and what was in the box the man was carrying. He got as far as deciding they were father and son, noting the similar ruffle of brown hair on the top of their heads, the hereditary cowlick more pronounced on the son than on the father, although even though the father tried to hide it, it was there. The angle of their chins was similar, though the son's was softer, it not yet chiseled with age and maturity. As the man glanced toward Cassie, Grady noted his eyes were brown. Grady glanced at the son. The son's eyes were green, telling the tale of a recessive genetic marker likely carried by the child's mother. Where she was, Grady didn't know.

The man glanced around the pit, staring at all of the open desks, his eyes shifting left and right, as if he was secretly disappointed that his tax dollars hadn't funded a more nicely appointed detective unit. If that was what he was thinking, then Grady seconded the thought, the smell of the old heating units pumping dusty warm air into the office, burned coffee lingering in the background, black streaks all over the dingy white linoleum.

"We wanted to file a report?" the man said, his voice hesitant and slightly hoarse.

Cassie looked at the man evenly. "A report about what?"

"A kidnapping."

5

"Why don't we go talk in one of the conference rooms?" Grady said, leading Cassie, the man, and the boy who Grady assumed to be his son, toward an open door.

Grady pushed the door to a gray painted room open. There was a long table with a fake wood top that was actually made out of some sort of plastic with shiny stainless-steel legs jutting out from it. For the purposes of taking a report, Grady called it a conference room. For the purposes of interviewing a suspect it was called an interrogation room. Grady blinked. It was a room. It would suffice for their needs. He closed the door behind him. "Have a seat. I'm Detective Max Grady." He pointed at Cassie. "This is Detective Cassie Reynolds. You said you want to file a report about a kidnapping?" The words came out even and calm, as if Grady was doing nothing more exciting than placing an order at a fast-food joint. He knew better than to get worked up from the jump.

Grady watched as the man nodded at the boy, set the box on the table, and then took a seat himself. He cleared his throat, putting a hand on his chest as if he was about to say the Pledge of Allegiance. "I'm Noah Chandler." He pointed at the boy. "This is my son Gabe."

Grady watched as Cassie took a seat at the other end of the table. She crossed her legs and leaned back in the chair, her face a mask of calm, the corners of her mouth tipped slightly upward as if she was about to smile.

"What can we do for you?" Cassie asked.

"My wife, Macy Chandler, has been kidnapped."

Grady pulled out a chair and sat down, folding his hands in his lap. He noticed the son was calm at the moment, only a flicker of his eyelids admitting he'd heard the words from his father. "She's been kidnapped?" he repeated. The thoughts started humming in his mind, the wheels and gears of analysis getting warmed up. Kidnappings could be motivated by many things — love, greed, extremism, jealousy, retribution. The list went on and on.

That was if this was a kidnapping. That was a big if in Grady's mind.

Grady furrowed his eyebrows. He sucked in a breath, getting ready to say something, but Cassie interjected, as if she was afraid of the next words that were going to come out of his mouth. She probably had every right to be, he realized, pressing his lips together.

"I'm so sorry," she began. "We want to help. Can you tell us what's going on?"

Noah Chandler's shoulders relaxed a little bit, the tension in his face softening. A small dose of compassion went a long way, was what Cassie had told him a few years back. He'd watched her empathize with people over and over again. He'd tried, on two separate occasions to replicate her technique, but it didn't work, at least not for him.

Grady noticed that Gabe looked up, his eyes wild, the rims red, like Grady's mom, Ann's used to after she'd been crying. He noticed the similarity and then pushed the thought away. Noah searched the room as if he was looking for something and then looked at Grady and Cassie. "Is it okay if Gabe puts in his earbuds and plays video games while we talk? I'm sorry, I probably shouldn't have brought him here, but I didn't want to leave him home alone, and given what we've been through, I didn't want to send him to school today."

Grady gave a short nod and watched as Noah put a hand on Gabe's arm. Within seconds, the boy had popped white earbuds into his ears and had his phone in front of him, his thumbs drumming rhythmically over the screen.

Noah sighed. "It's at times like these I'm very grateful for video games," he smiled weakly.

Grady frowned. He was beginning to wonder if there was actually a case or if Noah Chandler was there to waste his time. His chest tightened. "Well, now that we have junior all settled, how about if we cut to the chase."

"Grady," Cassie hissed.

Grady shot her a look.

Cassie blinked at Noah Chandler, her expression apologetic. "You'll have to excuse my partner, Mr. Chandler. The snow makes him cranky."

Grady pressed his lips together. He hated it when Cassie apologized for him. She didn't need to. He hadn't done anything wrong. And, it would have been more accurate to say most things make him cranky, but he didn't bother to correct her.

"No problem," Noah said, glancing at the surface of the table. He was gripping and ungripping his hands into fists as if he were kneading something. "As I said, my wife, Macy Chandler — she's a professor at Bedford College — she's missing."

"Hold up, you said before she'd been kidnapped?" Grady chewed the inside of his lip.

Noah nodded as if ceding the point. "Yes, that too."

Grady shook his head, feeling a surge of tension in his chest. "Which one is it, Mr. Chandler? Missing or kidnapped?"

"Let the man speak, Grady," Cassie said, rolling her eyes.

"It's both," Noah said with a sigh. He stood up from the chair where he'd positioned himself opposite of Grady and walked toward the back wall of the conference room. It was outfitted with a two-way mirror. If Grady knew anything about Williams, he was standing on the other side of the tinted glass, the room's microphones on, listening to every word that was going on between him, Cassie, and Noah.

"My wife, she hasn't been home in a while. This morning, I got a call, and it seems that instead of her just being gone, she's been kidnapped."

"And what makes you think that?" Grady said, narrowing his eyes.

Noah pushed the box he'd been carrying toward Grady. "Take a look inside."

6

Grady pulled the box toward him, giving Noah one last glance. Grady was by nature suspicious, and having an unopened box pushed toward him by someone he didn't know who could as easily be a suspect as a victim made the hair stand up on the back of his neck.

Grady studied the box. It was a typical shipping box, not much larger than a shoebox, but square rather than being rectangular. Made from brown corrugated cardboard, there were no brand markings on the outside of it, no black ink depicting where it had come from. There were also no shipping labels.

Curious.

As Grady lifted the flaps, he noticed Gabe giving the box a side eye, quickly returning to whatever was on the screen of his cell phone. Grady knew that look. There was something in the box the child didn't want to acknowledge, didn't want to think about. Grady cocked his head to the side, pausing for a moment, watching Gabe, whose attention was fixed on the screen, his thumbs still drumming on the images in front of him. Adults were good liars, but kids, not so much. Maybe having Gabe Chandler in the room would help him find out the truth of why the father and son duo had made their way from their home out in the snowstorm to bring a box to the Pittsburgh Bureau of Police.

Grady refocused on the box. He pulled it closer to him, peering inside. He glanced up at Noah, whose face had gone pale.

"It's a scarf I gave Macy last Christmas. She loved it. Wore it all the time. And her watch."

Grady didn't touch the items inside. He gave a nod to Cassie who walked out of the room for a moment and then came back carrying two sets of gloves. She handed them to Grady, then from under her arm, produced a clear plastic bag with a thick red tape seal at the top that had black writing, "Evidence — Do Not Tamper" on it.

After pulling on the black latex gloves, Grady carefully lifted the scarf out of the box from its folded position at the bottom. "Did you touch this? Take it out of the box? Fuss with it?" The words came out in a ramble.

Noah stammered, staring at the box and then at his lap. "I got the things out of the box. That's it, I think. I don't remember. This morning has all been a blur."

Grady narrowed his eyes at him and sucked in a breath, ready to tell Noah that he had to remember, when Cassie interrupted. "It's okay. It doesn't matter."

Grady shot her a look. It did indeed matter. Any forensic clues could be forever lost if Noah had messed with the scarf. But Cassie was too nice, too sweet to press him any further. Frowning, Grady took the scarf out, laying it across the length of the conference room table. He saw Gabe glance up, eye it, then shift in his seat and resume playing his game. The scarf clearly made him uncomfortable.

Grady scanned the length of the fabric. It was thin, almost

see-through, a light, dusty green with peach, yellow and red dappled flowers on it, giving the impression it had been woven by Monet himself. In the middle of the scarf there were a few dark brown stains. Grady looked up in time to see Noah's eyes widen, his hand covering his mouth. He pointed. "Is that?"

Grady finished his sentence for him. "Blood? Probably." He said it matter-of-factly.

"Grady!" Cassie hissed.

Grady shrugged. "What?"

Cassie didn't say anything more. She just shook her head.

Pushing the scarf off to the side, Grady reached into the box and drew out a slim gold watch. The face of it was six-sided, the background of the watch face in a dark burgundy. The band was tarnished, the glass to the bezel cracked as if it had been slammed against something. "And this is her watch?"

Noah nodded, his color even more pallid than it had been a moment before, mumbled, "It is. I gave that to her on our first anniversary. She's had it repaired so many times..." The words drifted off.

Grady matter-of-factly folded up the scarf and set the watch on top. He reached out his hand, in which Cassie put the open plastic evidence bag. He slid the two items inside, sealing it with the red tape and then pulling off his black gloves. "We'll need a bigger bag for the box this stuff came in, but we can get this processed for you." He sat down, spinning in the chair toward the wastebasket where he lobbed them in. "Two points." He looked back at Noah Chandler, whose eyes were wide, as if he was surprised by the interruption of discussing his wife's abduction with the announcement that Grady had made two points with his used gloves.

Grady ignored Noah's look. "Now, why is it you think this is a kidnapping?"

Noah blinked, clearly still processing Grady's casual attitude. “I got a call right before we came here. Whoever has my wife made a ransom demand.”

“Why didn’t you start with that?” Grady pressed. He furrowed his eyebrows. Maybe there was something to this case after all.

7

"The ransom demand? I was getting to it," Noah stammered, blinking. "I recorded it. I use a recording application on my phone so I don't have to take notes during phone calls with my clients."

Grady narrowed his eyes. Work issues could be a motive for a kidnapping. "And what is it you do exactly, Mr. Chandler?"

"I'm a marketing consultant." Grady pressed his lips together. That probably wasn't the type of job that would motivate a kidnapping. It wasn't as if Noah Chandler was a CEO of a Fortune 100 company, one that would have a hefty K & R policy — kidnapping and ransom insurance — on both he and his family members. At least it didn't seem so at the moment. "I work with companies bringing new brands and products to the market. I develop launch strategies. I help with the branding and even sometimes get involved with the product development."

Cassie cleared her throat, staring at Grady. He got the message. Focus on the call. Yes, the call.

"Okay, tell us about the call you got."

Noah rubbed the back of his neck. "I was sitting at my desk

doing a little work before I woke Gabe up to go to school. He's the only one home at the moment. We have another child. Kate. She's twenty-one — a junior at Bedford College where my wife works, so she doesn't live at home. And with Macy gone..." Noah stopped talking for a second, once again staring at his lap. He continued. "I've been making sure Gabe gets off to school. I was going through my emails and the phone rang. It was a strange automated voice. They said they have Macy."

Cassie cocked her head to the side, her voice soft. "Mr. Chandler, perhaps it would be easier if you played the call for us?"

Nodding, Noah seemed relieved at not having to talk. "Yes, yes. I'll play it."

Grady watched as Noah fumbled with his phone. His hands were shaking as he stabbed at the touch screen with his finger. "Here it is."

Grady leaned forward, listening. He heard an automated, tinny voice speaking. "We have your wife. We want the key."

Grady heard Noah reply, clearly confused, "The key? What key?"

"Don't play dumb with us, Noah. We know she has the key. She stole it. It doesn't belong to her. And now, we want it back."

At the end of the call, Noah shut his phone off and then looked at Grady and Cassie, his eyes darting back and forth between the two of them. "That's when we got the box. As soon as I hung up, the doorbell rang. We get a lot of early-morning deliveries. You know, people in my house are always buying stuff."

"Except for Macy."

Noah nodded. "So I went to the door and that's when I found the box."

"It was delivered as soon as the call was over?" Grady asked. That couldn't be a coincidence.

Noah nodded again.

With the timing, it was hard for Grady to believe anything other than what Noah Chandler had said. From what he was talking about, it definitely looked like a kidnapping.

Grady folded his hands in his lap. "Mr. Chandler, I need to ask you, how long has your wife been missing?"

"Four months."

8

"Four months?" Grady could feel his mouth hanging open. He closed it and swallowed, glancing at Cassie, whose eyebrows were raised.

Grady found a spot on the floor to stare at for a second, gathering his thoughts. He knew himself. If he didn't stop and think before the next words came out, he could turn this case into a hot mess. But the words "four months" echoed in his mind, bouncing along like a pinball in a pinball machine, ricocheting off his own experiences. How could Noah not know where his wife was for the last four months?

"You're only coming to us now after four months?" Grady said to Noah. He parsed the words deliberately, slowly.

Noah's eyes shifted between the two of them as if he just figured out the weight of what he'd confessed. "Well, no. I mean..."

Grady cocked his head to the side, placing his palms on the edge of the table and leaning forward. What had started as a conversation was quickly turning into an interrogation. "What exactly do you mean, Mr. Chandler? You come in here with a story about your wife being missing, then she's kidnapped, then you play a strange call for us, then you..."

Cassie interjected. "I think what my partner is trying to say, Mr. Chandler, is that we feel a little confused by your story. Maybe you could fill in some of the blanks?"

Saved by Cassie's compassion once again.

Noah squeezed his eyes shut for a second as if that would arrange the thinking in his mind. "I'm sorry," he said, holding up his hands. "I should've presented this in a more chronological order, but I've been so upset this morning. The call took me off guard, and —"

Grady narrowed his eyes, leaning back in the chair. "All right, why don't you give it to us in a more chronological order then." He glanced at Cassie. If he'd been close enough she probably would have kicked him under the table.

Noah sucked in a breath. "My wife, Macy, she's kind of a free spirit. She likes to disappear on what she calls her adventures. She goes to a cabin someplace, to write —"

Gabe looked up at the detectives, pulling one of the earbuds out of his ears. He was clearly listening to every scrap of their conversation. "She's working on a book of poetry right now. She's going to get it published!"

Grady frowned. "Go on, Mr. Chandler. You were saying that your wife likes to disappear on little adventures."

Noah nodded. "Yeah. She likes to be out in nature. Clear her head. Hike and walk. Unplug from technology and the stress of work. She needs time to be alone. So, when she packed up four months ago, I didn't really think much about it."

Grady raised his eyebrows. "Listen, I'm not married, but if my wife took off for months at a time, I'd be concerned. You weren't?" Noah's story sounded thin and implausible, like a cheap window blind trying to block out the reality of the harsh sunlight. Something didn't make sense.

Noah shook his head. "Not initially. Like I said, she did this pretty regularly — at least every year or two, less when the kids were little and they needed her home. But now that Kate is in college and Gabe is pretty self-sufficient, she just doesn't see the need to be there twenty-four-seven. Or at least she didn't."

Cassie shifted in her seat. "So, she packed up one day and took off? You haven't seen her since?"

Noah tilted his head to the side, chewing his lip. "Sorta like that. It was a little bit more intentional. I knew it was coming. We'd talked about it. Then, one day in July — I don't remember the exact date — she packed a bag and said she was going to go on one of her adventures and that she'd be in touch. When she left I heard from her a couple times and then I didn't."

Grady scowled. "You didn't think anything about that? It didn't occur to you that maybe your wife could be in trouble?" Grady could feel the tension building in his gut. Whoever this Noah Chandler was, Grady couldn't understand how he could be so cavalier about protecting the people in his family. It went against everything Grady knew.

"I guess I started to worry about her six weeks ago or so. I sent her some texts. She replied fine during the first month. She didn't say much, just that she was working on the book and it was coming along well and she would be home before the holidays. I didn't hear from her after the first few weeks. But then, today..."

"That's when you got the phone call, the scarf, and watch?" Grady grunted.

Noah swallowed, his Adam's apple bobbing up and down. "I guess I should have been more concerned. I did go to another police station and file a report, but they never got back to me."

Cassie leaned her elbow on the table. "You did? Where was that?"

"Thomasville Lake. I went a couple of months ago. At that point, we hadn't heard from Macy for quite a while. That's where she said she was last. Was renting a cabin near the lake. I was starting to get concerned. Something wasn't sitting right, but I didn't know what else to do."

Grady shifted in his seat. At least the husband had filed some sort of report. It helped to assuage Grady's concerns, but only a little. This strange case was becoming only slightly less strange. "What did the detectives in Thomasville say?"

"That's the thing, they didn't say anything. They never got back to me."

Grady stood up, lacing his fingers on the back of his head, his elbows winging out to the side. He started pacing. "You're saying your wife goes off on some adventure, as she calls it, you don't hear from her for a while, you go file a report with —"

"Thomasville Lake."

"Thomasville Lake. You never hear back from them and then all of a sudden today you get a call. In the call, the kidnapper, whoever it is, demands a key. Nothing else. No money. No timeline. Just a key, but you don't know what the key is. Do I have this correct?" The words came out slightly sarcastic, the expression on Grady's face stony. He didn't like the feeling of being played and for some reason, he felt like that was exactly what was going on.

Noah nodded eagerly, his eyes wide. "That's right."

Grady shrugged, looking at Cassie. "All right. We'll take a report and see what we can do." Not saying anything else, he got up and walked out of the room.

The door was just about to close behind him when Cassie blew through the opening, right on his heels. "Grady! What was that?"

He furrowed his eyebrows, turning back toward her. "What was what?"

She pointed back at the closed conference room doors. "You all but called those people liars."

Grady raised his eyebrows. "That didn't occur to you? I mean come on, Cassie, four months. Their dearly loved wife and mother is missing and they wait four months to reach out? Come on. I'm not sure I buy it."

Williams grunted as he limped past. "Doesn't matter whether you buy it or not, Grady. They filed a report someplace else and they have the call as proof. Just get to work."

Cassie stood in front of Grady, her arms crossed, a stony look on her face, speaking as soon as Williams disappeared. "You seriously don't believe them?"

"At this moment, I have no idea what to believe."

9

The ice snow mix dropping out of the heavy clouds was pelting at the single-paned glass window that separated Macy from the harsh winds blowing outside of the cabin. From her room, she had a single solitary view, though it wasn't a bad one, of the path down to the lake, stands of thick trunked maple and oak trees peppering the ground, their boughs almost devoid of leaves, what was left of the summer greenery now brown and crinkled on the ground.

Macy turned, hearing a whistle at the corner of the cabin window. Cold air had found a crack to play in. She picked up the paper napkin left over from her last meal and stuffed it in the corner of the pane where she could feel the cold air blowing into her small room. Shivering, she realized the thin pants and shirt she was wearing were better suited for warmer temperatures. She shrugged the blanket she'd pulled off the bed around her shoulders tighter, trying to fight off the chill. Walking over to the edge of the bed, she sat down, staring at the nearly empty room around her, her cell, her prison. She'd run out of new words to describe it.

Closing her eyes, she could visualize the room around her

without seeing it. It was small and spare. On any one of her other trips she would have gladly taken it except for the lock on the outside of the door that prevented her from leaving whenever she wanted. One night, desperate, she'd spent hours trying to get the window open. Her captors must have anticipated it. The window had been locked from the outside as well. Breaking the glass wasn't an option. A metal frame had been welded into place to block her escape.

The interior walls were wood, thin planks of siding, finished on the inside with cheap drywall and whitewashed. There were no pictures on the walls, no decor to speak of except for an old, dirty rug on the floor, so worn that it was nearly impossible to discern the pattern, although with all the time Macy had on her hands, she'd begun sitting on the floor, trying to trace it with her fingers. There was a twin bed pushed into the corner with a set of sheets and a single blanket on it, which Macy was currently using as a coat. There was a small desk and a chair in the corner, a notebook and pen placed neatly on the corner.

The first few days after her abduction had been nothing short of terrifying.

The day she'd been taken had been like any other. She'd gone to the lake during the day, sitting in a folding chair, working on her writing, walking and stopping into town on her way back to the small cabin she'd rented to get food for dinner. After she'd eaten, she took another walk around sunset, her final foray each day into nature.

That was when her life changed.

She didn't remember much about the abduction itself, even though she had spent months trying to piece it together. What she did remember was fragmented, like shattered pieces of glass — a feeling here, a smell there, with nothing concrete to hold them together except for the fear that held her so tightly it made her body ache. Her mind drifted back to the hike back to her cabin from the shore, the smell of the summer flowers around her added to the scent of the damp earth under her feet. A slight movement caught her off guard in the dusk, the shadow of a figure slipping behind her, a chill running down her spine.

Then everything went black.

Her captors had kept her blindfolded and tied to a chair for, as best she could tell, the first day or two. She'd fought a raging headache from getting slammed in the side of the face with an object she could only imagine was a gun, plus nausea from the constant fear and adrenaline surging through her body, wondering what would become of her. The room was silent and smelled of mold. Macy could remember the sound of a man sitting in front of her, his breath going in and out of his body but never saying anything. It was the only noise in the room other than the pounding of her heart, her body alternately cold and quivering and then sweating profusely. She'd pleaded and cried, but the man didn't do anything except tell her to be quiet.

After the fear had nearly destroyed her, they finally let her loose in her room. She would hear a voice from the other side of the door demanding she sit in the chair at the desk and face the other direction. Then she would hear the lock click in the doorframe, the door would swing open, giving a slight creak, the tinny noise of a metal tray being set on the door floor. Macy would hold her breath the entire time, knitting her fingers together in her lap, withdrawing inside herself, her hands shaking, sure they were going to attack her from behind. "Please," she remembered whimpering on more than one occasion. "Please, I just want to go home to my family."

"Shut up!" had been the retort from the male voice.

A few days later things changed. She'd heard a voice at the door — this time female — muffled by the wood, telling her to sit down. Macy did as the voice asked. It was lunchtime and although she didn't have much of an appetite, she knew she needed to eat to keep up her strength. She sat quietly in the chair facing the other direction, staring at her lap, a knot forming in her gut. She glanced over her shoulder, turning her head just slightly, dipping her eyes to the side, hoping to get a glimpse of whoever was holding her. Her fear, although still lingering in the periphery of her mind, had been replaced by a small dose of curiosity. Her heart started pounding in her chest as she turned her head, not sure if the person coming in the room was carrying a gun or a knife. Would they punish her for not doing exactly as they said?

But she had to know who was holding her.

Moving her head ever so slightly to the right, she saw a small figure of a woman open the door. She saw the curve of her nose and the rise of her cheekbone. For some reason the woman looked familiar. The smell of jasmine filtered through the room. Macy wrinkled her nose. That scent. She knew it. But from where?

Macy whipped around and stood up, staring at the woman, her mouth dropping open. "Lola? Why are you..."

The woman said nothing, closing the door behind her, the lock clicking in the door.

Macy remembered standing frozen in the middle of the floor, her whole body shaking, staring at the door that separated her from her freedom.

She'd been betrayed by the people closest to her.

10

Macy glanced toward the desk. After they'd taken her, they'd waited a few days and then given her the notebook out of her backpack as well as a pen. She kept herself calm by writing, doing the work she'd come to the woods to do. She still didn't know why they were holding her. A chill ran down her spine. Why had she been taken? What did they want from her?

Looking at the notebook now, seeing the wrinkled paper between the covers, she knew she only had a few blank pages left. If they expected her to keep her composure, they would have to provide her with the new notebook, otherwise she just might go crazy.

Macy walked back and forth in the little room. By her count it was eight short strides along one side or six long ones, depending on the mood she was in, with enough space for her to do push-ups, sit-ups and squats in the center. The meager exercise was the only thing that kept the blood moving in the long hours she was trapped inside. She had to knock on the inside of the door if she needed to use the bathroom. They brought her three meals a day, if they could be called that.

Usually toast and juice in the morning, a sandwich and fruit for lunch and dinner. If she ever got out of the cabin, she'd probably never eat a sandwich again.

Somehow, everything happened on a schedule, but Macy couldn't track the time. Her watch — the one Noah had given her on their first anniversary — had disappeared when she'd been abducted. She reached up, feeling around her neck. The light green scarf that Noah had given her for Christmas the year before had disappeared as well. Where it was, she wasn't sure. For all she knew it might still be on the trail where she'd been grabbed, now covered in a mixture of mud and wet snow. She reached up and touched her head. The cut on the side of her scalp from where they'd knocked her out had long healed.

After pacing back and forth a few laps trying to get her blood moving in the small room, Macy sat down on the edge of the bed, drawing her knees and feet up off the chilly floor, gripping the blanket tighter around herself. She shivered. Whether it was from the sudden drop in temperature and the snow blowing outside or from the fact that she was alone, she didn't know. The heaviness settled in her chest, her breath shallow. She wanted to be home. She missed her family, their yard, the smell of coffee perking in the kitchen, the noise of Gabe's bare feet on the wood floor. There were so many things she missed she couldn't count them all. Her eyes filled with tears. Would she ever see them again?

Macy reached up and touched the cross pendant around her neck, wrapping her fingers around it for a moment, feeling the heat of her body radiating through the metal. It had been a gift her mother had given her. It was no typical cross, like the ones so many people wore on thin gold chains. No, it was a cross inside of a circle, the hand-hewn metal thick and chunky, but by no means heavy, suspended on a black cord around her neck. Macy wasn't sure why her captors let her keep her necklace, but she was glad they did. It was one of her most prized possessions.

Macy pressed her lips together, allowing her tears to dry. She glanced toward the window once more, seeing the heavy white flakes of snow passing by, the occasional pelt of ice crystals pinging against the glass window. She pulled the blanket tighter around her shoulders and felt a pit form in her gut. Where was her family? Why weren't they coming to find her? Where were the police? It had been months. She knew she'd been on adventures before where they couldn't reach her for some time, but this was different. She felt her hands start to shake thinking about how badly she wanted to escape, but she was frightened.

An empty feeling washed over her, as if she was waking up from a nightmare. Why wasn't anyone coming to rescue her?

11

Lola Harrison pecked away at the keyboard of her computer, working on the schedules for the spring semester at Bedford College when the dean of the English department, a particularly annoying man in Lola's eyes, Rick Palmer, crossed the doorway. With his dirty blond hair, the bright white on-trend frames of his glasses, and his skinny jeans, he gave the impression that he was one of the students.

He wasn't, but he seemed to be the only one that didn't realize it.

Lola pressed her lips together, glancing up from her computer, trying to look busy so maybe he'd leave her office quickly. "Hello, Dean Palmer. How are you today?"

She had learned it was easier to be pleasant with the people in charge than grumpy. If she was pleasant, they ignored you. If you weren't, then everyone started to talk. Go along to get along was her thinking.

And Lola had every reason at that moment to want to stay invisible.

"Any news on Dr. Chandler?"

Lola's heart skipped a beat. She shook her head, painting a

saddened look on her face. "No, Dr. Palmer, I'm so sorry. I haven't heard anything since the last time you were here." She didn't add to the sentence, "Which seems like every day."

Dean Palmer leaned forward, his eyes bulging behind his glasses. "Are you serious? Have you reached out to her husband? We want Macy to know how much we love and care about her during this difficult time."

"I've reached out to Noah, but again, there's no news. The last I heard, Macy was doing a little better." The lie slipped out between her lips like it was coated in oil. She'd rehearsed it so many times it practically sounded like it was the truth. It wasn't. Lola hadn't reached out to Macy's husband, Noah. Not once. And she wouldn't.

Dean Palmer barely let her answer settle before he launched the next question. "But there's no timeline for her return?"

"I think," Lola tried to make her face look quizzical, "that he said something about Macy being ready to start for the spring semester. So, I've taken the liberty of working on her schedule so that it's in the portal when the scheduling window opens for the students in a few weeks."

Dean Palmer shook his head, "I suppose that will work. Now, if we could just get her back and working. I mean, I understand about all this family medical leave act stuff, but come on, it's been months with no word back. At least let us know what's going on!"

By the time Lola sucked in a breath to answer, it seemed that Dean Palmer had wandered away in a bit of a huff, muttering to himself. Lola got up from her desk and walked as quietly as possible to the doorway where he'd disappeared. She looked around the corner to see where he'd gone. Dean Palmer was halfway down the hallway, stopped by two other students, doing some sort of a TikTok inspired handshake and then clapping each of them on their shoulders as though they were all fraternity buddies.

Lola shook her head. Strange. Very strange.

As she sat down at her desk again, staring at the spring semester schedule she was working on, she realized it was hypocritical for her to point fingers at Dean Palmer for his behavior. Here she was, flat-out lying to his face. The request for emergency medical leave for Macy was nothing but a sham, a way to cover for her while she was gone.

Closing the document she was working on, Lola checked the time, logged off of her computer, stuffed the few personal items she'd brought to work with her — her water bottle, a bag of snacks, and her personal planner in a large floral tote bag and stood up. Slinging the bag over her shoulder, Lola slipped out of the office, walking in the opposite direction of Dean Palmer, who she was sure would have questions about where she was going in the middle of the day.

Out in the parking lot, the snow had collected on the sidewalk enough that it was slower walking than usual, not because of a vast accumulation, but because of the slush and ice forming the first crusty layers of the first late fall, early winter snow event. From across the parking lot, Lola saw another woman, huddled in a thick coat carrying a bag of food, heading her direction. Lola bristled, gritting her teeth. She wished anyone else was in the parking lot. Anyone else but Rachel.

"Hey Lola!" the woman called as she got closer, her face aimed toward the ground avoiding the pelting snowfall.

"Hi, Rachel," Lola replied, keeping her feet moving, shrugging her bag up higher on her shoulder.

"Where are you off to?"

Rachel Weiss was Dean Palmer's assistant. Working for the dean came with certain perks — lunch paid for every single day, additional time off, and travel with the dean to conferences if Rachel wanted to go. But one of Rachel's most profitable side gigs was peddling information around the college. Rachel loved to ask questions, trading juicy tidbits of gossip, conjecture and bald-faced lies with other assistants and professors throughout the college. Lola shook her head. She'd been witness to Rachel's antics on more than one occasion. Rachel had missed her calling. She should have been a spy.

"I'm headed out." Vague was always better when Rachel was around.

Rachel narrowed her eyes, a few flakes of snow landing on the shoulders of her gray coat. "Will you be back? I mean, in case Dean Palmer needs something, of course..."

Of course.

"I'll be back on Monday." Lola started walking toward her car.

"Wait! Where are you going? We still have half a day of work left for the week."

Lola sighed. As much as she wanted to stare at Rachel and scream, "It's none of your business!" she didn't. "I'm going on a little weekend getaway. But I'll have my cell phone with me in case you need me!" Lola tried to sound as happy and as cheerful as possible. There was no reason to get Rachel all worked up and start the gears of her information business churning in Lola's direction.

As Lola walked away, knowing exactly where she was headed, she heard Rachel mutter in the background, her frustration of not getting any information evident.

Lola looked over her shoulder when she got to her car and narrowed her eyes. Rachel's huddled form was at the other end of the parking lot. She needed to mind her own business, or she might get more than she bargained for.

12

By the time Lola got to her car and had ensured Rachel was heading the other direction, carrying her nosy questions with her, a thin crust of frozen ice and snow had covered the windshield. She slid inside, turning the engine on, flipping the defroster setting to high, and then getting out again, grabbing the snow brush from the trunk. She shivered against the cold as she brushed the slush off of her windshield and side mirrors. In just the last hour, the wet snow had managed to collect everywhere. She frowned. It was still fall. It seemed too early for snow in her mind. Worse yet, the drive up to the cabin would be a nightmare. She'd been doing it every weekend for months. Luckily she was driving during daylight hours. She couldn't imagine how the narrow twisting roads would be in the dark, covered by slush and sleet.

Done cleaning off her windows, Lola hurriedly put the snow brush back in the trunk of her car, slammed it shut, and slid into the driver's side, closing the door behind her. She sat for a second, waiting for the heat of the car to collect around her feet and finish defrosting the windshield. She shivered, shaking off the last of the cold. Early winter snowstorms were the worst. It wasn't cold enough to be real snow, just damp fat flakes, the harbingers of what was yet to come for the few months of the winter they suffered through each year.

A lot of people in the Midwest complained about the winter, but the way Lola looked at it, it really didn't last that long. There were only a handful of days when travel was difficult and Bedford College might be closed. And once it got cold enough, the snow was dry, not damp, which made everything seem warmer. She'd rather have a dry day with a twenty-five-degree high than a damp day with a forty-degree high, unless spring was coming, of course. Lola loved spending time sitting in front of the small fireplace in her house she had on the outskirts of the campus, building a fire in the fireplace, drinking a glass of red wine, and reading a good book that one of the professors recommended in the evenings. It was a simple life and she liked it that way.

But her life was no longer simple. She wasn't sure it would ever be again.

Thinking about it as she pulled out of the staff parking lot of Bedford College, she realized some of her favorite reading over the last few years had been Macy's poetry.

Guilt chewed at Lola's stomach. She thought about Kate, Macy's twenty-one-year-old daughter, who was a Junior at Bedford College. Lola didn't see her much. Unlike her mom, Kate was into math and IT. Lola remembered Macy joking one day, "She's probably the mailman's daughter. How she got so good at math and science, I have no idea. Noah and I are definitely not tuned up that way!"

Lola swallowed as she turned her car onto I-279, heading out to Thomasville Lake where the cabin was, her stomach sour at the trouble she couldn't seem to get herself out of.

Thomasville Lake was the main tourist attraction of the tiny township of Thomasville, about an hour outside of Pittsburgh. Pittsburgh as a city was sprawling, with the Monongahela,

Ohio, and Allegheny rivers joining each other downtown, legions of loyal gold and black adorned Pittsburgh Steelers fans trudging their way downtown to the football haven formerly known as Three Rivers Stadium every fall. The suburbs took up the space around the city, developments filled with kids and families going to their local school districts, junior football leagues and swimming teams keeping the families busy.

But on the weekends, many people would travel to small areas like Thomasville, wanting to get away from the city, away from the bustle and hubbub of daily life.

Thomasville itself was a small town, small enough that it didn't have a single stoplight, but a collection of stop signs that prevented people from flying down Arch Street, the main drag in Thomasville, too fast. But despite the small stature of the township, Lola had discovered it had everything anyone could need in order to stay at the cabins nearby long-term. There was a general store that carried everything from food to clothing to tools, a hardware store catty-corner to it run by the Nelson family, who had owned it for more than a century. Nelson's had plumbing supplies, lumber for projects, bricks, snowblowers, lawn mowers, siding, and a whole host of agricultural items, including a wide range of seeds, bulbs, and even an outdoor display of seedlings for vegetable gardens in the spring. Just past Nelson's Hardware was the local library, a small grocery store, and a meat market. And, with the advent of online shopping, people who wanted to order from the Internet could pick up their packages at the local post office or at one of the delivery lockers that was located outside of the building while they were in town.

But the most outstanding feature of Thomasville was the lake. It was a wide glassine body of water in the shape of a snowman, a large circle joined with a smaller circle, surrounded by tree-thickened hillsides, small cabins dotting the woodland among the herds of deer, foxes, wild turkeys, coyotes, and God knew what else. On the opposite side of the lake where Lola was headed was a waterfront pizzeria. In the summertime, pontoon boats puttered over to the restaurant where a pizza person would walk out with the pie delivering it dockside. There was water skiing, paddle boarding, kayaking, and lake tours given by the Pennsylvania Department of Natural Resources, if any visitors were interested.

But that wasn't the same area where Lola was headed.

On the other side of the lake, at the far end, where the body of water narrowed into a small oval, there wasn't much development. The people that wanted to visit Thomasville Lake wanted to be at the opposite end where the action was, where they'd have easy access to the recreation areas and restaurants that Thomasville had to offer. Lola shook her head. People were all about their comfort.

At the opposite end of the lake, there were only a few cabins, ancient hunting relics that had been added on, refurbished and remodeled by their succession of owners, a set of new shingles here, a new window there, never enough to truly update any of the structures, only to make them slightly more habitable.

As Lola pulled off the freeway and onto one of the rural routes, the drive in front of her ran through her mind. First, she'd stop at the market and pick up some food for the weekend, using one of the rusty, rattling shopping carts that the grocery store had by the door, smiling thinly at the people at the checkout, trying to avoid conversation. She'd listen to the wheel's clatter over the dirty linoleum, the vibration pulsing through her hands as she made her way through the space, picking up vegetables and snacks. She'd then have to load her groceries in the car in the cold and pelting snow and then drive around the edge of the lake on the narrow road that was barely wide enough for two cars to pass. Lola pressed her lips together and gripped the wheel a little tighter. She knew that section of the road would be icy. There would be no choice but to go slow. Thomasville wasn't exactly known for its snow removal prowess. Then, her car would have to make the final climb over the small gravel road that led to the cabin that overlooked the lake where she was due sometime in the next few hours.

Lola sighed. Part of her wanted to keep driving and never go back to Thomasville Lake, never face the cabin again or her part in what they'd done, but if she didn't, there was no guarantee what would happen to their prisoner. She felt like she was the one keeping the peace. If she disappeared, Macy would be on her own. A chill ran down her spine. No good would come of that.

13

After a predictably slow drive into Thomasville, the trip to the grocery store where she picked up not only groceries for the weekend but two extra blankets for the cabin, Lola got back in her car, ready to make the final push to her destination.

As she feared, the road circling the lake had turned icy. Normally at that stage of the drive, Lola was able to look off to her left and catch glimpses of the glimmering water in the distance. She'd never been down to the water. Dario wouldn't allow it. He was afraid they'd be spotted.

With the squalls of snow blowing overhead, the lake was shrouded in fog, the cool air clashing with the warm water. Within a month or six weeks, depending on how quickly the temperatures dropped in Thomasville, the water would ice over, all of the boats pulled out for the winter, but as Lola drove, she saw a few vessels still perched at their docks, the first snow squalls of winter catching people by surprise.

Twenty long minutes later, Lola pulled up in front of the cabin, got out of the car, and immediately began to shiver. She trotted to the trunk, grabbing the bags and headed down the slippery hillside.

Given the topography of the land where the cabin was perched, it was built a little differently than someone might imagine, as though it was leaning into the dirt, not standing free of it. Its foundation extended up the side of the hill, mirroring the curve of the land. The second floor of the cabin could be accessed as easily as the first, with screen doors on both levels.

Angling for the lower floor, Lola hiked down the hillside slowly, trying not to slip and fall. For a second, she felt one of her boots nearly go out from underneath her, but it stopped just as she was about to lose her balance and all of her purchases tumbled out of their bags. She got to the small door on the first floor of the cabin, pulled on the screen door and pushed open the door inside. A blast of warmth covered her face as she stepped inside. She sighed, immediately feeling more relaxed. She'd made it.

Lola glanced around her. The interior of the cabin was whitewashed and cheerful, but dated and certainly no reflection of Dario's hostile mood. A yellow-flowered wallpaper border ran around the kitchen area at the back of the large room where she was standing, the room divided by a long white Formica countertop into the cooking area and the family room. She listened. No noise. Her heart skipped a beat. Where was Dario? What was going on upstairs?

Lola looked toward a set of steps that jutted up on the side of the cabin just beyond the door where she'd walked in, an interior passage to the second floor that mirrored the curvature of the hillside. She liked to think of it as two ground-floor levels, although if the land had been flat, the cabin would have been a two-story structure. She glanced up the steps as she set the groceries down, pushing aside the thoughts about what was going on with Macy.

She looked around her. The television was on in the background, a commercial offering to solve acid indigestion once and for all, only with a few hundred side effects quickly rattled off by a fast-talking narrator who made the risk of cancer sound like nothing. Lola frowned. Where was Dario?

Leaving the groceries by the door, she kicked off her boots and headed up the steps, staring at the door at the top of the stairs. It was closed. Lola knew it was locked.

By the time she got back downstairs and dragged the groceries into the kitchen, she heard a truck outside. A minute later, Dario walked in, the screen door banging closed behind him.

"Where've you been?" Lola asked, pushing a bag of oranges into the back of the bare refrigerator.

"I had things to do," he said gruffly, shrugging out of his coat and hanging it on one of the hooks near the door. "What took you so long?"

Lola raised her eyebrows. "Did you not see the weather outside, cousin? The roads aren't exactly great and I only have my little car. It's not like I have a big truck with four-wheel-drive like yours."

"Yeah, well..." The words drifted off.

Lola stared at Dario for a moment. No one could ever claim they weren't family. The color of their hair matched, both of them of Spanish descent, related on their mother's side, with the same tanned skin and brown eyes. "What if our guest needed something? How long were you gone for?"

"Then she'd have to wait. I sit here all week waiting on her. And she's not our guest. I don't know why you keep calling her that."

Lola's face reddened. Macy was someone that Lola had considered a friend, at least before all of this happened. Lola looked down, pulling a package of ground meat from the bag and sticking it in the refrigerator on a different shelf from the bag of oranges. She swallowed. Lola, who had an idea what her life looked like before she'd gotten drawn into the mess with Dario, had no idea what the future looked like. None at all.

The one thing she knew for sure was that she and Macy would not likely be friends after this.

Lola spent the next few minutes unpacking the groceries and getting everything put away for the weekend. It was her job to, as Dario put it, "Mind the store," over the weekend, giving him a break.

With the groceries stowed, Lola glanced over at Dario, who had flopped down on an armchair, his feet up on the footrest. A scowl covered his face as he stared at the television. Lola was relatively sure by his expression he was once again running over the plan in his mind, or perhaps the lack of a plan was a better way to put it.

Dario had been asking Macy one single question for months — where is the key?

Lola blinked, thinking. Macy didn't have an answer. She claimed to know nothing about it. Dario didn't believe her, but Lola wasn't sure. The key was legendary in their family, the promise of a literal, life-changing fortune stashed away in a safety deposit box. Lola wasn't sure it was actually true, though Dario seemed convinced. It was something that only came up in whispered late-night talks over small glasses of anis, licorice-flavored liqueur, the story of it never spoke in the daylight.

From the corner of the kitchen counter, Lola picked up the blankets she'd purchased at the store. She pulled the tags off, shaking them out, seeing dust fly, little specks floating through the air. It looked like they'd been on the shelf for a while. But they were soft and warm, rustic red and black plaid. The room they had Macy in was designed for warmer weather. Lola knew she had to be cold. Her heart clenched. How had she gotten caught up in Dario's mess? She looked at the floor. The better question, one she'd been struggling with for weeks, was how she could get out of it. She had no good answer, at least not at that moment.

Dario glanced in her direction. "What are those?"

"I got a couple extra blankets. It's cold upstairs."

Dario's frown only got deeper. "Let her be cold."

Lola shook her head and rolled her eyes. "Dario, don't be mean."

Dario stood up and stared out the window. "Lola, we aren't running a hotel. We kidnapped someone. She's supposed to suffer."

A chill ran down Lola's spine. It wasn't from the weather outside. "Listen, I never agreed to help you do this. You forced me into it."

Dario threw his hands up in the air, his voice getting louder, his expression one of anger and frustration. "What was I supposed to do, capture her by myself? You just happened to be in the right place at the right time."

Lola looked down at the floor. The last thing she wanted to do was get into a shouting match with Dario. He was as stubborn as the rest of the Gilbert men were. Although they went by Gilbert, their original name Gilberto, from the Andalusia region of Spain, just outside of Seville. They were passionate, angry, hotheaded, and yet loving and loyal to a fault. Family was family. There was no arguing that to anyone in the Gilberto clan. It wasn't a war that could be won.

And in Dario's eyes, Macy had stolen their legacy. It wasn't an offense that could be ignored.

Without saying anything, Lola grabbed the two blankets and carried them up the steps. She'd packed extra pairs of sweatpants and socks and sweatshirts in her weekend bag and would pass those onto Macy when Dario wasn't looking. For now, the blankets would have to do. Lola knocked on the door to the room and unlocked it, stepping inside.

As Lola closed the door behind her, she found Macy sitting

on the bed, her knees pulled up to her chest, the single blanket in the room wrapped around her shoulders.

Macy looked up as Lola walked in. She didn't say anything, only peering at her with watery eyes, desperation on her face.

Lola swallowed. It felt like a crack was forming in her chest. She couldn't imagine how Macy was feeling. Her heart broke for her friend. How had she gotten in the middle of this mess? When Dario asked for help, why hadn't she said no? Why hadn't she warned Macy? She knew that at any time she could have gone to the police, but not only would she go to jail, but so would Dario.

And family was family. Go along to get along...

Lola swallowed the guilt back down into her gut and glanced away, setting the two blankets on the foot of the bed. "I thought you might be chilly so I brought you a couple blankets. We're getting an early snow. Wasn't expecting that."

"How are the roads?" Macy offered weakly.

Lola pressed her lips together. Macy was clearly trying to make conversation. Even though Macy was quiet by nature, Lola wondered if the torment of being by herself with her thoughts all the time for months on end had been torture. If nothing else, her friend had to be lonely. Macy didn't know the endgame. Neither did Lola. Only Dario did. And from what Lola could see, she wasn't sure what Dario was thinking, only that he became angrier and more impatient every single day.

Macy stood up, crossing the tiny room to where Lola was standing, haphazardly refolding the blankets for what felt like the thirtieth time. Macy reached out and touched Lola's arm. Lola felt the cool, clammy touch against her warm skin. "Lola, please. Just let me go. I won't tell anyone. I want to go home and see my family. Please..."

The words nearly cracked Lola's heart in half. She pressed her lips together.

Searching Macy's face, she shook her head. "Macy, just give Dario what he wants."

"I can't." Macy sat down on the edge of the bed, staring at the floor. "I don't have it."

14

Dario had moved silently up the steps, waiting outside of the closed door where Lola and Macy were talking. He'd become good at going up the treads as silent as a cat over the last few months, knowing exactly where the haphazardly built wooden steps would creak and pop.

He moved across the landing, where there was a small sitting area. An olive-colored loveseat with rough burlap fabric and spindly legs stood against one wall, a wood-backed chair tucked in the corner, another dirty rug covering the rough wood floor. Dario moved slowly and quietly to the room where Macy and Lola were talking. He leaned his ear toward the door, cocking his head to the side.

As Dario listened, he frowned. He couldn't hear the words they were saying. They must have been whispering. He didn't like secrets. Worse yet, he didn't like the way that Lola had been behaving for the last few weeks. Narrowing his eyes, he wondered what the women were talking about. It made him think Lola's resolve was cracking. He'd have to watch her. Closely. She always said family was first, but Dario was beginning to wonder if she actually meant it. Maybe it had been a mistake to involve her.

Creeping back down the steps, Dario started to pace in the family room, the television noise murmuring in the background. "Folks, we have an unexpected winter storm arriving here over the next few days. Looks like the squalls are going to continue coming out of the northwest, blowing over the Canadian border into parts of northwestern Pennsylvania. This will continue for the next day or so. We can expect accumulations of…"

Dario tuned out the man's overly cheerful voice in the background. How one person could get so excited about a storm blowing in, Dario wasn't sure.

He had his own storms to deal with.

Still pacing, his arms crossed in front of his chest, Dario looked out the window.

The little plot of land where the cabin he'd bought with the last of his money had a direct line of sight down to a dock with two stations for mooring a boat. A small power boat, an eighteen-foot center console, was tied off at the dock, the cover protecting it from the majority of the storm. From where he was, he could just barely make it out, bobbing up and down at the dock on the waves kicked up by the storm. On the other side of the cabin, he had a trailer for it. Getting it out of the water for the winter was one of the chores he was planning on doing the following week while he watched Macy.

Macy.

Every moment of his life over the last few months had been watching and waiting for her, like an overgrown babysitter. He'd given up everything — his life, his job, his friends — everything. He'd disappeared to the cabin with no warning, dumping his cell phone and everything he knew. And despite every tactic he could think of, Macy hadn't cracked. He'd had a lingering realization over the last few days — was it really possible she didn't know about the key?

Staring out the window and shaking his head, Dario wondered if perhaps cracked was too strong of a word. Maybe shared was the better option. Although he'd had his hand forced when he kidnapped her, hitting her over the head in order to knock her out long enough to bring her to the cabin, Dario hadn't laid a hand on her since. He couldn't. It wasn't that type of incarceration in his mind. He considered it more of a persuasion.

Unfortunately, it wasn't working and time was running out.

He thought back to the call he'd placed earlier that morning to Noah Chandler, Macy's husband. It was a final move, one he hadn't wanted to make. He'd told Noah of his demand for the key that was missing, the key that would restore his fortunes and his family's good name. It was simple in his mind. As soon as he got the key, he'd let Macy go. No harm, no foul.

But like Macy, Noah acted completely innocent when it came to the key. Dario dropped his hands to the side and balled his fingers into fists. How could they not know about the key? Were they just playing him, pretending to be dumb?

Dario began to pace in front of the television again when Lola came down the steps. He charged over to her, his face reddening. "What were you talking about in there?"

Lola's eyes got wide. She took half a step back and stammered. "I don't know. Nothing. She was cold. I gave her the blankets. She wants to go home."

Dario threw his hands in the air and stormed to the other side of the room. He spun around, staring at Lola again. "What do you not understand about this? She can't go. Not until she gives me the key."

Lola shrugged. "I don't know what to tell you, Dario. All these months have passed by. She doesn't know anything about a key. Maybe there isn't one. Maybe it was just some fable in the family. Or maybe, just maybe, you got it wrong and we kidnapped her for no reason."

The words stung like a slap in the face. The fact that Lola was accusing him of getting his information wrong was like pouring gasoline on a fire. "You've got to be kidding me!" Dario pointed his finger at Lola. "You might be happy living your small little boring life, but I'm not. And we're owed more. We deserve to have back what was stolen from us!"

Lola sighed and then held her hands up like a stop sign in front of her, "Listen, Dario, I don't want to fight. Maybe you're right, maybe you're not, but either way, this is getting out of hand. We've got to let her go. She's got children and a husband. They have to be scared to death for her. People are starting to ask questions at work. I'm covering the best I can, but if Dean Palmer calls Noah directly, the sham is over. They will know I lied. This just isn't right."

Dario wheeled around staring at Lola, his face a stony mask, his fists gripped into tight balls. "Her family should be scared for her. I want that key and I'm going to get it. And you're right about one thing — time is running out, and so is my patience with both of you. Make no mistake, Lola. Macy better be here when I get back. Don't get any ideas about letting her go or you won't like the consequences."

Dario stormed out of the cabin, slamming the door behind him.

15

After two more cups of coffee and a great deal of grumbling under his breath, Detective Max Grady finally worked up the strength to go to Williams's office to talk to him about the Chandler case.

Crossing the office space filled with mismatched desks and chairs, Grady approached the lieutenant's office seeing his door was open. That was a sign Williams was at least open to receiving visitors. Grady rapped on the open door and waited for Williams to glance at him.

"What do you need?" Williams grunted, his gaze returning to the pile of files on his desk.

"The Chandler case. Wanted to see what you want Reynolds and I to do about it, Lieutenant?"

Williams looked up slowly over a set of silver-rimmed half-moon glasses that made him look ten years older than he was. The glasses, combined with his bad attitude, gave Grady the impression that Williams was at least a hundred years old. Crotchety didn't begin to describe the man, not that Grady was a ray of sunshine himself. Williams narrowed his eyes. "Do about it? Fix it."

"Fix-it" was the lieutenant's way of telling Grady to go do something and stay out of his hair.

"Yeah, sure. What kind of fixing do you have in mind? The Chandler's already filed a report with Thomasville PD. Technically, this isn't our case."

Williams stripped the half glasses off his face adding them to the same hand where a pen sat between his fingers. "Why is it that I always have to spell things out for you, Grady? You've been here long enough. Take Reynolds. Get in your car. Drive to Thomasville and figure it out."

It might have seemed clear to Williams, but it didn't to Grady. Clarity was his friend. "Do you want us to take the case, Lieutenant?"

Williams shook his head, looking back down at the paperwork in front of him. "Not if you don't have to," he muttered.

Grady spun on his heel, feeling singularly unsatisfied by the answers he'd gotten from the lieutenant. Per police protocol, he and Reynolds were supposed to check in with Williams, ask for his direction and input on cases, and then execute his wishes.

The problem was, Williams didn't have any wishes other than all of their cases would go away.

But that would put them all out of a job.

Acid eating away at the inside of his stomach, Grady walked past Reynolds, who was perched at her desk, jotting down notes on a pad of paper. She'd drawn one heel up to the seat of the chair, her knee pointing towards the ceiling, her other leg dangling down to the floor. She was in a twisted position, a pen in her fingers, staring at the paper as if she was waiting for inspiration. If Grady had to guess, it was about the Chandler case. He grunted as he passed. "Let's go."

She hopped up out of her seat, gathering her things as he watched. "Where are we off to?"

"Thomasville."

Cassie raised her eyebrows. "You decided to go have an actual conversation with Williams?"

Grady shrugged. "Actual is a strong word. I don't know if I'd go that far."

After waiting for exactly four minutes, which Grady timed on his watch while Cassie gathered her things, poured a fresh cup of coffee into her thermal mug, used the restroom, and logged out of her computer, they were finally ready to go.

The two of them stepped into the elevator that dropped them down to the first floor of the police headquarters and then headed out the front door.

As soon as they walked outside, a cold wind whipped around the corner of the building, coming down Western Avenue, cutting through the layers of clothes and coat that Grady had on. He shrugged against the wind, pulling up the collar and checking both ways. His car was parked across the street, not his personal car, but the black sedan owned by the department he and Cassie used for work.

Seeing the road was all clear of traffic, the two of them trotted across the slushy roadway, popping up on the sidewalk on the other side of the street just as another cluster of traffic passed behind them. They walked to the car in silence, Grady using the key fob to open up the sedan and start it, watching as Cassie jumped inside, slamming the door behind her.

Grady frowned, the icy snow pricking at the skin on his face. Typical girl. She was waiting for him to clear the windshield.

Grady opened the door to the back seat and grabbed the snow brush from inside. Cassie was hunched over the dashboard, fiddling with the heat, twisting and turning knobs like a mad scientist. He shook his head as he walked to the front of the car. By the time he got in the car, she'd probably have the heat turned up to a tropical eighty-five degrees, the defroster blasting on high. He'd have to get inside and reset everything where it should be, otherwise he'd be coated in sweat by the time they got to Thomasville.

It only took him a minute to wipe the wet snow from the windshield. At the last moment, he took a second to lift up the wipers and clear the snow and ice from underneath them, letting them snap back on the glass so they would work better. There was nothing worse than driving in a snowstorm and not being able to see in addition to slipping and sliding all over the road. It was like adding insult to injury.

Tossing the wet snow brush back onto the floor of the backseat, Grady opened the driver's side door, taking off his coat. Cassie yelled from inside, "Come on, close the door. It's cold."

"Gimme a sec. You'll live."

With his coat safely stashed on the backseat of the sedan, Grady slipped into the car and slammed the door. As expected, Cassie had that heat and the defroster running full blast. But instead of an expected setting of eighty-five degrees, it was only at seventy-five. For that, Grady was grateful.

While Grady cleared the windshield, Cassie had taken the liberty of programming the onboard GPS to get them to Thomasville. Grady glanced at the screen and saw their arrival would take an hour. That was in good weather. He pressed his lips together. They'd be lucky if they got there in an hour with how people drove in the first snow of the season. He was glad he was no longer on patrol. The calls of cars off the side of the road wouldn't stop until the snow did. Worse yet would be dealing with the people — crying, frustrated, angry people. Too much emotion for a little snow.

While they drove, Grady and Cassie alternately spoke about things that were not important, or nothing at all. Cassie told Grady about the new toy she had gotten for her dog, Happy. "I saw it online on one of those top ten dog toys sites, you know the kind I mean, right?"

Grady grunted.

"Anyway, I thought it would be great for Happy. I mean, he's so active. He loves doing things and he's such a good boy, so I thought he needed a new toy."

Grady grunted again.

"It's called a giggle ball. Isn't that great? It's green and it has this mechanism inside that when it rolls it makes a funny noise. Now, I wouldn't say it actually sounds like a giggle, but it definitely makes me want to giggle, which I guess is a good thing."

Grady grunted for the third time.

Cassie didn't miss a beat. "And Happy loves it. He loves it so much I have to keep it in the closet. As soon as I put it on the ground he chases it and then it makes all these strange noises. Honestly, he spent twenty minutes the other night chasing this thing around the house."

Clearly, Cassie was as happy about the giggle ball as Happy was, Grady thought.

After her report on Happy's latest toy, Cassie was quiet for a second and then looked at Grady. "Did Williams say what we're supposed to do when we get to Thomasville, other than talk to these guys and find out what happened?"

Grady chewed the inside of his lip. "Not really. I think he wants us to kick the case back to Thomasville, though, since that's where the first report was taken."

"Well, if that's what the lieutenant wants..."

"...then that's what the lieutenant will get." Grady finished. It was something they had said over and over again to each other.

But somehow Grady wasn't certain that was how things were going to work out, at least not on that day...

16

The drive to Thomasville had been predictably nightmarish with the swirling snow collecting on the roads. It only worsened as they got into town. Once they got into town, locating the police department turned out to be more frustrating than the drive itself.

After circling the block a couple of times, grumbling under his breath, Grady finally figured out where the Thomasville police station was. They'd passed Nelson's Hardware, the Thomasville General Store, and the library twice before figuring out that all of the municipal buildings were clustered in one spot down a side road. Though the GPS had gotten them close, it hadn't provided an exact location. Grady could feel the tension building in the back of his neck, threatening a headache of gargantuan proportions.

"There it is!" Cassie pointed through the snow-streaked windshield, as though she'd just found a lost relic.

Grady narrowed his eyes. "That little tiny sign? How in the Sam Hill is anyone supposed to find that?"

Cassie shrugged. "I guess it doesn't matter. We found what we were looking for." She was predictably resilient.

The Thomasville police station was in the same building as the road division for the township, a smallish red brick building with a single floor and a large garage attached to the side. What the garage was for, Grady wasn't exactly sure. He drove around the corner of the building finding two empty parking spots marked for police parking only and pulled in. Hopefully, some bored Thomasville police officer wouldn't decide that Grady's detective vehicle was a civilian car and tow it, but he was willing to take the chance.

Getting out of the car, Grady nearly slipped on a patch of ice, having to grab at the driver's side door to keep himself upright.

"You okay over there?" Cassie grinned, her eyes raised, already on the sidewalk. "You looked like you were trying out for the Olympics there for a second."

"I'm fine. They need to salt the road."

Grady followed Cassie as she made her way up the short sidewalk to the door of the police station. Outside were a collection of plants in white plastic tubs, their leaves and stems brown and drooped as though they had been put there for the summer and then someone had forgotten about them as the days became shorter and the weather colder.

Cassie, leading the way, pushed the door to the police station open. Grady trailed her through a white painted door with a nondescript plaque that said Thomasville Police on it. There was no lock and no buzzer. Grady shook his head. Typical small-town policing. They'd probably never survive in a bigger city with that relaxed attitude.

Brushing the snow off the shoulders of his coat as they stepped inside, Grady could feel the warm air touching his face. The lobby of the Thomasville police station smelled a little funny, like burned coffee mixed with the metal odor of a furnace that had recently been turned on, the dry heat sucking all the humidity out of the air. Grady licked his lips and looked around.

The interior of the Thomasville police station was not much different than any other small-town police department Grady had visited during his career. They all had the same hallmarks — scuffed paint in some version of a neutral color — a dirty gray, or off-white, or beige — plus the same drab flooring, either tan carpet or tile, and the same art on the walls, a few posters of things to do in the area they patrolled, plus a few plaques for good measure, demonstrating the prowess and authority of the department.

Grady knew it was all a front, a ploy for the department to look their part of the civil Thomasville society.

A frosted glass window slid open, revealing a woman probably around Grady's age with stringy blonde hair caught back in a tortoiseshell clip, sad brown eyes wearing an oversized blue dress. She was chewing gum, her mouth slightly open every time she chomped down on it. "Can I help you?" She glanced between Grady and Cassie. Cassie shot him a look as if to tell him not to speak, at least not yet. Cassie sucked in a breath, holding up her badge. "I'm Detective Reynolds and this is Detective Grady. We're from Pittsburgh. We wanted to talk to someone about a report that was filed on a missing person a few months back."

The unnamed woman at the front desk raised her eyebrows, her sad brown eyes widening and bulging as if Cassie had said something that was completely shocking. "A missing person? I haven't heard anything about that," she stammered. "Come right on in," she said, pointing to the door on the other side of the lobby.

Her surprise was no shock to Grady. He pressed his lips together. It would be a miracle if they could get anywhere in Thomasville. Maybe Williams was right, maybe they should just let the locals handle it.

But then again, Macy Chandler had been gone for four cold months...

17

By the time Cassie and Grady had made it through the door, the woman sitting behind the desk at the Thomasville police station had stood up and crossed the ten feet or so between her desk and the door to the lobby. She motioned for them to follow her.

Grady scanned the room in front of him. Apparently whoever had acquired furniture for the Thomasville police station was on the same buying plan as Pittsburgh. The desks were only slightly more matched than the furniture in the pit, where he and Cassie worked. There were fewer of them too, a cluster of four desks in the middle of the station, newer flatscreen monitors on each desk, a long wall of wooden cabinetry built into the side of the room. The cabinets housed a variety of items, including a paper cutter, a pile of copy paper, and a commercial-sized coffee maker that was burbling in the background. The woman who'd led them through the station must have seen Grady staring at it. She blinked and then pointed, sounding more like a den mother than a police administrator. "Would you like a cup? I just put a fresh pot on."

Cassie shot Grady a look and then cleared her throat. Grady

bit the inside of his lip and then answered, his voice gravelly, "Sure."

The woman's face brightened. "Great! Let me get you settled in the meeting room and then I'll go get your coffee. I'll get someone to help you, too, of course."

A second later, the woman led Cassie and Grady into a brightly painted room. "We just painted this," she said, lifting her chest as if she was proud of the accomplishment. "There's a plan to redo the whole station, but we have to do it in bits and pieces. We don't have as big of a budget as I'm sure you folks have in Pittsburgh." She pointed to the chairs that were stationed around a six-seat conference table in the center of the room. "Why don't you find a place to sit and I'll let the detectives know that you're here. I'll get your coffee on the way. Be back in a moment," she said cheerily.

"Great. Thank you," Cassie said encouragingly. Grady didn't bother to answer.

Grady surveyed the room. It was a far cry from the interview/interrogation rooms they had in the pit. This one was much more welcoming, almost as though he'd stepped into someone's kitchen without the appliances. The walls were painted white, the trim stained in a medium oak color. It looked like new dark brown flooring had been put down to match the trim. Whether it was tile or vinyl, Grady couldn't tell, but he didn't care enough to reach down to touch it to find out. The table didn't have a single scratch on the surface, no dents or marring from years of reports being taken on it. Grady sat down in the chair at the far end of the conference table, feeling the firm cushion push up underneath him. It was clearly new.

A moment later, the woman who had greeted them came bustling back into the conference room carrying two cups of coffee. From a pocket in her dress, she pulled out a handful of creamers, two napkins, two stirrers, and four packets of sugar.

"I didn't know how you like your coffee so I brought this with me. Hope you don't mind I stuck it in my pocket?"

Cassie shook her head. "No. That's perfectly fine. Thank you." Cassie looked up at the woman from where she'd taken a seat next to Grady. "I'm sorry, I didn't catch your name."

"Sorry," she put her hand on her chest. "Becky. I'm the department's admin."

"Nice to meet you. I'm Cassie."

"Nice to meet you, too," Becky said with a smile.

Grady was silent.

As the pleasantries subsided, two men walked into the room. Grady looked up, staring at them. One of them, a shorter man with brush-cut brown hair and skin that almost matched, glanced at Becky. "Thanks, Becky," he grunted, clearly letting her know it was time for her to go.

Grady took stock of the two men. The one that had already spoken couldn't have been more than five and a half feet tall, short and stocky with thick arms and a square face. The one that hadn't spoken yet was probably the same height as Grady, about six feet tall. He had dark hair and smooth skin. He looked young, or at least younger than Grady by probably ten years. Grady glanced at his left hand. No ring on either of them. If Grady had to guess, the older one was divorced at least once, the younger guy probably still looking for the woman of his dreams somewhere in the backwoods of Pennsylvania.

The stocky man spoke first. "I'm Detective Andy Bennett. This is Detective Hunter Franco. Heard you guys drove in from Pittsburgh in this horrendous weather. What can we do for you?"

Grady took a sip of his coffee and then looked at Andy, who had taken a seat at the other end of the table. "I'm Detective Max Grady. This is Detective Cassie Reynolds. Pittsburgh Bureau of Police. We're here following up on a case we caught this morning. Supposedly, somebody came to you and reported that a woman was missing in the area a couple of months ago. Macy Chandler. That ring a bell?"

Andy looked at Grady and then back at Cassie, shrugging as if it was no big deal. "Yeah, it rings a bell, if there was a bell to ring."

Grady narrowed his eyes, trying to keep his voice even. He'd only met Andy a minute before and he was already irritated. "What does that mean?"

Andy didn't respond for a minute, crossing his arms in front of his chest. He glanced at Hunter, who was still standing in the doorway. "We might have a file with some notes on that. Can you go check? I think it's at the bottom of my pile on my desk."

Hunter nodded. "Sure. I'll be right back."

Grady cocked his head to the side. They might have a file? Might? "You said the case might ring a bell, but you didn't answer my question. What does that mean?"

Andy shrugged and then started picking at the skin at the edge of one of his fingernails. "Out here we get all sorts of crazy stories. People go missing, things go missing. People around here don't have enough to do so they assume it's some huge crime or a major conspiracy. We've even got some of those alien enthusiasts out here who stop in the office every now and again to tell us stories about how their body has been taken and then returned to earth after some ridiculous medical experiment." He scoffed. "We see a lot of crackpots. We take some notes, make it look good, if you know what I mean, then stick the file on the desk in case they come back. I'm sure you guys do the same thing in Pittsburgh, right, Max?"

Grady bristled, pressing his lips together. It was at moments like those it was best he didn't speak.

Fortunately, before Grady could formulate a response, Detective Hunter Franco came back into the brightly decorated room with a single manila file in his hand. "I think I found what you wanted." He handed the file to Andy. "Is that it?"

"Yeah, I think so," he frowned, opening it up. He shook his head, staring at the contents, then sliding it across the table to Max. "Honestly, I don't have too many notes on this page."

Cassie drummed her fingers on the table, "Now that you've looked at your notes, can you remember anything about the situation?"

Andy shrugged from where he was seated at the other end of the table. "There wasn't much to tell if I remember correctly. A man came in. Said his wife had been traveling in the area and he hadn't heard from her for a while. Was concerned she'd gone missing or been kidnapped or something. We sat down with him, gave him a cup of coffee and listened to his story, same as we do with everybody."

Listened, yes. Took action, not likely, Grady thought.

"Did he have anything for you to go on?" Cassie probed.

Andy shook his head. "No. Not really. When he was pressed, the guy wasn't even sure his wife was in the area. For my money, I bet she ran off with some other man, you know what I mean, Max?"

Grady kept his hands under the table where Andy couldn't see him gripping his fingers into fists. There was no reason for Bennett to keep repeating Max's name. Grady licked his bottom lip. "So, there wasn't really any cause for concern on your part?"

Andy rubbed his chin. "In my mind, no. Maybe Hunter felt differently, but if he did, he didn't say anything to me at that time."

Grady shot Hunter a look, whose face remained completely blank. Grady chewed the inside of his lip. If he had to guess, Hunter didn't take a breath without Andy's approval. It was collusion, the worst kind. A complete lack of action.

Cassie's voice interrupted his thoughts. "Did you guys end up filing a report?"

Andy shrugged. "No. I just kept the notes on my desk. Figured if there was anything to it the man would come back."

Grady narrowed his eyes. It was time to press the youngster. "How about you, Hunter? What do you think? Did you end up filing a report?"

It was clear from the look on Hunter's face that he was surprised Grady had addressed him. "No," he stammered. "I sat in the interview with Detective Bennett. Like he said, there was no real evidence. There wasn't even any proof that the woman had been in the area. After the man left, the whole thing kind of slipped my mind, to be honest."

Grady shot up out of his seat, turning toward the back wall of the newly painted conference room trying to push back the surge of anger in his gut. Everything in him wanted to punch a hole through the drywall. He spun back, looking at the two detectives at the far end of the room. "Are you kidding me? So you two couldn't be bothered to do any follow-up at all? Is that what you're telling me?"

Andy held his hands up in front of him. "Don't get your panties in a twist, Max. We're just doing what we do here at Thomasville."

Grady stared at Andy, towering over him from the other side of the table. "You're just doing what you do? What does that even mean? Every department has standard policies and operating procedures set out by the state. What we do in Pittsburgh should be no different than what you do here in Thomasville. You get me?"

Andy frowned. "I don't get why you're so mad about this. You always this grumpy?"

Cassie raised her eyebrows. "He is."

"I'll tell you why I'm feeling a little cranky around the subject of Macy Chandler. I had the same man and his son in my interview room this morning that you did a couple of months back. There's been a ransom demand and I've got a bloodied scarf and a watch that have been positively identified as belonging to the woman. And now, because you guys 'do what you do,' the woman has been gone for four months." The words rang with anger and sarcasm.

Andy shot Hunter a look and then turned his head back towards Grady, "Four months? I didn't have access to that information. There was no ransom demand when he came here." Andy's face furrowed defensively as he glanced up at Hunter, who hadn't left his post against the wall of the conference room.

Hunter shook his head no. "I agree with Andy. We didn't have any of that information."

Grady balled his hands into fists, staying at the far side of the room. He didn't trust himself if he got closer to the detectives and what he might do. He glared at Hunter, feeling like a fighter before a brawl began. "You always agree with Andy, Detective Franco? Are you that kinda guy? The one that just does what he's told?" He shoved the file back toward the other end of the table.

Cassie shot up out of her seat. "Grady, I think it's time we get going. Clearly, these guys don't have any information on this case." She glanced at the Thomasville detectives. "If you don't mind, I'd appreciate a copy of your file."

Andy shrugged, still not moving from his position at the far end of the table, "Do you want us to follow up on the information? I mean, now that there's more to it..."

"No, don't bother," Grady grunted, walking out of the room. "Cassie, I'll be in the car. I need some air."

Andy yelled behind him, his voice dripping with sarcasm. "Nice to meet you, Max!"

18

By the time Cassie made it out to the car, Grady had cooled off a little bit. He'd been sitting with the driver's side window halfway open, sucking in the cold air, watching the snow accumulate on the edge of the window, trying to calm the rush of emotions in his gut. He couldn't stand it when people didn't do their job.

He blew out a breath as he saw Cassie stride out of the Thomasville police station, her head down against the wind and the snow, trotting the last few steps to get to the car. There was a blast of cold air that filled the interior of the vehicle as she opened her door and then closed it again, settling herself on the seat, putting a manila file on the dashboard. Reaching for her seatbelt, she glanced at Grady. "How about if we get some heat going in here? This is like sitting in an icebox."

Grady grunted, grudgingly rolling up his window as he watched Cassie adjust the heat. As he pulled away from the front of the Thomasville police station, Grady could have almost sworn he saw Detective Andy Bennett leering at him from one of the windows. Grady gritted his teeth. Andy Bennett may have won the first battle, but he wasn't going to win the war.

As the car rounded the corner away from the Thomasville municipal buildings, Cassie reprogrammed the GPS to take them back to Pittsburgh. She settled in her seat, unbuttoning her coat and leaning back. "Well, that was interesting."

"I hate it when people call me Max," Grady grunted.

"That is your name."

"No, that was my father's name," Grady said firmly.

Cassie quickly changed the subject. "Hunter ended up giving me a copy of the notes from the initial interview they had with Noah Chandler, plus both of their business cards in case we need to follow up."

"I'm sure that won't be necessary," Grady scoffed, staring straight ahead at the road. There was no way somebody as inept as Detective Andy Bennett or Hunter Franco would be touching any work that Grady was involved in.

"They seemed nice enough to me. Maybe they really didn't have any inkling that Macy was actually gone." Cassie shrugged. "What are we going to do about the case, Grady? Remember, Williams wants us to kick it back to Thomasville."

Grady shook his head. "Turn it over to those two knuckleheads? Are you kidding me? Williams just wants his desk clear. That's all. If I had to guess, Andy Bennett is probably less than a year from retirement, probably has some plans for what he's doing after already..."

"He did invite me to stop by his food truck..." Cassie smiled weakly.

"And Hunter Franco is as green as any detective I've ever seen. If I had to guess, he probably spent less than a year on the road and got promoted quickly because he was the only one available to fill Andy's spot when he retires."

Cassie shrugged. "I don't know, Grady. All I want to know is what we're going to do about the case."

Grady paused for a moment, staring out ahead of the car, watching the snow gather on the side of the road. “I don’t care what Williams says. We're taking it.”

19

Detective Hunter Franco had indigestion, and it wasn't from anything he'd eaten.

As he watched the black sedan that carried the two detectives from Pittsburgh drive away, their car quickly obscured by the squalls of snow blowing overhead, he swallowed, chasing the bile at the back of his throat. "Watch and learn, watch and learn," Andy had said to him over and over again.

Hunter had watched, and from his perspective he'd been given a clinic on exactly what not to do.

From what he could tell, Detectives Grady and Reynolds from Pittsburgh had come looking for their help. Detective Grady had clearly seen a lot. That was obvious from his serious expression to his dark hair with the slightly gray temples, and his nearly immediate frustration with Detective Bennett. It didn't help that Andy had insisted on calling him Max, something Grady hated, although he didn't know that until Cassie told him after their meeting. She didn't fill in the blank as to why, but it didn't really matter. The fact that Andy kept leaning on Max's first name didn't make the meeting go any better.

In fact, it probably couldn't have gone worse.

As the sedan pulled away, Andy nodded at Hunter. "Those big city cops, they always feel like they know everything. You can take that file and throw it in the shredder. If they come back, there won't be any paperwork for them to reference." Andy said, walking to his office in a huff.

Hunter knew what Andy would do now. He would sit in his office playing on his phone for the next couple hours, go out for a late lunch, come back to the office for another couple of hours, using the browser on the department's computer to research recipes and locations for the food truck he was building in his garage for after his retirement. At the end of his shift, he would stand up, take a thick black magic marker and cross off one more day closer to retirement. The calendar in his office was numbered like an Advent calendar counting down the days before Christmas. Then, Andy would surge out the door like a raging bull at one minute before four o'clock giving Becky a brief wave as he left.

Hunter stood near his desk, watching as Andy lumbered his way back to his office mumbling about the meeting they'd had with Grady and Reynolds under his breath. Hunter waited for a second as the door closed to Andy's office. With their chief out on a medical leave, nothing was getting done.

Nothing.

Hunter looked at the file in his hand and took two steps towards the shredder, then stopped. Grady's words hung in his head. Hunter's imagination ran wild, thinking about the man and his son that had shown up at Pittsburgh's police department that morning, distraught about their wife and mom. Hunter had a brief memory of the man, his brown hair hanging over his forehead, his expression tight and pained as he explained to them that he couldn't find his wife. Noah Chandler had never come back after that day. Until that morning,

Hunter had totally forgotten about the case. A knot formed in his gut. What was he doing?

Hunter glanced down at the manila folder in his hand. If he shredded the document inside, there would be no official record of Noah Chandler's original report to the Thomasville Police Department. There'd be no paper trail other than the copy of the sketchy notes Andy had taken during their initial meeting with Noah Chandler two months before.

Hunter licked his lips, glancing down at the manila file folder again. Andy might be ready to hang it up, but Hunter wasn't. Not by a long shot. He was just getting started. He might as well start with the Chandler case and handle it right.

By the time he got back to his desk, Hunter had fairly assumed that Reynolds and Grady had figured out the situation in Thomasville. Andy had all the hallmarks of someone who was ready to retire, the surrendered posture, the angry look on his face, as though every question was an imposition, the slight bulge of his belly over the belt of his pants, no longer worried about department physical fitness standards or being able to run a perp down as they sprinted across the street.

Detective Andy Bennett was a man who had already given up.

But Hunter hadn't.

Sitting down at his desk, Hunter wondered if his greenness showed. He hadn't even bothered to sit down, almost like he was a butler waiting to execute every wish of the seasoned detectives who'd been seated around the table. He shook his head to himself. Never again would he do that. From now on, he'd take a seat at the table. He'd earned his place.

After getting a criminal justice degree from the University of Pittsburgh, with a minor in German, Hunter had paid his own way to go through the police academy, spending six months learning weapons skills, legal terms, proper arrest and interview techniques, and even going through a massive obstacle course that included ropes and walls in record time.

Thomasville had been the first department to offer him a full-time position so he'd taken it, happy to have the steady pay and benefits even if it was a smaller department. He'd told himself it was an opportunity for him to learn at a slower pace, to not be thrown to the wolves like he might be in a bigger department, like Pittsburgh.

Now he wondered if his assessment had been wrong.

Based on Grady's and Reynolds's reactions to Andy's decision-making, they clearly hadn't agreed with the way that Andy had handled the Noah Chandler interview. Hunter shook his head. He knew better. He should have at least filed a report, gotten something official into their system in case anyone came looking. And they had. To Grady and Reynolds, Hunter was sure he and Andy looked lazy, like a bunch of hacks, not concerned for the people that came into the building. That wasn't who Hunter was. Andy might have given up, but Hunter was just getting started.

Logging into his computer, Hunter pulled up an online report form and opened the file they had on Noah Chandler and his missing wife, Macy. "Better late than never," he muttered under his breath. He hoped that was the case.

Hunter spent the next few minutes filling in the blanks as best he could, glancing at Andy's door from around the edge of his computer monitor. As he copied the information into the computer, he wondered about Macy Chandler. Questions started to roll through his mind like waves. Was she really missing? Grady and Reynolds had mentioned she'd been gone for four months. How was that even possible?

A knot formed in Hunter's stomach, the details of the day surfacing in his mind as he typed. Hunter remembered the faraway look Noah had on his face when he was unable to answer Andy's questions and the shrug he'd gotten from Andy as soon as Noah walked out the door. "His wife probably left him and the poor guy has no idea," Hunter remembered Andy saying as he retreated to his office for another round of recipe research.

But if what Grady and Reynolds had said was true, then Macy Chandler might be in real danger.

The two detectives from Pittsburgh had mentioned a ransom demand and a bloodied scarf and watch, but hadn't said anything more than that. Hunter's natural curiosity was piqued. He'd been the kind of kid who would stumble onto something interesting and then read and research everything he could about it. His mom and dad had both been teachers, so as much as they let him use the computer when he was growing up, they forced him to read books too. Real books. Hunter remembered an entire summer where he'd gotten fascinated by IndyCar racing. He couldn't have been more than about ten years old. He and his mom spent that entire summer walking back and forth to the Thomasville library, getting stacks of books they dragged home in a backpack, Hunter sprawled out on the floor of his bedroom, flipping through the pages of the tattered books, reading about drivers like Mario Andretti and Bobby Unser, reading stories about the history of the race tracks and the way the cars were developed. As his research expanded, he learned how other legendary drivers like Carroll Shelby and Bob Bondurant had helped develop speed and traction, some of them even losing their lives on the test track. By the end of that summer, Hunter's curiosity led him into science and physics as well. His parents were thrilled at his interest. What would they think now of the way he'd mishandled the case? Hunter swallowed, a lump in his throat.

He felt that same itch now, only it was slanted toward the case that was evolving right in front of him, the one of a missing, now kidnapped woman, Macy Chandler, who'd been gone, as best he could tell, for four months. Four cold months.

As Hunter finished the report, he checked off the box that it was to be entered in their system as information only, not actionable. As much as he felt strongly about trying to help, he wasn't in a position to cross Detective Bennett, at least not while their chief was out on medical leave. The last thing Hunter wanted to do was get caught in Andy Bennett's crosshairs. The guy was grumpy enough. Hunter didn't need to make his training with Andy any worse than it already was, especially if it meant that it might hamper his ability to take over as the next detective for Thomasville PD.

He glanced towards the door, to where Reynolds and Grady had left a short time before. Grady was rough around the edges, that was for sure, but something in Hunter knew that Detective Max Grady had seen his fair share of action and his fair share of cases.

Something in him knew that if Max Grady was concerned about Macy Chandler, then he should be too.

20

"Where to now, Grady?" Cassie said, speaking as she chewed a bite of a chicken wrap they'd gotten from a fast-food place on the way back from Thomasville to Pittsburgh.

Grady shoved a few french fries in his mouth as he drove, chewing slowly. The road conditions had improved only slightly since their trip to Thomasville. At least on the way home, it seemed as though the Pennsylvania State Road Department had finally managed to get their trucks filled up with salt and hit the interstates, scraping the slush and snow mix off the freeway coating it with a heavy crust of salt that Grady knew would leave white marks all over his black sedan by the time they got back to the office. It was too early for this much snow, he thought, not yet quite replying to Cassie's question.

Grady glanced over at her. She was perched on the edge of the passenger seat closest to the window, her thin frame curled up near the door, her long fingers wrapped around the filmy waxed paper the chicken wrap had come in. He shook his head a little. Cassie always ordered the same thing whenever they got take-out — some variety of chicken and vegetables. One time, he tried to get her to eat a cheeseburger with him. She complained that the heavy food made her groggy and bloated. She seemed to have a fondness for vegetables, one that Grady didn't share.

Grady shoved a few more french fries into his mouth and took a sip of the syrupy soda that had come with his meal. "I say we go to the Chandler house. Let's take the notes those morons from Thomasville PD gave us and go at Noah Chandler again. Let's see if there's any inconsistency in his story."

Cassie shot him a look. "You think he's lying?"

Grady shrugged. "Someone is or we don't have the full picture yet. This whole thing doesn't feel right. If there was an actual case here, why didn't the Thomasville guys do anything about it?"

Cassie rolled her eyes. "I think you know the answer to that question."

Grady nodded, keeping his eyes on the road. "Yeah, clearly they are inept at best, lazy at worst. But, as much as I wanted to rip Andy Bennett's head off his shoulders, if Noah Chandler didn't give them anything to work from, then it's kinda hard to blame Andy and Hunter for not taking action."

"Yeah, but they should've at least filed a formal report. I mean, a missing person is no joke." Cassie shifted in her seat, grimacing. "I can't believe you're defending these guys?"

Grady bristled, raising his eyebrows. "Oh, believe me, I'm not. That Andy Bennett is the worst kind of cop. There's a little part of me that feels bad for the other guy."

"Hunter."

"Yeah, Hunter. He's clearly being groomed to take over Andy's spot. He's gonna learn a lot of bad habits in the process. But, no matter how bad their police work is, the reality is we still have a missing woman. The initial notes Hunter gave you might have something in it that helps us with this case."

"Honestly, I already looked at them. There's not much there." Cassie glanced Grady's direction. "You're thinking the next step is to go see the Chandlers in their natural habitat?"

Grady raised his eyebrows. Sometimes the way that Cassie phrased things almost made him laugh. Almost. "Yeah. In their natural habitat. I like that. Let's go see if visiting their house gives us any different information."

An hour later, after navigating a few slippery back roads, Grady pulled the salt and slush covered black sedan up the driveway at the Chandler household. As the wipers pushed the flakes of snow off the windshield, he stared at the house.

The Chandler's lived on the outskirts of Pittsburgh. A couple more miles to the west and they would have been in a completely different jurisdiction and they would have been someone else's problem. As it was, the area of Pittsburgh they lived in was far different than the downtown version where the police headquarters was. Grady looked around him before getting out. The development where the Chandlers lived had wide lots and mature trees in it, clearly built decades before. The house itself was well maintained, an old farm style, two-story home, white with black shutters around each window and a covered front porch that looked like it had been added on relatively recently. The way the exterior looked reminded Grady of a home remodeling television show. The driveway held two cars, an SUV and an older sedan. It certainly wasn't the way he was raised, but he had no feelings about it. His history was just that. History.

Grady parked right behind them, blocking both cars in case anyone decided they wanted to make a hasty retreat. Grady had questions and he needed answers. Leaving before he got them wasn't an option.

Getting out of the car, Grady realized the weather had improved, if only slightly. What had been a nearly constant snowfall a few hours earlier had changed to a few occasional flakes here and there, a mist of freezing rain dropping down over the area. The clouds had thinned as well, the heavy cover lifting leaving behind a thin gray haze obscuring the sun. Grady thought back to the weather report he'd seen earlier. The snow would be on and off for the next few days, the precipitation reminding everyone that the nice weather was always punctuated by at least a few months of dreary weather in anticipation for the explosion of color in the spring. Grady didn't mind. He liked the change of seasons. The weather wasn't something he could change and the gray usually matched his mood.

Making his way up the front walk, Grady led, leaving fresh slushy footprints on the unsheltered front walk. He stepped up on the front porch, followed by Cassie, faced with a red door decorated with a grapevine wreath filled with pink, yellow and blue flowers, much more appropriate for the spring than the snow they were facing right now. He imagined Macy Chandler outside switching over the front porch decor, hanging the wreath she probably made herself a few months before.

Grady pressed his lips together. If she was home now, she probably would be the kind that would change it out for something more appropriate for late fall. A lump formed in his throat.

But she wasn't...

Grady reached out a thick finger and pressed the white button for the doorbell, hearing it chime inside. A moment later, he heard footfalls approaching the door. He stood directly in front of the peephole, relatively sure that whoever was inside would look out before opening the door. A second later, he heard the locks on the door pop, the door swinging open with a slight creak. Noah Chandler stared at him. "Detective Grady? I didn't expect to see you again today."

Without asking, Grady stepped inside, wiping his shoes on the front mat. "We had some follow-up questions. Thought it would be easier to swing by your house then have you come the whole way back down to the station again." It was only a partial lie. It would be easier for Noah, but Grady had ulterior motives.

Noah closed the door behind him and Cassie. "Well, that was nice of you. Come in. Can I get you something to drink? Coffee? Tea?"

"No, thanks," Grady said, answering for both of them. "We won't be here that long."

Noah waved Grady and Cassie forward into the kitchen. On the way, they passed a dining room that had six high-back chairs and a dark mahogany table, a credenza jammed against the wall filled with shiny decorative dishes and crystal glasses. Grady narrowed his eyes, wondering how many times the Chandler family had actually sat in the dining room and shared a meal. If Macy was as free of a spirit as Noah said, it would be more likely they'd sit on the floor and eat than anything else.

Unlike the dining room, which looked barely used, the kitchen looked homey and lived in. The walls were painted a neutral beige, warm oak cabinets surrounding the space, a basket of apples and oranges on the center of the kitchen table, a stack of unopened mail on the edge of the kitchen counter. Noah held out his hand, "Please, sit down. Let me know if you'd change your mind about something to drink?"

"We will," Grady answered.

Grady settled himself down at the kitchen table and looked at Noah, starting the conversation before Noah sat down. "We're on our way back from Thomasville PD."

Noah raised his eyebrows, a hopeful expression on his face. "Oh? Did they have anything? Any news about my wife?"

"No. In fact, they didn't have much at all."

Cassie laid her hand on Grady's arm. "Now, Grady, that's not Noah's fault."

From Noah's shifting glance, Grady could tell he sensed the

tension between the two of them. "What do you mean? What's going on here?"

Grady crossed his arms in front of his chest. "It seems that the two detectives at Thomasville PD —"

"Bennett and Franco, right?"

Grady nodded. The two men must have made an impression of some sort on Noah. "I see you remember their names. Well, they didn't do anything with your case, to be blunt."

Noah ran his hand through his hair. "What does that mean exactly? I told them Macy was missing."

Grady gave a single nod. "They didn't believe you."

Noah jerked up from his chair, folding his arms across his chest. He started pacing. "This is what I was worried about. I told them I thought she was somewhere in Thomasville. That was two months ago. Why didn't they look for her then?"

Grady narrowed his eyes, watching Noah carefully. It wasn't what Noah said that interested him, it was his body language. Noah was clearly upset. It seemed as if he had made a good faith effort to report his wife being missing, but the ineptitude of the Thomasville detectives had slowed the case down to a grinding halt. Without the ransom demand, the bloody scarf and the broken watch, Grady might have felt the same way, but at least he would have followed up. He grimaced. While Macy might have just been missing before, now she was the victim of a kidnapping scheme. And that was a whole different thing.

"What I was wondering was if you could go through what led you to go to Thomasville in the first place for us again?" Grady said, pulling a notepad and pen out of his pocket.

Noah walked into the kitchen, pulling out a glass from the cabinet and filling it with water. He took a sip and then set the glass of water down next to the sink. "I mean, I already told you..."

"Tell us again. Any small detail might be helpful." Cassie encouraged.

"Okay," Noah sighed, turning to face them, leaning against the counter, his palms resting on the edge behind him. "As I said, I knew Macy was gonna go on one of her adventures and when she did, I heard from her a couple of times at the beginning. But after I hadn't heard from her for three or four weeks..."

"Which one is it? Three or four?" Grady pressed.

Noah shook his head. "I don't know. Everything's a blur right now."

"Keep going," Cassie nodded.

Grady frowned. They were working at cross purposes. Grady wanted Noah off balance so he'd expose himself. Cassie wanted him comfortable so he'd talk. They would have to have a discussion about that later.

Noah sighed. Grady tapped his fingers on the table. Cassie's tactics were getting him to relax. "Like I said, she'd been gone for a while. I wasn't all that alarmed until I hadn't heard from her for a few weeks. I tried texting her a bunch of times but she never responded. I didn't know if she had lost her cell phone. With the way she is, it's entirely possible she didn't remember my phone number. You know, everything's programmed into our cell phones now. It's not like it was when we were kids and we had to memorize our phone numbers. I thought if she lost it, then maybe she got a burner phone and I just didn't have the number. She does have my email address though. She could have reached out that way. She should have." There was a flash of anger on Noah's face that evaporated almost instantly. He took another sip of water. "I know it sounds crazy, but that's how Macy is. She's different." He shook his head, as if he was taking a minute to gather the thoughts in his mind, "Honestly, she should have been born in the sixties. She would've been a perfect hippie. Probably would have crisscrossed the country going to music festivals in some sort of a camper."

"Nice," Grady grunted. In actuality, it sounded perfectly

abysmal to him. Grady much preferred his own house and his own bed with his own things. No one would ever accuse him of being a free spirit, that was for sure. "Can you get back to the part about when you went to Thomasville?"

Noah nodded. "Yeah. Like I told you this morning, I went to Thomasville first because that's where Macy told me she was. She didn't give me a specific address or location, only said she was headed that way. I didn't really feel like I needed one as long as I heard her voice here and there. I've been so busy with work and the kids and all that..." His voice drifted off as if he was suddenly distracted by a long to-do list looming over his shoulder. "I mean, I guess I should have been more concerned. She is my wife, after all."

Grady watched as Noah's face paled. It was as if the realization that his wife had been kidnapped was landing on him in bits and pieces. He'd take a hit, recover, take another hit and then recover. From his years of being a detective, Grady knew that people processed information in different ways — two, primarily — either they took it all at full force immediately assuming their loved one had already died and they were preparing for the funeral, or it hit them like it was with Noah, in waves, the reality of their situation settling in on them like a slowly sinking ship. A creak here, a groan there, a gush of water, all of it piling up over hours or days when they finally realized the life they had was well and truly underwater.

Noah was, at that moment, a sinking ship, whether he realized it or not.

"What about your kids?" Cassie asked. "We met Gabe this morning, but you said you have a daughter too? Neither of them was concerned about their mom? Have they heard from her?"

Noah scratched his forehead. "Yeah, they've been concerned, but they know how she was. Kate especially has a good idea about her mom's personality. She's tuned up completely differently. Kate is a lot more cynical and analytical. She's twenty-one, so she sees things differently than Gabe does at twelve. But yes, they've both been concerned. They are the ones that finally told me I needed to come and see you."

Grady narrowed his eyes. "I thought the kidnapping call was what motivated you to show up at our office?" Grady waited for the answer, his heart skipping a beat. Was this the first hole in Noah Chandler's story? What was it that actually motivated Noah to come to the office and ask for their help?

"Oh yes, that, well... Right," Noah stammered, running his hand through his hair and starting to pace. "Yes, while I was planning on coming to see you anyway, the call I got this morning from the kidnappers, plus the scarf and the watch, kind of hurried the process along."

Grady frowned and glanced at Cassie, who raised her eyebrows. Grady turned back to Noah. "And if you hadn't gotten that call this morning, just out of curiosity, how long would you have waited?"

"I don't know..."

21

"You don't know?" Grady said gruffly. What Noah Chandler had just said was unthinkable in Grady's mind. Noah didn't know how long he'd wait to track down his wife? Grady stared at Noah. Cassie was silent, scribbling notes on her pad.

Noah stopped pacing and was looking at the floor, his face twisted in a mask of guilt and grief. What exactly Noah was looking at, Grady wasn't sure. What he was sure of was that at every turn, things got stranger. He was starting to lose his patience. "Man, this is your wife. You're telling me you weren't concerned? You can't tell me her disappearance just slipped your mind. She's already been gone for four months. How long were you going to wait? Six months? A year?"

"I... I don't know," Noah stammered.

Grady sucked in another breath, getting ready to pummel Noah with the reality about his missing wife when a young woman came into the kitchen from the other side of the house. Grady watched her as she hovered near the edge of the room, seemingly surprised there were visitors in the house. While there was a striking resemblance between Noah and the Chandler's youngest son, Gabe, Kate looked like she was cut from a different cloth. With dark hair and dark eyes, she was strikingly beautiful, almost exotic. She was wearing a pair of wide leg jeans, cut off to just above her ankles, the hems tattered, heavy black Doc Martin boots on her feet, an oversized sweatshirt covering her upper body. Her dark hair was long and shiny, her eyes intense and intelligent.

"You must be Kate," Cassie started.

Kate didn't move for a second, staring at the two detectives sitting at her kitchen table. "Who are you?"

Noah stepped forward and put a hand on her shoulder. "Honey, this is Detective Grady and Detective Reynolds. They're from the Pittsburgh Bureau of Police. They're gonna try to find Mom for us."

"Try to?" Kate shot a look at her father. "What are you talking about? Someone has to do something. You know she's been kidnapped, right?"

"Yeah, we heard that," Grady said.

Cassie extended her hand across the table, pointing at one of the chairs surrounding the table. "Kate, could you sit down and talk to us for a few minutes? We just have a few questions."

Grady watched. Kate glanced at Noah. He gave her a nod encouraging her to cooperate. Realistically, since Kate was an adult in the eyes of the law, Grady could've thrown her in the back of their sedan and dragged her downtown to question her in one of their dingy interrogation rooms, but there wasn't any need for that... At least not yet.

"So, Kate," Cassie started, the words coming out slowly. "We're just getting our bearings. We only met with your dad and your brother a few hours ago, so this case is new to us."

The compassion thing again, Grady thought to himself.

"From what we've gathered, your mom's been gone for a total of about four months. When was the last time you heard from her?"

Kate shrugged, looking at the top of the table, picking at the edge of the placemat in front of her. "I don't know. Probably a couple weeks after she left. I think she texted me to wish me good luck on some exam I was taking or something."

"You're a student at Bedford College where your mom works?" Cassie asked.

Barely making eye contact, Kate responded. "That's right."

"Your dad said you're an IT major?"

Kate pressed her thin lips together, nodding.

Cassie continued. "At what point did you start to get concerned about your mom's whereabouts?"

Grady watched as Kate's eyes shifted back and forth between the two of them. She glanced at her dad, but didn't say anything. Noah's face was blank. Something wasn't right. Grady looked at her. "Kate, if you know something, you need to tell us."

Grady's words must have shocked Kate out of her thoughts. She straightened up, her expression stony, "Know something? All I know is my mom is gone and my dad got some crazy call about a key this morning."

"You don't seem all that concerned about your mom." Grady stared at the young woman, his eyebrows furrowed. There was no emotion coming from Kate, no sadness, no fear — only anger.

Kate crossed her arms in front of her chest and leaned back in the chair, cocking her head to the side. "You do know my mom does this every year or so, right? She goes off on some expedition to find herself. She leaves all of us at home. I swear to God I think she's been gone more than she's been home in the last few years. For all I know, she could walk in the door any minute now, flowers woven into her hair, singing some song she made up. It's ludicrous."

Grady glanced at Noah. Although he couldn't be sure, he thought he saw a sheen of perspiration on Noah's forehead.

Noah looked down at his daughter, setting a hand on her shoulder. "Now, Katie, that isn't true. Your mom has always been here for you. She loves you!"

Katie spun in her chair, looking up at her father. "Dad, you know as well as I do that Mom's gone a lot. When she is here, she's not present. She tinkers around in her office or goes and plays in her garden, maybe makes dinner once in a while. That's it."

Noah turned away from his daughter. "Your mom is a good woman, Kate."

"Well, she's a horrible mother. I mean, look at Gabe. He's only twelve. She disappears on him and leaves us here to take care of everything. What am I supposed to do? I'm at school all the time. As far as I'm concerned, she might as well be dead!"

As soon as the words came out of her mouth, Kate shot up out of her seat and stormed out before Grady or Cassie could say anything. Noah looked at the floor for a second shaking his head and then looked at the two detectives. "I'm sorry about that. Katie's tuned up a little differently than Gabe. She has more of a temper. I have no idea where she got it from because her mom and I are pretty peaceful. But man, when Katie gets mad, she gets mad."

Cassie started to push her way up out of her chair. "I can go talk to her..."

Noah held up his hands. "I'd suggest you leave her alone. It's better if you don't. She needs time to cool off. She'll be okay in a couple of hours. Macy's disappearance has been harder on her than she lets on."

From the other side of the house, Grady heard the door slam as if someone had gone outside. A moment later he heard an engine start. Kate was leaving. He got up and walked to the front windows, seeing the small, worn sedan that was sitting in the front yard drive through the snow over the grass passing his car, bumping back up on the paved driveway, the tail spinning slightly as Kate hit the snow-covered road and sped away.

Grady went back into the kitchen. "She's gone."

After watching Kate make a hasty departure, Grady and Cassie asked Noah a few more questions, attempting to firm up the timeline around Macy's disappearance. As best they could tell, it looked like Macy had left sometime in late July. The family had heard from her until about the middle of the next month, at which point she'd gone dark. There'd been no news from her since. Then, based on the information they got from Noah, they went to Thomasville to report her missing in September. Two months had gone by since then.

As they were standing up to leave Noah's kitchen, Cassie looked at Noah. "One final question, Mr. Chandler? You said Macy is a professor at Bedford College?"

"That's right. She teaches literature."

"What did she do about her fall class load?"

Noah shook his head and blinked. "I asked about her fall classes when she was packing. She said it was handled. I figured she took a sabbatical or something." He put his palm on his forehead. "I've been so busy with work and Gabe. Honestly, I don't know."

Cassie and Grady thanked Noah for his time and headed out to the car. Inside, Cassie stared at Grady. "Was that strange or was that just me? Who leaves their family, disappears for months on end, and no one seems to blink an eye until there's a ransom demand? Definitely not the way I was raised."

"Definitely a ten on the strange meter. Your last question was good though."

Cassie smiled, giggling. "Gee, thanks! Does that mean we're gonna take a field trip to Bedford College now?"

"You've got that right."

22

Bedford College was a collection of small red brick buildings on the outskirts of Pittsburgh. Completely overshadowed by larger, more notable schools like the University of Pittsburgh and Carnegie Mellon University, Bedford College seemed comfortable with its identity as a small, local school.

True to its roots, the small college had been started in the late 1800s by the Bedford family, immigrants from England, who wanted to offer higher education to people in the Commonwealth of Pennsylvania. Over time, the college had withstood several world wars, numerous economic declines, nearly dozens of blizzards, protests, and even an occasional minor earthquake.

Grady found a spot for the sedan in one of the staff parking lots after winding his way through red brick buildings that looked nearly identical to each other. The parking lot was almost completely abandoned, the tracks of the vehicles leaving the parking lot on that snowy Friday afternoon covered over with a new layer of wet, slushy snow. From the glove compartment, Grady pulled a placard that read, "Emergency

Vehicle — Do Not Tow," and set it on the dashboard in case any overeager campus traffic monitor decided to target his vehicle for removal. That was the last thing he needed, he thought. It was bad enough to have to trudge around in the snow trying to figure out what happened to Macy Chandler, let alone have the hassle of dealing with the parking people on campus.

Once they got out of the car, Cassie pointed the way, using her phone's GPS to send them to the correct building. With all of them looking the same, Grady wasn't sure how the students discerned which building their classroom was in. He certainly couldn't, but then again maybe when they weren't in a shroud of snow, it would be easier.

The first thing Grady noticed when he stepped inside of the Baldwin building, the home of the English Department, was the smell. It was a rough combination of dusty books, which didn't seem to exactly match where they were given they were nowhere near the library according to Cassie's calculations, a concoction of perfume from passing students and burned coffee, leaving the building smelling strangely homey.

"The academic offices should be just up those steps," Cassie pointed, turning to her right.

Grady followed Cassie as they went to the second floor, their boots leaving a few wet footprints on the tile floor as they trudged up the tile-covered steps. Putting his hand on the stair rail, Grady realized the wood had been worn smooth by decades of students going to and from classes. How many generations had gone to Bedford College? How many of those students had sat under Macy Chandler's teaching? Where was she now?

That was the question he needed to answer.

The second floor of the Baldwin Building was a singular long hallway, wide and carpet covered, with a series of doors on either side of it. Staring down the length of the building, Grady noticed there was an opening on either side of the hallway about halfway down. Narrowing his eyes, he followed Cassie as they walked through a few clusters of students, their backpacks on their shoulders, hats pulled down around their ears, their shoulders already slumped against the storm outside even though they were still in the warmth of the building.

At the end of the hallway was Macy Chandler's office, or at least what was supposed to be, announced by a small black and white sign attached to the wall outside the door. The door was open. Grady followed Cassie inside. The first part of the office was what looked to be a reception area. There was a desk facing the open door with a computer monitor on it, an inbox at the corner, and an overfull cup of pens and pencils.

At the back of the office was another door, this one with another placard that read Macy's name once again. Grady looked at Cassie. "This must be for the receptionist or something." He twisted the knob for Macy's office. It was locked.

Before they could do anything else, an auburn-haired woman wearing a droopy dress over a pair of black leggings stuck her head in the doorway. "Can I help you?"

"We're looking for Macy Chandler. Is she here?" To Grady, the question seemed reasonable. Just because Macy hadn't been at home in four months didn't mean that she hadn't been at work. Stranger things had happened.

"Macy?" The woman shook her head. "She hasn't been here in months. She's out on medical leave."

"And who are you?" Grady pressed his lips together. They hadn't heard anything from Noah Chandler about Macy having a medical issue. His gut tightened. There was a lie somewhere in what was going on. He just had to find it.

"I'm Rachel, Dean Palmer's assistant. He runs this department. Who are you?" The words came out as a little bit of a challenge, the woman making it clear that Grady and Reynolds were on her turf.

"Detectives Grady and Reynolds. Pittsburgh police." Grady

pulled his coat aside showing his badge. "We need to talk to your boss. Is he around?"

The woman's face paled and then her cheeks reddened as if she had gotten her hand caught in the cookie jar. "Yes, yes of course. I think he's finishing a meeting. If you'll stay here, I'll bring him to you. His office is just down the hall."

As Rachel disappeared out of Macy's office, Grady lifted his chin towards Cassie. "Watch her." There was no telling what Rachel was doing. Given the fact the case was getting stranger by the moment, they needed to tighten things down. They'd let Kate go, but Grady wanted to make sure they had a chance to talk to Macy's boss.

A moment later, Cassie slipped back inside of Macy's office. "They're walking this way now. Rachel, or whatever her name is, is bringing some dude wearing white frames."

"On his glasses?" Grady frowned.

Cassie nodded, raising her eyebrows, a grin tugging at her cheek. "Yeah. They're in style right now. Maybe you should try it."

"Not a chance."

As described, a man wearing glasses with white frames, a pair of torn skinny jeans, an olive-green T-shirt, and a sport coat walked into Macy's office. He pressed his lips together looking at Grady and Cassie. "Hello," he said formally, "I'm Dean Rick Palmer, the head of the English department here at Bedford College. Rachel said you are detectives?"

Grady nodded. "Where's Macy Chandler?"

Cassie held her hand up, glaring at Grady. "Forgive me, we skipped the introductions. I'm Detective Reynolds, this is Detective Grady. Pittsburgh police. We've gotten a report that Macy Chandler is missing. We wanted to stop by, check her office, and speak to anyone who might have any information about her whereabouts. Are you her boss?"

Once again, Cassie's soft pedal approach interrupted getting to the point. Grady bristled, but kept his mouth shut.

"The police? I'm not sure why you're here," he scowled. "The last we heard, Macy was out on medical leave. We're expecting her back. Her assistant was working on her spring class schedule just this morning."

"And where is her assistant?" Cassie asked.

"Lola?" Rick Palmer glanced over at Rachel, whose face instantly appeared at the doorway, as if she had been listening outside the entire time.

"She left a few hours ago," Rachel nodded, a smug grin on her face. "Said she was taking the afternoon off."

Grady pulled the notepad out of his pocket. "Any idea where she was headed?"

"Some sort of cabin for the weekend. She didn't say where. We were talking outside when I was bringing lunch back in for Dean Palmer. It was snowing. She seemed like she was in a hurry. To be honest, I think she's got a boyfriend. She's been sneaking in and out of the office a lot over the last couple months," she said conspiratorially.

Grady furrowed his eyebrows. "Why is she on medical leave?"

Dean Palmer's eyes widened. "Because that's what the paperwork she gave us says." He glanced over his shoulder, looking at Rachel. "Can you go get those papers for me?"

While they were waiting, Grady walked over to Macy's office door tapping it with a single finger. "This is her office?"

"Yes," Dean Palmer said.

"We're going to need to get inside."

Dean Palmer reached into the pocket of his shredded jeans and pulled out a ring of keys, taking a couple steps toward the door. "I have a passkey for all the rooms on campus," he mumbled, fumbling with the lock on Macy's door. "This should open it, but if not, we'll have to call one of the maintenance staff."

As the door popped open, Grady stepped inside. At least they didn't have to get into an argument about search warrants. That was something.

A moment later, Rachel returned carrying a manila folder in her hand, extending it towards Cassie, peering into Macy's office as if she was looking for something. Absentmindedly, she handed the file to Cassie. "Here it is. Here's the paperwork for Macy's medical leave."

Grady stood just inside the doorway of Macy's office scanning what was in front of him. There was a wide wooden desk in front of an enormous window that looked out onto either a parking lot or a lawn area. With the snow, Grady couldn't tell which. On either side of the office were tall bookshelves packed with books that looked to be in no certain order. If Grady had to guess, Macy knew exactly where every volume was, the books filed in some order only she would know or understand. There were two chairs in front of Macy's desk. In Grady's mind, he played a scene where a student was sitting in front of the desk, notebook or laptop computer in front of them, talking to Macy Chandler about a project, or an essay, or an upcoming exam. Though he hadn't met Macy, the profile he had in his head was of someone who cared about other people, but not so much for social conventions, schedules, and the things that seemed normal to the rest of society.

Grady walked behind Macy's desk, sitting down in her chair, pulling open her drawers. Inside, there were sheaves of paper with notes scrawled on them, plus a stack of forms half filled out with the Bedford College logo on the top. Cassie came over to the desk, opening the file folder and setting it in front of Grady. "I just asked Dean Palmer. He said the paperwork seems to be in order."

Grady narrowed his eyes, cocking his head to the side.

Something didn't seem right. From Macy's drawer, he pulled out a requisition form on the top of the pile. Grady glanced from the medical leave paperwork back to the paperwork from Macy's desk.

He looked up at Cassie, his face stony, his gut in a knot. "They might look like they're in order, but she didn't sign this." He pointed to the page. "That's not her signature."

23

"What do you mean she didn't sign this paperwork?" Dean Palmer exclaimed, glancing over his shoulder at his assistant, Rachel, who shrugged, her face almost smiling, as if she was happily watching a soap opera unfold right in front of her.

"The signatures don't match," Grady grunted. He pointed to the two sheets of paper in front of him. They were close, but one of the signatures had letters that were rounded and more looped than the other. It was a fake and a poor one at that. "We're going to take these with us." Grady stood up from the desk, sliding the requisition form he'd found with Macy's signature on it next to the forged medical leave forms. He looked at Dean Palmer, whose mouth was hanging open as if he was in shock. "Where is Macy's assistant?"

Dean Palmer blinked. "Like we said, she left at lunchtime."

Cassie raised her eyebrows. "Is that normal?"

Grady already knew the answer, but he waited for Rick and Rachel to answer.

Dean Palmer threw his hands in the air, completely flustered by the question. "No, of course not. We expect all of our employees to work a full week unless they decide they're going to take vacation time." He looked over at Rachel as if he was trying to pass the buck. "Did she fill out a leave request in the online portal?"

"No? I don't know!" Rachel stammered. "It happened the way I told you. I saw her in the parking lot walking to her car. She had a bag with her. I didn't think to ask her about the paperwork. I just assumed she did what she was supposed to do."

Yeah, right, Grady thought. The dean and his assistant were both sporting flushed cheeks. Grady narrowed his eyes, thinking for a moment. He didn't think that they were actually involved in the disappearance of Macy Chandler, but they were certainly guilty of bad management. "I need contact information for the assistant. Her name, address, cell phone number, email — the works. Now."

Rachel ran out of the office and was back a second later holding a slip of paper in her hand. She practically threw it at Grady. On it was scrawled the name, Lola Harrison. "This is Lola's information. Do you want me to call you or something if she shows up?"

Cassie glanced back at Grady who didn't move. Nothing in him wanted to talk to Rachel again. She used too many words. It was sucking the life out of him. Grady didn't move. Cassie must have gotten the hint. From out of her pocket, Cassie handed Rachel one of her business cards. "Yes, feel free to give me a call if you think of anything else."

Dean Palmer stood in the office staring at Grady and Cassie as they left, his mouth hanging open. "What about Macy? Where is she?"

"That's what we're going to find out," Grady said in a gravelly voice as they walked away.

24

Grady didn't talk much on the way back to the department. They'd pretty much spent all day long trying to track down what they could on Macy Chandler. The lack of information made Grady feel like he was grasping at straws flying through the air during a hurricane. It was frustrating, to say the least.

By the time they got back to headquarters, the snow had let up, a slushy mix of half frozen ice and crusty flakes coating the ground. Trying to be a gentleman, Grady pulled up in front of the entrance to headquarters and let Cassie out. She protested for a minute, then must have seen the expression on his face. Although he was trying to be a gentleman, it was more that he was done talking for the day. She leaned back inside the car before slamming the door shut. "I'll let Williams know you're headed home," she said without asking.

Grady didn't answer, grateful he didn't have to explain himself. He just nodded.

After dropping off the salt-stained black sedan in the police-owned parking lot, Grady walked straight to his personal vehicle. He slid inside the black SUV, turning the defroster on full blast and running the wipers, seeing the wet slush slide off the side of the windshield, the heat from the engine quickly melting what was left of the slushy mix on the hood of his car. He knew he should probably have taken the keys for the black sedan back upstairs in case someone on another shift needed to use it, but he didn't care. There were other cars in the lot. He wanted to get home.

As he drove, questions from the day ran through his mind. There were gaps in the story to be sure. Macy Chandler was missing or kidnapped or something. What had happened exactly, he had no idea. The timing was problematic. Macy had been gone for four months. The case was a lot more like a cold case than anything else. Time wasn't on their side, especially now that there was a ransom demand. There was no way to tell if Macy had been beaten, injured, starved or tortured. The sheer fact that so much time had gone by made the case critical in Grady's eyes.

The thing he really couldn't understand was the lackadaisical attitude of the officers in Thomasville. Were they lazy, ill-equipped or perhaps they just didn't care? Sure, Thomasville was known to have a transient population with vacationers and summer residents, but there had to be a core of people in the community that were worth taking care of. And it didn't matter whether or not the people in the township were transient. The job of a police officer was to take care of the people in front of him — protect them, serve them, or conversely, protect the rest of the community from them.

Walking into the kitchen at his house, Grady tossed the keys on the counter, rubbed his forehead and leaned his palms against the edge of the counter, closing his eyes for a second. The same image kept popping up in his head over and over again of the police officer that had dragged him away from his dad's dead body. Something about this case was bringing up memories, and a lot of bad ones.

It had been so many years since he pulled the trigger and killed his father that much of the actual incident was a blur, washed away by time and space, other less traumatic memories softening the edges of that day though it still lingered, like indigestion the morning after Thanksgiving. Grady remembered cradling his left arm against his body, watching his father continue to torment his brother and his mother, feeling a surge of pain from the cracked bones in his arms as he sprawled on the floor in his parent's bedroom. He remembered the feel of the cool metal against his hand as he pulled the pistol out of the drawer of his father's nightstand. All he wanted was his father to stop. He remembered opening his mouth to say something, the gun extended out in front of him. And he remembered the noise, the sound of the gunshots hitting his father square in the chest as his father turned toward him, his eyes black with rage. His last memory was of a scream from his mom and a guttural yell from his brother bouncing off the ceiling, just after the shots.

Then there was a black hole in his memory.

What happened next, he couldn't remember. And although he'd tried to get his mother, Ann, to talk about it multiple times when he visited her, to fill in the pieces of the puzzle he couldn't remember, she wouldn't. Without fail, every single time she simply looked away and took another long drag on the cigarettes she chain smoked, her hands still shaky after all these years any time Grady mentioned his father. Grady didn't mention it anymore.

What he did remember was an older man wearing a suit and tie, a shiny badge hanging around his neck calling to him, as he sat crumpled on the floor of the bedroom. "Max? Max? Everything's okay. You are all right."

Grady remembered looking up at the detective, the man's face calm and gentle. "But I..."

The man shook his head, holding his hand out toward Max.

"We don't need to talk about that now. What I need you to do is leave the gun on the ground, grab my hand and walk out of this room with me. Okay? Your mom and brother are outside. I bet you want to see them."

Grady remembered looking down and seeing the gun in his right hand resting on the ground, his hand limp but his index finger still looped around the trigger. He looked up at the man, blinking quickly, letting go of the gun. "I can't use my left arm. I think it's broken..."

The detective looked at him nodding. "That's okay. We can get that fixed. Just listen to my voice. I need you to give me your hand, stand up, and walk out of this room." The man held out his hand again. Max remembered taking it, stepping over his father's dead body and walking away.

To this day, Max wondered if that moment was the one where he decided to become a police officer.

From the freezer, Grady pulled out a frozen dinner, piercing the plastic with a fork from the drawer and throwing it in the microwave as he walked to the bedroom. He tugged at his tie, taking it off, quickly changing into a T-shirt and a pair of sweatpants, padding back into the kitchen, barefoot by the time the microwave beeped. He slid the black tray out of the microwave, cursing under his breath. The plastic was hot. He slid the black microwavable tray onto a paper plate and carried the whole mess into the family room with him, popping on the television.

There was a basketball game on TV. Grady didn't really watch, not even paying attention to who was playing. He shoved large bites of food in his mouth and swallowed mostly without chewing, the Salisbury steak, mashed potatoes, and vegetables all somehow having the same mushy consistency. The entire time, questions ran through his mind.

There was one fact about the Macy Chandler case he just couldn't process. Why had it taken four months for her family to come forward? It was unthinkable in his mind. There was no doubt that valuable time had been lost. Macy's trail was completely cold.

A four-month absence led to a whole other series of questions — why had the kidnappers waited until that very moment to issue a ransom demand? How long had they held Macy? Why hadn't they reached out sooner? And the key — that was another mystery entirely. Noah Chandler didn't seem to know what key they were referring to. Was that actually true, or was he hiding something?

Grady tossed the empty plate down on the coffee table, put his feet up and grabbed the clicker, scrolling through the channels. He needed to stop thinking and get some sleep.

If Macy Chandler had been gone for four months, one more day wouldn't hurt.

Blinking, a chill ran down Grady's spine. Or would it?

25

By four o'clock in the morning, Grady had been up and down out of bed more times than he could count. He'd tried sleeping on the couch which didn't work, transferred to the bed, went back to the couch, and finally went back to bed where he guessed he got about an hour of sleep. Something about the case wasn't sitting right with him. There were too many unanswered questions, the tangle of them getting knotted in his mind as he tried to sleep, the casual attitude of the Thomasville officers and the lagging timeline plaguing him.

By seven AM, Grady had gotten out of bed, ran two miles on his treadmill, taken a shower, and eaten a bowl of cereal. He looked out the window. The snow had started again. It wasn't the same fat snow as the day before, but smaller crystalline flakes floating down from the sky. It looked like he was living in a life-sized snow globe. As he got in his black SUV, ready to go to headquarters wanting to take another look at the notes they'd gotten from Thomasville, he decided to make a detour first.

The Oakview Center mental health facility had been his brother Ben's home for the majority of his life. Grady pulled up in front of the doors, grabbed a parking spot and walked inside, feeling the warmth of the heat soaking through his clothes. The nurse behind the desk, a woman named Darlene, waved at Grady. "Hey! You're here early today. I think Ben just finished breakfast. If I had to guess, he's probably in the game room."

Grady nodded. "Thanks. I know the way."

After the night Grady had killed his father, Ben's mental condition had declined precipitously. He went from speaking to not speaking and began having violent outbursts that reminded Max of the way his father had treated the family. Though he had the mental capacity of a five-year-old, at that time, Ben already had the strength of a full-grown man without the control to know when to use it or not. After two months of battling with Ben pretty much every single day and their mother ending up in the hospital with a black eye and a fracture to her eye socket, the county interceded, removing Ben from their house, placing him in the Oakview Center for intensive care. At the time it happened, Grady felt like it was a tearing away, yet another part of his family destroyed by violence. But over the years he'd come to understand that keeping Ben at a facility that could treat him, care for him, and keep him safe was probably for the best.

The game room at Oakview was spacious, flanked by a long wall of windows that filled one side, multiple tables set up around the room as well as a spot for watching television at the far end. Grady walked in, stopping in the doorway, and looking for Ben. His brother was at a table in the corner, staring at the surface, his tongue sticking out, his fingers moving slowly across the table. In his quarterly meetings with the psychologist who managed Ben's care, ones that their mom refused to go to, she would say how Ben had learned to enjoy putting together puzzles. They'd even managed to get him into their work program, which was housed at the back of the facility, assembling bags of parts for a plumbing manufacturing company that needed some extra hands.

Grady strode over to the table, pulled off his coat and draped it across the back of one of the chairs. He put his hand on Ben's back and kissed the top of his older brother's head before sitting down. "Hey, buddy. How you doing?"

Ben didn't say anything, just giving Grady a lopsided smile and pointing to the puzzle. His verbal skills had returned after three years of speech therapy after the accident, but had never returned to where they were. Ben only spoke rarely and even then it was only one-word sentences. It was yet something else their father had stolen from them.

Grady looked down at the puzzle. It was a garden scene with flowers in a million different colors popping off the pieces. Ben proudly pointed to the box lid which was standing up on its end so he could look at the picture. "Pretty!"

Grady nodded. "Yes. It is pretty. How've you been? Are you enjoying work?"

Ben made eye contact briefly, gave a few bobs of his head and then stared back at the top of the table again. He pointed to a piece that was closer to Grady. Grady picked it up and handed it to his brother, watching as Ben carefully fitted it to the edge of the puzzle where he was working. Somehow, Ben had found peace in sitting and staring at the picture, trying to put things that were torn apart back together again.

It occurred to Grady that perhaps he was doing the same thing. Even though his own family had been shattered by tragedy, it was his job to put the Chandler family back together again.

A couple of minutes passed and a male nurse, a tall man with dark curly hair and matching skin, wearing a pair of green scrubs, approached the table. "Hey, Ben! How you doing today? You know what? It's time to go to work!" he said enthusiastically.

Grady looked up at the man, whose name badge read Marcus. "I thought they were only working in the afternoons?"

"That's right, but we have a special party this afternoon for all of our residents. We're gonna get our work done this morning, have lunch, and then spend the afternoon having fun."

Hearing the word fun, Ben scrambled up from the chair, wrapped one arm awkwardly around Grady's neck in a half hug and charged down the hallway, Marcus trailing behind, leaving Grady by himself in the game room. Silence settled over the empty space. He looked out the window for a moment, staring at the melting snow outside.

Grady sighed, stood up and put on his coat. He wondered what Macy Chandler was thinking at that moment. Was she terrified? Lonely? Despondent? Four months was a long time. Longer than Grady could imagine. Grady frowned, walking toward the front door. Ben wasn't the only one who needed to put pieces together. Grady had a set of his own to wrestle with.

26

Macy started off her day the same way she started off all of them since she'd been locked up. She knocked quietly on the door and waited for someone to let her out so she could use the bathroom. She'd learned to not drink too much. There was no telling how long it would take someone to get to her. Her captors had given her a bucket and a roll of toilet paper in case of an emergency, but she preferred not to use it, the idea of staying in the small room so close to her own excrement turning her stomach.

After Macy went to the bathroom and brushed her teeth, Lola brought breakfast, a single piece of toast and a glass of lukewarm orange juice. Macy hadn't had coffee in months, no pizza or pasta either. But she missed candy the most, some days wishing for nothing more than a few of the miniature chocolate bars to enjoy. Showers were irregular and she wore the same outfit sometimes for an entire week. Macy tried to tell herself that it was like camping. She was roughing it for a little while. Eventually, somehow things would end — either they would let her go, she would escape, someone would rescue her or, she'd die in the process. There weren't that many options.

A lump formed in her throat as she tried to chew the dry bread. She pushed it away after only taking a few bites. She glanced at it, knowing she needed to eat to keep up her strength but having no desire to do so. Macy sighed. Based on the way her clothes were hanging on her she knew she'd lost weight, but she didn't have any appetite, and the food they offered her wasn't exactly gourmet. Macy stood up to get her journal, hoping that putting pen to paper would help smooth out the rough edges of her emotions. She had no idea how she was going to survive another day locked in the room. Staring out the small window for a moment, she thought about Dario. He kept asking her about a key over and over again with an ever-growing anger and intensity. There was no request for money, just a key that he insisted she had. He promised to let her go if she gave it to him. She'd racked her brain, but she didn't know anything about it.

Leaning over the desk, she felt something shift at the back of her neck. The cross necklace that she'd worn since she was a teenager fell off and hit the floor. Quickly grabbing at it, and glancing at the door, hoping the noise of it falling didn't alert her captors, Macy scooped it up, holding it in her hand.

The cross was hammered silver strung on a black cord. Macy frowned, looking at it. The cord had frayed at the end near the clasp and had come off. She flipped the pendant over in her hands a couple times, staring at the design. She never took it off — not on the day she was married, not on the day she'd had Kate and not on the day she'd had Gabe. It was part of her, something she wore no matter what.

Macy rubbed the metal between her fingers, remembering the day her mother gave her the pendant. She'd turned sixteen years old. She was living in Texas with her family, a bright sunny day in June. It was her birthday. Her mother came to her room, quietly knocking on the door and sitting next to Macy on her bed. "I have a special gift for you, one that you must promise me you'll never take off. It represents your future."

Macy opened up a small red velvet box to find the hammered cross pendant strung on a black cord. It was beautiful.

Her mom had hung it around Macy's neck and then looked at her sternly. "You must promise me you will always wear this. You can't give it to anyone else and you can't throw it away. It must stay with you. Do you understand me?" Her mom had passed the year after, her warning lingering in Macy's mind. Why her mother had been so stern, Macy didn't know.

Staring at the pendant now, Macy held it in the palm of her hand, flipping it over. She looped a finger in one of the gaps in the design and then ran her fingers around the edge of it again, her finger hooking onto the bottom of it. As she pulled her finger away, it got caught. She felt a pop, as though something had given way. For a moment, she was concerned that the pendant itself had cracked as it had fallen off her neck, the old metal brittle from years of wear.

Staring at it, Macy realized that the bottom section of the cross had separated from the circle that it was held in. Macy cocked her head to the side, narrowing her eyes. She used her fingers to pinch at the bottom of it and gave it a tug. As she did, the entire bottom of the pendant came undone, revealing a metal section that was cut like a key.

Macy's heart started to pound in her chest. Was this the key Dario had asked her about? She looked over her shoulder toward the door and then quickly went and sat on the bed, her back to it in case Lola should walk in unexpectedly. Macy turned the key over and over in her hand, her breath catching in her throat. Was this what Dario had wanted? Had she been wearing it all along? Macy stared at the key hidden in the palm of her hand. It was engraved with an address and numbers on it, barely visible. She stood up, walking to the window, hoping that the bright daylight would help her see exactly what was on it. It read, "1787 E. Diamond Hill Road, Fort Worth." There was a set of numbers listed after it — 73521.

Macy stared at the key in the pendant for the longest time. It had to be why her mother had said not to take it off. But what was in Fort Worth?

Her stomach tightened into a knot realizing she'd had what her captors wanted on her the entire time she'd been trapped, Macy snapped the pendant back together again, making sure it was secure, fixed the cord for the pendant and tied it back around her neck, never taking her eye off the door. Dario had asked her over and over again about a key. She pressed her lips together. She'd had no idea what he'd been talking about.

Until now...

27

Macy spent the next hour pacing back and forth in the cramped room where she was being held, thinking, her breath shallow. A limited number of options and a whole host of questions rolled through her mind, as they had for months. If Lola was the only one at the cabin at the moment, Macy could ask to go to the bathroom, push her way past Lola and try to run out into the woods, but the reality was she had no car and based on where she thought she was at Thomasville Lake, it could be miles in the bad weather before she might find anyone that could help her, miles that Dario would have a chance to catch up to her.

Worse yet, in the cold she'd have a limited amount of time. She had no boots and no coat. Hypothermia would be a real possibility. Macy shivered. Was it worth the risk? She couldn't stay trapped forever. Her sanity was dwindling away day by day. Macy grimaced. Though Dario hadn't laid a hand on her as of yet, she wouldn't put it past him. She could almost feel his thick hands grabbing at her, dragging her back to the cabin if she tried to escape. Her body quivered as she reached up and touched the spot on the side of her head where he'd hit her and knocked her out cold when he'd abducted her. If he was capable of that, she had no idea what else he was capable of. Her imagination ran wild. It was more. Much more.

She looked around the room. She had no access to technology. No way to get a message to her family.

Or did she?

Macy stopped in the center of the room, staring at the ceiling, chewing her lip. She went to her notebook and scrawled a quick note and then knocked on the door. A moment later, Lola appeared, the lock from the outside of the door clicking open.

"Are you okay? Do you need to use the bathroom again?"

Macy waved Lola inside of the room. Lola frowned, but complied, closing the door behind her. At first, when Macy had been taken, their interactions had been very superficial, focused on what Macy needed at that moment — a new roll of toilet paper in the bathroom, a box of tissues, a drink of water — but as time had gone on, the normal relationship between Macy and Lola, the one they'd had before she'd been abducted, resurfaced, albeit in a somewhat awkward form. Somewhere underneath the circumstances, they were still friends, or at least Macy was banking on that fact.

Macy took a deep breath, trying to calm the butterflies in her stomach. She had to be careful with the words she used next. She'd heard Dario and Lola fighting on more than one occasion through the vents in the floor. If she pressed her ear down to it, she was able to make out most of what they were saying, eavesdropping on their conversations. It was clear, based on what she'd heard Lola say, that she wasn't one hundred percent in agreement with Dario's plan, whatever that was.

"Lola, I have to get out of here. I can't do this for one more day." Macy reached out and grabbed both of Lola's hands. Lola looked away.

"I know, Macy. I know how hard this is for you, but there's nothing I can do. Dario is in charge."

"Please, Lola? Is he even here right now? I've been locked up here for months. All you have to do is put me in your car and drive me into town. Just drop me off somewhere. You can come back to the cabin and lock the door or tell Dario I managed to escape somehow. I promise I'll never tell anyone that you were involved. You can go back to the college and work just like you always have. No one has to know."

Macy watched as Lola blinked, instantly wondering what Lola was thinking. There was no doubt Lola was in a difficult situation. After Macy had been locked up for about a month, she'd heard Dario refer to Lola as family. Macy had quickly figured out that Lola was Dario's cousin. How they were related exactly, Macy still wasn't sure, but she knew Lola was loyal. It was one of her best traits. And now that loyalty had her stuck between her friend and her family, both of whom were desperate. All Macy could hope is that she had at least a little pull left as Lola's friend.

Lola pulled her hands away. "No, I'm sorry. I can't. You know I can't."

Macy looked at the floor for a second and then grabbed a piece of paper from her desk. "Then will you do me at least this one small favor? Will you get this note to Kate? My family, they don't even know if I'm really alive or not. And if there's something that Dario wants — that key he keeps mentioning that I don't have any idea about," she lied. "Then if they know I'm alive, they'll try to cooperate. They'll try to get you what you want. I know Noah, he doesn't want any trouble." She searched Lola's face, which had softened just barely. "Please?"

Macy held her breath. She waited, watching Lola's expression. The easiest thing would be to admit she had the key and give it to them, hoping they'd hold up their end of the bargain and set her free. But something in her gut told her they wouldn't, the image of her dead body floating face down in the lake surfacing in her mind. Macy blinked, pushing the thought away, staring at Lola, who looked frozen. She hadn't expected Lola to agree to drive her into town, but maybe negotiating for a smaller favor would be easier for Lola to say yes to, especially if Lola was feeling guilty about her part in the kidnapping.

Macy held the piece of paper out in front of Lola. "You can read it. You can see it doesn't say anything about where I am. It just tells them that I'm alive."

Lola glanced down at the piece of paper in Macy's hand, chewing her lip. Macy couldn't breathe. She waited for another second.

Without any warning, Lola snatched the sheet of paper from Macy's hand, quickly read it, folded it and stuffed it into her pocket. Without saying anything, Lola turned on her heel and walked out of the room, slamming the door behind her. Macy stood still, her body shaking from head to toe as she heard the lock click close again.

Now, all she could do was wait.

28

Kate had put the meeting with the detectives the day before out of her mind and had gone about her business. Her mind worked that way. She could compartmentalize. Other people might have wondered how she was able to continue going to classes not knowing where her mother was, but it wasn't an issue in Kate's mind. Her mom would have expected her to continue moving forward and not sit around the house crying and whining. That wasn't who she was.

After a morning filled with classes, a study group that took a couple of hours, greasy pepperoni pizza and pop included for lunch, Kate finally made it back to her dorm a little after three PM. She stopped at the mailbox downstairs in the lobby and opened it, pulling out a sheaf of papers. She curled them in her hand and carried them upstairs.

As a Junior at Bedford College, Kate had been given the opportunity to become a resident assistant. She got paid a little stipend each month, not much more than would cover coffee, pizza, and beer, to sort through relationship issues on the floor she managed and keep the peace. The side benefit was she got a single room. Having the privacy was golden, especially with a newer boyfriend, one who wasn't accustomed to sharing space with a bunch of twittering young freshman girls.

As Kate got back to her dorm room, unlocking the door, she checked down the hallway. All was quiet. That was good. Normally, if there was drama, it would crop up between nine PM and midnight. Luckily, she had time to relax and study before the latest skirmish over who got to use the bathroom first would erupt.

Closing the door behind her, she shook her head, shrugging off her backpack and tossing it on her bed. The room Kate occupied was a small single on the second floor of Oliver Hall. It had a built-in twin bed on one wall, a desk, and a small spot of open floor on the other side with a rectangular window set in the middle. The view was of a chunk of lawn, newly covered with snow. Kate tossed the flyers from her mailbox down on her desk watching the papers land next to a pile of notebooks, noticing a white sheet of folded paper with a torn edge slipping out between two of the pages. Kate frowned. She walked closer to it, using her index finger to push it away from the rest of the sheets and then picked it up, opening it.

Her hands started to shake as she read it.

"Katie, I'm okay. I'm very sorry I haven't been in touch. I'm hoping to come home soon. I was thinking this week about that little snow globe we got you when you were a kid. I always think about that when the first snow hits. Please tell your dad and your brother how much I love them. DGU — your mom."

Kate stared at the paper, the breath ragged in her throat. Her heart pounded in her chest. She flipped the paper to the back side to see if there was anything else. It was blank. Questions pounded through her head. How had her mom gotten the note to her? Where was she? When was she coming home?

Kate felt like the earth was shifting underneath her. She sat down on the edge of her bed, her legs wobbly. She'd put her mom's disappearance out of her mind, but now it hit her full force in the face. Her mom was gone. Something about the note told her Kate was her only hope.

Taking a couple of deep breaths, Kate stared at the paper again. DGU meant "don't give up." It was something that her mom used to say to her when she was on the swim team in high school. Her mom would yell it right before Kate hit the water, knowing that the last lap would cause her lungs to burn and her legs and back to hurt, but that she could get through it. The letters DGU hung in her mind. It had become an anchor in her life whenever things got hard.

And now her mom was asking her not to give up once again, but this time, it wasn't something Kate was trying to accomplish. Her mom was asking Kate not to give up on her.

Kate stared at the sheet through tears. She didn't know what to do. She'd just chalked her mother's absence up to bad parenting, but now it seemed like she was in trouble. Thoughts ran wild through her mind. Should she call her dad or the police? Kate read through the note again. Her mom hadn't said to do anything like that. She just wanted Kate to know she was alive. A chill ran through her body.

If Kate knew her mother, there was something more to it...

Kate pulled her legs up on her bed, leaning against the pillows, taking the note with her. She read through it again twice more, trying to absorb all the details. She frowned. There had to be more to it than her mom just letting her know she was alive and telling her not to give up. Her mom lived in a colorful world of images, symbolism, and allusions. If her mom only had one shot to communicate with the family, she would have chosen her words carefully, intentionally.

Kate ran her finger across each line of the text once more. She glanced up at the shelf above her bed. There was a picture of her and her mom above her. Macy was hanging over Kate's shoulder, a big goofy grin on her face. Katie had gone home for her twenty-first birthday and her mom surprised her with the most lopsided chocolate cake Kate had ever seen. Her mom was no baker, but it was the thought that counted. Next to the picture was the snow globe Macy had written about in her note. Kate reached up and grabbed it off the shelf, giving it a shake as tears stung her eyes. Her mom must have seen the snow. That meant she was alive, didn't it?

Kate's stomach sunk. What if this was the last note she ever got from her mom?

Hot tears rolled down her face. She was terrified for her mom and frozen on her bed, not sure what to do. She set the snow globe down next to her, grabbing a tissue from the box she kept within reach for the girls she watched over. They were criers. Kate was not, at least until that moment.

Blowing her nose, she noticed that the snow had settled down in the snow globe. She picked it up, ready to give it a shake again when she glanced inside. Kate frowned, holding it close to her face. It had been a long time since she had looked at it in any detail. There was a scene of a lake inside, the blue body of water shimmering against the coating of snow. In the background was a little brown cabin with a piece of plastic sticking up out above where the chimney would be, curved to look like smoke. Next to the cabin there was a tiny crooked sign with something painted on it. Kate squinted, frowning. There were letters on it, but she couldn't quite read it. Grabbing her cell phone, she turned on the flashlight and pointed the beam inside the scene. With a little more light, she was able to read the letters.

Thomasville Lake.

Kate's heart nearly stopped in her chest. Was her mom trying to tell her something? It couldn't be a coincidence that she'd mention the snow globe in her note. Kate remembered hearing her father say that Macy was staying at a cabin somewhere when she first left them in July. Kate hadn't paid that much attention at the time, getting ready to go back to school. Her mom left home a lot. At the time, Kate didn't think anything about it, assuming her dad knew where her mom was. Apparently, she'd been wrong.

Kate grimaced. Thomasville Lake was filled with cabins. Kate had been there when the spring semester had ended with her boyfriend and a group of other friends. They'd rented a cabin for the weekend and gone hiking. Little cabins were peppered all over the hillsides. There had to be hundreds of them.

Until that moment, Kate didn't even realize that the snow globe had come from Thomasville Lake. She frowned, trying to remember when her family had been there, but no memories came to mind. She'd had the snow globe since she was a child. They must have stopped there at one point or another.

Kate shot up off the bed and began to pace again. Was her mom being held at Thomasville Lake? Is that where she'd been the entire time?

Kate stopped, staring out the window in her room, wondering if her mom was watching the snow at that moment too. Her heart sunk, her hands clammy. A knot of dread curled in her gut. She glanced at the note sitting on her bed again, wondering if it was the last time she'd ever hear from her mom.

29

At midnight, Kate opened the door to her dorm room and stared down the hallway. She heard the quiet thump of music at the other end of the hall, but other than that, the floor was silent. Her students were either sleeping, hunkered down in their rooms, or still out for the night. At that moment, she didn't care where they were.

Shrugging the backpack up higher on her shoulders, Kate headed to the stairwell and trotted down the flight of steps out into the night. The cold caught her off guard. She sucked in a breath and zipped up her jacket higher, pulling a hat out from her pocket and jamming it down over her ears. The snow had stopped temporarily, but she'd gotten a weather warning on her phone that more was coming.

Going out to the little sedan that her parents had given her to drive to school, Kate jumped in, turned on the heat and grabbed the ice scraper from the backseat. She took a second to scrape off the ice crystals that were frozen onto the windshield so she could see where she was going, her fingers quickly turning numb from the cold. Getting back inside the car, she blew on her fingers, trying to warm them up. She locked the doors and sat in the parking lot for a second, pulling the note her mom had written out of her pocket. From inside of her backpack, she pulled out the snow globe and set it in one of the cupholders, staring at it. It would have to be her good luck charm. She would need a lot of luck if she hoped to find her mom.

Attaching her cell phone to the charging cable, she keyed in the location for Thomasville Lake. She glanced at her backpack as she put the car in gear. She had nowhere to stay when she got there, but she'd have to figure it out. She had no plan other than getting herself to Thomasville Lake. After that, she was on her own. But something in her knew that she was her mom's only shot, her only path left to freedom. There had to be a reason her mom had reached out to her and not to her dad. Kate's skin prickled. Her mom needed her. Just her.

Now, if she could just find her in time...

30

After his brief visit with his brother, Grady had gone straight to work, settling in at his desk with a cup of average tasting coffee. Grady had just finished going over the notes from the Thomasville Police Department when his phone rang. He lifted his eyes from the notes. There was nothing there, save for the date and a few basic comments on who Macy was and how long she'd been gone. At least Detective Bennett had been honest about not doing his job. Grady could give him that. Grunting, he looked down at his phone. Part of him hoped it was good news, but his gut told him it wasn't. "What can I do for you, Mr. Chandler?"

"It's Kate. She's gone!"

Grady frowned, closing the file in front of him. He twisted in his chair away from his desk and pressed the phone closer to his ear, not sure he understood what Noah was saying. "Kate, your daughter, is gone?"

"Yeah. Oh my God. You have to help us."

"Slow down, Mr. Chandler. What happened?"

"I didn't hear from Kate yesterday at all after you were at

our house. That's not like her. I texted her but she never called me back. I couldn't sleep. I was so worried. I drove over to the college in the middle of the night, thinking if I could spot her car then I would know she was fine. It wasn't there."

Grady cocked his head to the side. "Did you leave Gabe at home by himself?"

"Yes, yes, I did," Noah stammered. "But he's twelve. He was okay. I left a note on the counter for him."

Grady wandered over to the coffee pot, setting the phone down and putting it on speaker. "All right, we'll table that for a minute. Kate's car wasn't there?"

"No!" Noah yelled. "I called campus security. I made them take me up to her room. I figured she was sleeping and didn't know I was texting her, or maybe her phone was broken and she didn't know it, or maybe it ran out of charge. I don't know."

Grady furrowed his eyebrows. "All right, Mr. Chandler. Take a breath. You were with campus security and then what happened?"

"They took me upstairs and opened her door. She wasn't there. Her backpack was gone. I even texted her boyfriend. He said he hasn't seen her in a couple days."

Grady frowned. There was a boyfriend involved. This was news to Grady. "A boyfriend?"

"Yeah. Chris Talley. They've been going out for like a year or so. He's older, already working. Seems okay, but..."

"Is there any chance she went to stay with a friend? Could she be traveling somewhere? Maybe you just forgot?"

"No!" Noah bellowed, Grady blinking at the sudden increase in volume. "She's gone, Detective. I'm telling you. You have to help us."

Grady hung up the phone with Noah Chandler with a promise to get back with him in a couple of hours once he had a chance to contact Bedford College campus security and get a hold of Cassie. Noah hung up reluctantly, seemingly unsure that Grady would do as he promised.

Grady, after hanging up the phone, stared off into space, his hands clammy as he stood next to the coffee pot in the pit. Both Macy and Kate were missing? How was that possible?

31

After making a quick call to Cassie, updating her on Kate's disappearance, Cassie told him she was already on her way. They could talk once she got to the office. Grady heard a bark behind her. Happy the dog must have been on his way to day care.

Scenarios ran through his head as quickly as the ticker from the Dow Jones. Grady watched the morning news as he sat back down at his desk. If what Noah Chandler was saying was true, it was a worst-case scenario — both the mother and daughter from a single family abducted at the same time.

But were they really abducted?

That was the question, Grady thought, loosening the charcoal gray tie around his neck. Before visiting Ben, he'd put on gray pants and a light blue shirt and grabbed a gray blazer. His only nod to comfort was he put on comfortable work boots with a thick tread. With the weather, it was hard to know what he would end up getting himself into and he didn't want to take any chances.

Grady closed his eyes for a moment, wondering how long it would take Cassie to arrive. The drive downtown to the office hadn't taken as long as it normally did. The streets were temporarily clear, the majority of people home for the weekend, happily avoiding what would have been a messy late day rush hour traffic jam if it had been during the week.

Sometimes Grady wished he had that opportunity, but police officers were like the postal service. It didn't matter what the weather was, what mood he was in, or how inconvenient it was, there was a job to do.

Grady sat down at his desk with a grunt. He logged into the department's website and thumbed through his emails. He got an alert from Thomasville PD. Narrowing his eyes, he realized someone had entered a report on Macy Chandler's disappearance. It was postdated, of course, for two months previous. Grady pressed his lips together as he opened the file. Hunter.

From what Grady could tell by the brief notes in the report, Hunter had typed in the information that Detective Andy Bennett had given to them while they were visiting Thomasville the day before. Grady sighed. Whether detective Hunter Franco had decided to do that on his own, guilt gnawing at his gut after Grady and Cassie's visit, or Andy had told him to, that was another question for another day.

Grady scanned the notes. There was nothing added to them that he didn't already know. He drummed his fingers on the desk, staring at the screen. To make it worse, Hunter had entered the details as an information report only. What that meant was that it was simply background material, a heads-up of something that might or might not be going on, with no action requested from the department. Nothing more than an FYI. Grady shook his head, mumbling under his breath. "Nice try, Hunter, but not enough."

Bookmarking the report so he could show it to Cassie when she got to the office, Grady stared at his computer for a second and then typed in the name Kate Chandler. He took a sip of lukewarm coffee as the database searched for reports that might be related to her. A second later, a whole list of Kate Chandler related arrest records came up from across the state. Grady blinked and then filtered out any Kate Chandlers that were not of college age.

If anyone had asked him a few seconds before if he expected to find a report that included Kate Chandler, he would have said no. Although she seemed a little emotional and dramatic, she was, after all, a twenty-one-year-old college girl coming to grips with her mother's disappearance. Drama was a specialty of twenty-something females. Or at least, that had been his personal experience, though he hadn't dated someone that young in a long time. It wasn't a mistake he'd make again. What he'd seen on the job, of course, was a completely different issue. There was no person, as far as Grady was concerned, no matter their age, that didn't have the capacity to harm someone else. It was a reality of life. Only the strong survived.

A moment later, the list narrowed, only a few records left. Grady blinked. Apparently, Kate Chandler was someone who had been involved in a bit more than a few emotional outbursts.

Staring at the results on his screen, Grady shook his head. After meeting with the mild-mannered Noah Chandler, the last thing Grady expected to see was a domestic violence report between Kate Chandler and her boyfriend. Leaning closer to his computer, Grady clicked on the single report in front of him, whispering under his breath, furrows forming on his forehead. "What the —?"

After scanning the document, Grady read the final line of the report by the officers involved in the call. "The couple reported getting into an argument. The female, Kate Chandler, picked up a vase and threw it against the wall next to the boyfriend, Chris Talley, shattering next to his head. No injuries reported. The victim did not want to press charges. We did escort Mr. Talley out of the area and advised Ms. Chandler that she was receiving a written warning. The next incident would require a court visit."

Kate Chandler was violent?

Grady tried to picture the scene in his mind as Cassie walked into the office. She was toting a cardboard cup holder with two white paper cups in it. It was coffee from BrewMasters. She only got coffee from BrewMasters when she was worried about his mood. She set the tray down on Grady's desk, dislodging one of the cups from the holder and handing it to him. "Thought after the start to this day we might need a little something stronger than the sludge we brew here."

Grady nodded, tossing the swill he'd been drinking in the trash and lifting up his cup in a silent cheers. "I'll drink to that." He paused for a moment, weighing his words. "You're never gonna believe what I found."

Cassie took a sip of her coffee and cocked her head to the side. "What's that?"

Grady pivoted his monitor toward Cassie, who plopped down at the chair next to his desk. She leaned forward, staring at the screen, her lips parted. Grady watched for her reaction. It came a few seconds later. He saw the muscles of her face tighten, her eyebrows furrow. "Domestic assault? What is going on here?"

Grady shrugged his shoulders, every muscle in his body tightening. "I have no idea, but we need to get to the bottom of this. My gut tells me we are running out of time."

32

After a hushed conversation with Cassie, against Grady's wishes, they decided to loop in Lieutenant Williams. Williams was hobbling through the office, pouring himself another cup of coffee when Cassie waved him over. "Lieutenant, do you have a minute?"

Grady and Cassie quickly explained the call they'd gotten from Noah Chandler, Kate's disappearance, and the domestic assault case file they'd found on her. Williams scratched the side of his face and then looked at the two of them. "I thought I told you two to dump that case off on Thomasville. They took the initial report, didn't they?"

"If you could call it that," Grady grumbled under his breath.

Cassie cleared her throat. "Sir, Grady just told me they only filed an information report. And, they only did it last night."

Williams grunted, looking at the floor. "I don't know how to make this more clear. This isn't your case, at least the Macy Chandler part. If Kate Chandler's missing and in our jurisdiction, that's another story. That's my final word on the issue. Let Thomasville handle the kidnapping." He stared at them, his expression pinched. "That's an order."

Grady pressed his lips together, trying not to speak, a lump forming in his throat. As he looked up at Williams, the lieutenant caught his eye and then looked at Cassie. "Kate Chandler is likely to pop up any minute now. Her dad sounds paranoid. Don't spend a lot of time on this. But before you start working on the pile of other cases you have to close, you'd better tell Noah Chandler to get his other kid someplace safe until Kate pops up, in case there's something more to this than I think there is."

Grady hadn't exactly gotten the stamp of approval from Williams to take the case. In fact, he'd gotten the exact opposite, at least as far as Macy was concerned. Every case that the detectives brought in meant it was another one they needed to clear, another one cluttering up Williams's desk. But Grady knew he couldn't let what was going on in the Chandler family ride until something horrible happened to Macy Chandler. The ransom demand had been made, but now things were even more complicated. Not only was Macy missing, but Kate too.

Grady picked up his phone. He dialed Noah Chandler.

Noah picked up after the first ring. "Detective? Do you have news? Where's Katie?"

Grady put the call on speaker. "Noah, we don't have any news on Kate yet." Grady glanced at Cassie wondering if he should tell him about the domestic assault case that had been opened involving his daughter. Cassie pressed her lips together and shook her head. It was a warning. In a split second, he knew she was right. Kate was an adult. There was no way to know if she'd told her dad about the argument she'd had with Chris or not. They still didn't have a full picture of what was going on in the family. "We just got to the office and talked to our Lieutenant. Is there a place you can take Gabe so he'll be safe?"

"Safe?" Noah stammered, his voice shaking. "What do you mean? You think someone is coming after my kids, too?"

Cassie was the next one to speak. "Noah, I want you to stay calm. This is only a precautionary measure. The reality is we don't really know what's going on here and we'd hate for things to become more complicated. You are under enough stress as it is and you're alone. I'm sure you could use some help. So I'll repeat Detective Grady's question. Is there a place you can take Gabe for a few days while we figure out where Kate is?"

Somehow, the way Cassie said things always sounded more pleasant, like it was the Disney version of whatever Grady was saying.

There was silence on the other end of the line. The only thing Grady could hear was Noah breathing heavily in the background as if he'd been running or had just gotten punched in the gut. "I guess so," he said slowly. "My sister, she lives in Erie. I can take Gabe there for a few days. But what about Macy? Are you still looking for her?"

Grady nodded, grimacing. The idea of letting Thomasville run with the case didn't sit right with him. "Right now we are focused on Kate. Hang in there. We'll find them. Hopefully, they are together." Grady skipped the part about how Williams had ordered them to let Thomasville handle the case.

As Grady hung up the phone, the memories of his own shattered family rising in his mind, he knew there was no way he could live with himself if he didn't see the case through to the end.

33

Noah had taken the call from the detectives while he was in his home office, pacing back and forth. His entire body felt like it was electrified, his skin tingling, his stomach tightened into a small ball. He was almost used to the idea that Macy was gone at that point, but Kate was a completely different story. Now the two most beautiful and precious women in his life were gone. It was as if Kate's disappearance had magnified the fact that his wife had been kidnapped. It felt like his whole life was coming apart at the seams.

And he had no idea where either of them could be...

Noah stopped for a second, staring out the window of his office. There was a crusty layer of snow over the still green grass, a rim of flakes building up on the edge of the garden fence at the back of their property. From where Noah stood, he could see the drooping plants. His heart sunk. If Macy had been home she would've pulled the plants the month before, bringing in the final harvest, carefully repotting a few of the plants to try to nurse along on the windowsill in their kitchen. He'd been so absorbed with work and Gabe and just trying to get dinner on the table that he hadn't noticed them dying day by day. A pit formed in his stomach. He hoped it wasn't the same for Macy.

Striding out of his office after sending a quick text to his sister, Noah yelled upstairs. "Gabe?"

His heart skipped a beat, waiting for Gabe to respond. There was silence. What if he was gone too?

A moment later, Gabe responded. "Yeah, Dad?" Gabe's round face and flap of light brown hair appeared at the top of the steps. "We don't have to leave for school already, do we?"

"No. No school today. It's Saturday, remember? I'm gonna take you to Aunt Lisa's house for a couple of days. Thought maybe we should go for a visit," Noah said quickly. He hadn't told Gabe that he couldn't find Kate. Not yet, at least. It might break Gabe. He idolized his big sister. A lump formed in Noah's throat. If he was having a hard time adjusting to the idea that both his wife and his daughter were missing, he couldn't imagine how terrified Gabe would be.

Gabe frowned, then he shrugged, as if his momentary complaint had been solved by the idea he wouldn't have to go to school. "Okay. I'll go pack."

"Good. We'll leave here in about an hour. That'll give you time to have breakfast before we go. Don't forget to pack your warm clothes. Doesn't look like the temperature is going to go up over the next couple of days."

With Gabe off packing on his own, Noah stared back at the phone. It pinged. Lisa. "Of course. Are you coming this morning?"

"Yeah. We'll be there in a few hours. I'll send you a text when we leave."

The next hour or so was a blur for Noah, his mind bouncing back and forth between Macy, Kate, and the things he needed to do to get him and Gabe out the door. Confusion nipped at his heels as his brain tried to process all three things at one time. Four separate times, he'd walked into his office to retrieve his computer to take with him and four separate times he'd forgotten to grab it, walking out of the office with a file, his planner and a pen instead. He stopped in the doorway and sucked in a deep breath, balling his hands into fists. "Get it together, Chandler," he mumbled under his breath. He had to be strong. He couldn't crumble. Not now. Gabe needed him. His girls needed him.

Forty-three minutes later, and relatively sure, but not certain they had packed everything they needed for their trip to Erie, Noah ushered Gabe out to the white Mazda SUV he drove. They tossed their bags in the backseat, Gabe sliding into the passenger side, Noah taking a minute to adjust the mirrors and the seat. For some reason, although it was his car and he was the last one to drive it, they felt uncomfortable. Chewing the inside of his lip, he realized everything in his life at that moment felt like a pair of shoes two sizes too small.

Pulling out of the driveway, Noah could hear the crunch of the crusted over snow, his tires grinding and slipping a little as he made his way out of their development.

Once on I-79, Noah knew it would be a straight shot north toward the shores of Lake Erie to get to his sister Lisa's house. As they drove, Noah chit-chatted a little with Gabe about school and his friends and then watched gratefully as Gabe put in his earbuds and started playing his video game. Sighing, Noah leaned back in his seat. He had two hours to go, two hours to be lost in the maze of his thoughts. Staring at the road in front of him, his mind bounced between Macy and Kate and the demand from the kidnapper. He hadn't heard back from them. Pushing the thought out of his mind, Noah realized at that moment, he was more worried about Kate. He'd almost become used to the idea that Macy was gone, part of him processing that she might never come back again, but his daughter? That was another matter entirely.

He swallowed. In his heart, he knew both Kate and Macy were alive. Or at least he thought so. If they came back, no, when they came back, things would be different. They'd have to be. He couldn't go through this again. Not ever.

Noah's mind went back to the call from the kidnappers once again. Whoever had been at the other end of the line had demanded a key. Noah shook his head, a wave of nausea running over him. He'd almost forgotten about the call in his agitation over not being able to find Kate. Did the same person have Kate that had Macy? And what was this nonsense about a key? Noah racked his brain, thinking about all the keys that he had access to as he drove. He and Macy each had a personal set of car keys, which included a house key and keys to their vehicles, but other than that, they didn't have any other keys. They had a small safe at their house so there was no need for a safety deposit box. Even if they had a safety deposit box, there would be nothing of value in it, other than copies of their insurance papers and their passports. And neither of them had keys to their parents' homes. Macy's dad lived in the Upper Peninsula of Michigan in an expansive home right on the water, a good fourteen-hour drive away, and his parents lived in Florida, in an enormous retirement city called The Villages.

Noah's mind drifted. Macy's dad knew she'd been missing, but didn't seem concerned. He knew how Macy was. She'd started her "excursions," as her family called them, when she was in high school, disappearing for days at a time, only to be found on another ranch, sleeping in someone's barn.

But if he knew about the ransom demand? That would change things, not that there was anything they could do. The kidnapper wanted a key, one he was sure Noah knew about. This didn't have anything to do with Macy's dad and he didn't have the heart to tell him. The last thing he wanted to do was put any more stress on him. No, Noah would keep the information to himself until everything was resolved. He thought for a minute about calling his own parents, but knowing Lisa, as soon as he dropped off Gabe, she would call them and give them every last nitty-gritty detail. The good news was, if he knew his parents at all, Lisa would end up being the go-between, ferrying tidbits of information to them as soon as Noah turned his back. He'd never hear from them, not until he called and was ready to talk about it.

And he wasn't.

He sighed, gripping the wheel a little tighter. He needed to stay focused. There was a simple path in front of him. Drop Gabe off, get him situated. Stay for a few hours at Lisa's house, and then head back to Pittsburgh to try to help with the search for Kate and Macy and wait for the kidnapper to call again. As the thoughts organized themselves in his head, he realized once he was home, he didn't have the first idea of where to start or how to help.

Noah glanced at Gabe. He was so young to have to deal with all of this. Although Gabe had shot up two inches in the last year, he still had the round curve to his cheek of a child, puberty not getting a full grip on his son yet as it had done with Kate. A lump formed in his throat as he remembered Kate as a child. She'd been full of life, rambunctious, with a stream of dark hair trailing behind her everywhere she went, a glint in her eye that Noah couldn't explain but loved. Her chubby cheeks and square body had transformed into a young woman right before his eyes, boys appearing at the door nearly at the same time, that same glint in her eye now used on them instead of the mischief she was causing around the house.

And now she was gone.

As the thought hit Noah, his SUV fishtailed on the freeway, the tires skidding on a patch of untreated ice. Noah took his foot off the gas and held onto the wheel tight, feeling the vehicle straighten out, the tires gripping again. He put his foot back on the gas, nudging the Mazda forward again, the vehicle shuddering. He glanced up at the sky. The snow had resumed, heavy bands of snow drifting south off of Lake Erie, thick flakes drifting down from the sky.

Shaking his head, Noah slowed the Mazda down, reaching for the heater in the car and turning it up. It was going to be a long drive.

34

Grady grudgingly complied with Lieutenant Williams' order to limit the search to Kate Chandler, who had disappeared in their jurisdiction. It didn't sit right with him, but an order was an order. Three hours went by before Grady could locate Kate's boyfriend, Chris Talley. Chris finally picked up the phone after Grady had called no less than five times. "Chris Talley?"

"Yes? Who's this?"

Grady frowned. There was a good deal of crowd noise behind Chris. Where was he? "This is Detective Grady from the Pittsburgh Bureau of Police. I've been trying to call you."

"I've been on a plane for the last few hours. What's this about?"

A plane? That would explain why none of Grady's calls went through. "It's about Kate Chandler. Do you know her?"

"Yeah, she's my girlfriend. But I suspect you already know that if you're calling me. Why? Is there something wrong?"

Grady intentionally ignored the question. He'd learned that one of the best ways to get information from someone was by ignoring their questions and only asking another one of his own. Grady wasn't in the mood to give out much information, not that he had a lot to give. "I was wondering if you could swing by the police department? We have a few questions for you."

Chris sighed, sounding impatient. "Listen, I've been on a plane for the last four hours. Took the redeye back from Los Angeles. I'm exhausted. I don't know what this is about, but can we do this another time?"

"No," Grady growled. "Here's the situation, Chris. Either you can come to the department, or I'm going to come and find you. Believe me, things will go much more quickly if you could stop by for a few minutes. I get aggravated when I have to chase people around."

There was silence at the other end of the line for a minute. "All right. I'm leaving the airport now. I'm heading your way."

"Thank you for your cooperation," Grady said grimly.

Twenty-two minutes later, Grady got a call from the desk sergeant on the first floor that Chris Talley had arrived. "Send him up," Grady replied. He glanced at Cassie. "Chris Talley is here."

"Oh, you got him to come to us?" Cassie had just returned from the other side of the building. Grady had no idea what she'd been doing, although she seemed to be sporting a fresh coat of lipstick after her initial two cups of coffee.

"Yep. So far, his story is he just came back on the redeye from Los Angeles. Sounded pretty grumpy."

Cassie raised her eyebrows, staring at Grady. "That's okay. I'm good at dealing with grumpy."

"I hope you're not talking about me," Grady blinked.

Cassie shook her head slowly, her eyes widening. "Of course not. I'm talking about Williams."

Grady looked away. "Yeah, right."

The arrival of Chris Talley interrupted their sparring match. The elevator doors slid open revealing a young man who looked to be in his mid to late twenties with a long loping stride, his blond hair cropped at the sides and longer on the top. He was wearing a charcoal gray suit and a white shirt, the tie drooping and loosened around his neck, a backpack looped over his shoulders. A rolling overnight bag clattered over the tile floor as he approached. If he hadn't been at the airport, he was certainly making a good show of it, Grady thought. He got up from his desk and intercepted the man as the elevator doors closed. "Chris Talley?"

The young man nodded.

"I'm Detective Grady. Right this way."

Cassie trailed behind them as Grady led Chris Talley into one of their interview/interrogation rooms. Which one it would end up being, Grady had no idea. As they walked inside, Cassie disappeared for a second. He knew she was going into the adjoining room to turn on the surveillance video and the microphones, recording the conversation in case there was anything they wanted to review later on. As soon as she returned, she closed the door behind her, the noise echoing in the hollow, dingy gray room.

"Sorry about the accommodations," Grady started. It was his best effort at making Chris feel comfortable. "You can toss your bags on the chair over there. There's nothing inside of them we should know about, right?"

Chris blinked and then looked at Grady, "Not unless you're concerned about some dirty clothes or my laptop."

Grady didn't bother responding, pointing to a chair.

Cassie interrupted, "Detective Grady tells me you were on a long flight. Can I get you a bottle of water or a cup of coffee?"

Chris shrugged as he sat down. "Both would be nice, actually, if you don't mind."

"Sure."

The pleasantries out of the way, Grady sat down and stared at Chris Talley. He could see why a young woman like Kate

Chandler would be attracted to him. Chris was around six feet tall, with a medium build. He had bright blue eyes and high cheekbones, his cheeks flushed from the cold outside. Grady bet Chris Talley was the kind of guy who had no shortage of dates, no shortage of young women who would happily throw themselves at him at bars and in hotels.

Grady played with the pad of paper in front of him on the table, waiting for Cassie to come back. He didn't want to start the interview without her, at least not this time.

A second later, Cassie came back into the room, setting a cup of coffee and a bottle of water in front of Chris, and then produced a protein bar from the vending machine out of her pocket. "I'm always hungry when I land after a long trip," she nodded. "Can't promise it's the best meal you'll ever get, but it'll hold you over until we're done here."

Chris looked up at Cassie, seemingly a little confused by her hospitality. "Thanks," he said awkwardly.

Grady cleared his throat, impatient to get started. "Again, thanks for coming in. We appreciate it."

"Yeah, sure." Chris shifted in his seat uncomfortably, his hands folded in his lap. "I don't understand why I'm here. What's this about?"

Cassie sat down next to Grady, across from Chris, pulling her chair out at an angle so she wasn't staring straight at him, crossing her legs. Grady glanced at her. She had on a variation of the same outfit she usually wore, except that this time, the suit was black. It had a long double-breasted jacket. She'd put on an olive-green turtleneck underneath the blazer and paired it with black pants and heeled boots. Her strawberry blonde hair was pulled up in a topknot at the top of her head, tiny earrings puncturing each ear lobe. "We just have a few questions for you. This shouldn't take too long," she said sweetly.

Grady tapped at the paper with the tip of his pen and then

looked up at Chris. "You said you just came back on the redeye from Los Angeles? Is that right?"

"Yeah, you see my bags over there, right?"

Grady bristled. He already didn't like Chris's tone. "Can you grab your phone for me and show me your boarding passes?"

Grady watched Chris carefully for his reaction. He narrowed his eyes just slightly and then cocked his head a millimeter. If Grady hadn't been looking for it, he would have missed it. The movement was nearly imperceptible. Grady knew what it meant. Although Chris was trying to keep a game face on, he was unsure about why he'd been called to the police department. His expression spoke of suspicion. Grady started to wonder how many interactions Chris Talley had had with the police in the past. Grady had pulled Chris's background information before he arrived, but there wasn't much to see, the only things in Chris Talley's record were a speeding ticket, two parking tickets, and him named as the victim in the domestic assault case with Kate Chandler. Was there more to the story that Grady didn't know about?

After fumbling with his phone for a second, Chris shoved it across the table at Grady and Cassie. Grady stared at the screen. Based on the boarding passes in front of him, it appeared Chris Talley had been on United flight 1792 from Los Angeles to Pittsburgh, boarding at eleven the night before, which was three o'clock AM Pittsburgh time. If that was true, then that verified Chris Talley's whereabouts, at least overnight, which was exactly the timeframe they had for Kate's disappearance.

Grady leaned back in his chair as Cassie took a picture of the boarding pass with her phone. She gave Grady a quick nod and then sat back down again.

Grady cleared his throat, "Why were you in Los Angeles?"

"For a pharmaceuticals conference."

"You work in pharmaceuticals?" Grady said, raising his eyebrows.

Chris nodded. "Yeah. I'm a rep. I have a piece of the Pittsburgh territory. I was out in Los Angeles for one of my company's conferences. They're rolling out some new diabetes drugs."

"And which company is that?" Grady asked, jotting the information on his pad of paper.

"Bell Pharmaceuticals." Chris glanced at the two of them, his eyebrows knitted together. "Why am I here? Why do you care where I was?"

Without looking up, Grady held his finger in the air. He was in no hurry to tell Chris why he'd been called to the pit. "We'll get to that in just a second." He looked up at Chris after taking his time making a few notes. Grady wanted him impatient and off-balance. "And when did you leave for your conference?"

"A week ago. We were there all week and then worked through the weekend. Lots of team building hogwash."

"And do you happen to have a receipt from your hotel that details your stay?"

Chris frowned and then fumbled with his phone again, tossing it down on the table with a clatter, clearly annoyed. Grady leaned over, looking at it. There was a receipt from the One Palm Hotel and Conference Center that matched exactly what Chris had said. Grady glanced at Cassie, who stood up and took another picture.

Chris leaned back in his seat. "So, now you know where I have been for the last week. I'm gonna ask this one more time or I'm going to get up and walk out. Since I clearly haven't done anything wrong, why am I here?"

Grady narrowed his eyes. He didn't like Chris's attitude. Sure, he was impatient, but they were getting to it. And yes, as much as Grady wanted to question him, technically Chris had every right to walk out. They had nothing to charge him on, at least not yet...

Grady set his pen down and leaned back in his chair, crossing his arms in front of his chest. "Fair enough. I know you had a long night. Me, personally, I avoid planes at all costs."

"Good for you, but it's kind of required for the work that I do."

Grady nodded, trying to ignore Chris's sarcasm. "When we spoke on the phone you said you know Kate Chandler. What's your relationship with her?"

"She's my girlfriend." Chris looked back and forth between Grady and Cassie, his head on a swivel, "Why do you keep asking about Kate? Is she okay?"

"That's what we're trying to find out. She's missing."

35

"Missing? What are you talking about?" Chris Talley's face had paled considerably upon hearing the news.

Grady swallowed, laid his elbow on the table in front of him, and leaned forward. "Yeah, we got a frantic call from her father this morning. He can't find Kate. You wouldn't happen to know anything about that, would you?"

Chris furrowed his eyebrows and then stood up from the chair he was sitting on, running his hand through his cropped blond hair. "I have no idea what he's talking about. What do you mean she's missing?"

Cassie cocked her head to the side and looked at Chris. She didn't answer his question. "When was the last time you talked to Kate?"

Chris blinked, dropping his hands limply to his sides. "I don't know. It's been a couple of days, I think. When I go to these conferences they keep me busy twenty-four-seven. She knows that. I think the last time we talked, I told her we'd do something this weekend after I got a chance to regroup."

Grady stared at Chris. From what he could tell, Chris was

telling the truth. His shoulders were relaxed, his eye contact steady. There was no tightness along his jawline and no narrowness in his eyes. Grady would accept that answer, at least for the moment. "How has Kate been recently?"

Chris sat down in the chair again, folded his arms across his chest and frowned. "Fine, I guess. You know about her mom, right?"

Grady nodded. "She's been gone for a while, correct?"

"Yeah."

Cassie interjected. "Did Kate seem concerned about her mom at all?"

Chris looked up at the ceiling for a second as if he was trying to remember and then leveled his gaze back at the detectives. "Not really. I mean, a little, maybe. She said her mom has done this a bunch of times, but I think with how long she's been gone it has started bothering Katie some. Why?"

Grady considered for a moment letting Chris know there had been a ransom demand for Macy, but he hesitated, stopping as he sucked in a breath to speak. He wasn't willing to play his hand, at least not yet. If Chris was somehow involved in their abductions, the less Grady and Reynolds revealed, the better. Grady folded his hands on the table in front of him, interlacing his fingers. "You have any idea where Kate could be?"

"No," Chris said, shaking his head. "Last time I talked to her, she was at school, getting ready for some exam or something. I think she's in the middle of midterms or just finished them. He put his hand on his forehead. "Sorry, my brain is swimming. Between the conference and all the travel, I'm not sure I'm even thinking straight."

"That's all right, Chris." Cassie said encouragingly, "You're doing fine."

Everything in Grady wanted to yell at Cassie. In reality, other than the fact that they'd verified Chris had been out of town, they'd gotten nothing from him. It was time to cut to the chase. "Tell me about the incident between the two of you that required a police visit over the summer."

Chris's face paled, his mouth going slack. "Yeah, I guess you would know about that, wouldn't you?"

Grady nodded, his expression stony.

Chris looked down at the table, shaking his head. "We got into a fight. It was right after Kate's birthday. We'd both been drinking."

Grady raised his eyebrows. "You say that like it's a regular thing. Is Kate a regular drinker?"

Chris shrugged. "Yeah. Most college kids do. I'm not gonna lie about it."

Grady gave a short nod.

"Anyway, we'd gone out to dinner. The waitress was cute. I may have flirted a little bit with her after a couple glasses of wine. I shouldn't have done it, I know that," Chris said, holding his hands up, accepting his error. "Then when we got back to Kate's dorm room, I took her upstairs to make sure she got home safe. We were gonna hang out for a little while and then she turned on me. She got ticked, really ticked."

Cassie said quietly. "And that's when she threw the vase at you?"

Chris nodded. "Yeah. I got her flowers for her birthday. She was so mad at me for flirting with the waitress that she chucked the whole thing at my head. It hit the wall — the flowers, the water, the vase. Shattered into a million pieces. I guess one of the girls down the hallway heard us yelling and called the police." Chris looked back and forth between the two of them. "But you need to know, I didn't touch her."

Grady nodded. "We saw that in the report. What happened when the police got there?"

Chris shrugged. "They took me down the hallway to the lounge. Took my statement and then put me in the back of a police cruiser and drove me home. I talked to Katie later on that night. She was upset, crying. Said she was sorry for losing her temper. Said the officers had issued her a written warning and that next time she would go to jail. I guess they cut her a break."

"I guess they did," Grady said, his voice gravelly. "You guys have any other problems after that? Anything recently?"

Grady was still inching his way around the topic of whether or not Chris had anything to do with Kate's disappearance.

"No. I mean, we have disagreements about stuff, for sure. But what couple doesn't?"

Cassie drummed her fingers on the table. "Can you give us an example of the stuff you fight about?"

Grady glanced at Cassie. Where she was going with this, he wasn't sure.

Chris pressed his lips together. "Well, we haven't been fighting much since then, I guess. We did have a disagreement a couple of weeks back. Katie wanted to do something, but I needed to get a workout in. She wasn't happy that I wasn't available. We were fine, though. No big deal."

"And how did you meet?"

"At a Bedford College football game. It was homecoming, last year. I used to play lacrosse. Midfield. I was there hanging out with some of my lacrosse buddies and saw her with her friends. The rest, as they say, is history."

Grady frowned. "Is it now?"

36

"Hang here for a little bit for me," Grady said, getting up from his chair in the interview room, gathering his pad of paper and his pen and walking out, trailed by Cassie. He'd decided he didn't like Chris Talley.

Cassie closed the door to the interview room where they'd left Chris Talley sitting by himself, nursing his cup of now lukewarm coffee and his bottle of water. "What do you think?" Cassie asked, resting her weight on one hip and crossing her arms in front of her chest.

"I think we should hold him," Grady said, setting the pad of paper down on his desk.

Cassie frowned. "I wanted to know what you thought about what he said. Hold him? For what? He alibied out for Kate's disappearance. He was in Los Angeles."

Grady flopped down in his desk chair and stared up at the ceiling for a second. "There are some gaps there. Why hasn't he talked to Kate in the last couple days? Didn't he seem a little too lackadaisical about Macy's disappearance? He didn't say anything at all about the ransom demand. Does that mean Kate didn't tell him? Or is he involved? And, he doesn't seem at all concerned about Kate being gone."

"Sounds like you have a lot of questions."

Williams wandered over to Grady's desk. "What are we doing here?"

"Just discussing what to do with Kate Chandler's boyfriend."

Grady held his breath. Was this when Williams was going to tell them to get back to their other cases? Williams shook his head. "I watched some of that interview from behind the glass. Not much there if you ask me. He was in L.A. Sounds like their domestic issue was a one-off. I fight with my wife all the time. Doesn't mean he doesn't love the girl."

Grady wasn't surprised that Williams had watched the interview, nor was he surprised that Williams didn't think that there was anything there. Par for the course with the Lieutenant. He was always breathing down their necks, ready to rush cases out of the detective's unit and off his desk.

Shaking his head, Grady said. "Lieutenant, there are just too many holes in what he said. I think he knows something he's not telling us."

Williams grimaced. "What holes? Grady, he answered all of your questions and gave you documentation that he was out of town. Maybe, if you're grasping at straws, which you are, you could say he's involved somehow in the disappearance of Kate, but they're in a consensual relationship. Not much of a disappearance there if you ask me. Even if he was involved, with the timeline, he wasn't hands-on. It would've had to be an accomplice. Do you have any evidence of that?"

A knot formed in Grady's stomach and heat rushed to his face. "No. But that doesn't mean there isn't someone."

Williams stared at Grady, his head cocked to the side, his face sagging, his jowls covering the worn white collar of his shirt. "You seriously want me to buy that?" Williams looked at

Cassie. "Detective Reynolds, go cut your suspect loose. Now. Then the two of you, get back to work. We shouldn't even be looking at this Kate woman until she's been gone for twenty-four hours. I've given you some room to move, but it's over. You've got other cases to solve. Let Thomasville pick up the slack."

As Williams limped back to his office and Cassie got up to escort Chris Talley out of the building, Grady sat and stared at a blank spot in the wall on the other side of the pit. Fury rose up through his gut. Sure, Williams was right that they didn't have any evidence, and that technically, they really couldn't open a missing persons case on Kate until she'd been gone for twenty-four hours, but that didn't mean there wasn't a case. Grady rubbed his chin. Statistically, the most likely suspect for any murder or an abduction was a spouse, a lover or a family member. No matter what Williams said, Grady knew that was the reality. And Chris Talley was the perfect suspect. Handsome, professional. And he was dating a younger woman. A student who didn't have her life in order. From what Grady could see, Chris Talley was the kind of guy who should be dating other fast-moving professional women, not a hotheaded IT student from the local college. Maybe Kate's disappearance had something to do with Chris's desire to move on?

Grady surged up from his desk and stomped out of the pit, heading for the stairwell, anger filling every inch of his body. He ran the two flights of steps up to the top floor and pushed his way through the fire door down the hallway to where it ended. The entire top floor of the building was nothing more than storage. It had become Grady's refuge when he needed a minute to think or a moment to get away from the nonsense that Williams shoveled at him. At the back of the building there was a set of large windows that took in the skyline. Off in the distance, on a clear day, he could see the water glinting off of the Monongahela River.

But not today.

The weather was as cloudy as his thoughts. The snow has started falling again, exactly as the weather forecasters had predicted. Looking up at the sky, he could see the snow coming down in sheets, a squall dumping a pile of flakes and then passing over, the sky brightening for just a moment until the next heavy set of clouds appeared.

Grady pounded his fist on the window ledge, feeling the cold metal soak through his skin. He pushed himself away, pacing back and forth a few times. Thoughts raced in his head, his breathing shallow. This case was too complicated. It was bad enough that they had a woman who was gone for four months, her family so lax they didn't even pay attention to her disappearance.

But now the daughter was missing too?

From the back of his mind, memories of his own home life began to surface. Were the Chandlers actually that different from the Gradys? Did any of their neighbors know what was going on in the Chandler household? When Grady was young, very few people realized there was anything unpleasant happening in his household at all. His mom had always done a masterful job of hiding the bruises from his father's fists, gripping his hand and Ben's hand tightly anytime they were out in public, his mother pasting a semi-relaxed half smile on her face anywhere they had gone.

Grady shook his head. He knew he could drive down any side street of any neighborhood anywhere in the country and there would be stories to tell — adultery, financial problems, arguments, abuse. The list went on and on. He remembered in high school, an English teacher had made them write a paper on the theme, "Man's Inhumanity to Man." The paper had been overwhelming for Grady to write. He'd seen too much inhumanity in his life by the time he was a teenager just in his own household. He'd refused to write the paper and ended up getting an F. He didn't care at the time and he didn't care now.

Even with the drama of his own upbringing, that was nothing compared to what he'd seen during his career as a detective.

He gripped the ledge of the window hard, the tips of his fingers paling under the pressure. He gritted his teeth, staring down at the ground, feeling the frozen air from outside the building soaking through the glass in front of him. A chill ran down his spine. Whether it was from the cold or from the case, he wasn't sure.

Grady shook his head and turned around, leaning against the wall, crossing his arms in front of his chest. He would've liked to have Chris Talley sit in the interview room for a while, sweat him out, give him time to think about his story. Maybe, even if he wasn't involved, maybe he'd have more details that would help them figure out what in God's name was going on.

Grady bit the inside of his lip. That was the crux of the problem. Grady had no grip on what was going on... and that's what scared him the most.

poisoning. He'd refused to write the [illegible] ground and [illegible] and he didn't [illegible] now.

[illegible] with the warmth of his own upbringing. [illegible] compared to what had sent him out the door as a [illegible].

He gripped the edge of the window hard, the tips of his fingers going under the pressure. He'd had nightmares, staring down at the ground, feeling the [illegible] the building sinking through the [illegible] down [illegible] whether it was from the cold or from the [illegible].

Grady shook his head and turned [illegible] that [illegible] gone [illegible] dead. He [illegible] like [illegible] Old [illegible] sweat [illegible] to think about his story. Maybe [illegible] solved [illegible] would [illegible] not [illegible].

Grady [illegible] That was the [illegible] of the problem. Grady hadn't [illegible] what [illegible] in the [illegible].

37

Although Grady's goal in going upstairs to the storeroom had been to settle down, it didn't work. By the time he got back to the pit, Chris Talley was long gone. Grady glanced around the half-empty desks, acid eating at the back of his throat. Williams was locked up in his office and Cassie was sitting at her desk, staring at her computer. Grady charged over to Cassie's desk and stood in front of her. "We need to go back to Thomasville."

"Why?" Cassie asked, glancing up at him as she typed.

"That's the only lead we have. What if Macy's been there the entire time?"

"We don't know that," Cassie said calmly, still typing on her keyboard, barely looking up at him.

The fact that Cassie wasn't taking Grady seriously only added fuel to the fire. "Reynolds, what other information do we have? So far we've got an assistant that took half a day off from work, a professor who is missing under forged medical leave papers, and a family that thinks that their mother might be in Thomasville, not to mention a missing daughter. I'm telling you, Thomasville is the center of this."

Cassie stopped typing for a second, sighed and looked up at Grady. "We don't have jurisdiction, Grady. You heard Williams. He isn't really even into us following up on Kate Chandler until tomorrow at least. You're going to have to let the detectives up there handle it. You want me to call them for you and let them know about Kate?"

Grady felt his face redden. "Those two morons? Are you kidding me? Bennett and Franco, whatever their names are, they aren't going to lift a finger." Grady threw his hands up in the air. "And what if Kate Chandler is there too? I'm telling you, those guys aren't going to do anything."

Cassie leaned back in her chair. "It's not up to us. The Lieutenant gave us a direct order. I don't think I have to remind you, Grady, that this isn't the way things work. He could write you up and it wouldn't be the first time. Our job is like Chris Talley's. He has a territory to work in, and so do we. This is called a jurisdiction."

"I know, you just said that!" Grady exploded.

Cassie looked over her shoulder, her eyes wide, and then looked back at Grady. "Keep your voice down, would you? Williams is going to come out here and get ticked at us."

"You think I care about Williams at this moment? I've got two people from the same family that are missing. We've got no leads. And the only option we have is one you don't want to take advantage of."

Cassie's mouth hung open. "Excuse me?"

"You heard me!" Grady yelled, seeing a few heads turn in the pit. "If it was up to me, we'd be back in Thomasville already. We'd be hunting. We would turn over every rock and every stone, search every cabin around that lake until we figured out if Macy was there or not. And once we did, we'd find leads that would get us both Macy and Kate back."

"On what? On a hunch that her husband has that Macy was headed to Thomasville? You're talking about the same man who seemed to have no idea his wife was even missing until she'd been gone for over six weeks. Even then, he didn't do anything until there was a ransom demand. I'm telling you, Grady, we don't have much to go on. Even if we did, it's not our case."

In his fury, all Grady heard was "not our case." "Maybe you don't think this is our case, but I do."

Grady stomped over to his desk, pulled his badge and gun off of his belt and slammed it down on top of a pile of files. Cassie looked over at him, her mouth open, shaking her head. "What do you think you're doing? Why are you being so dramatic?"

"There is one thing you are right about, Cassie, and that is that we don't have jurisdiction. No badge means no problem. I just fixed that."

38

Grady was so furious by the time he left the pit that he only heard the muffled yells of Reynolds and Williams behind him as he grabbed his coat and strode towards the stairwell. The two of them might have the patience to wait for some magical lead to appear that would bring Macy and Kate home, but he didn't. He was tired of being hamstrung by Lieutenant Williams.

He'd had enough.

Outside, the cold air stung his reddened cheeks as he ran across the street, jumping in his black SUV and starting the engine. He tossed his wallet and his cell phone in the center console, pulled his backup pistol out of the locked compartment under his seat and backed out of the spot where he was parked. He slammed the SUV into drive, angling for the freeway.

A minute later, his phone rang. Grady glanced at the screen. Williams. He hesitated. Against his better judgment, Grady stabbed at his phone with his finger, taking the call. It was time to face the music. "Yeah?" he answered.

"Grady, I thought I told you to hand the case over to Thomasville?"

"You did," Grady grunted, his voice like steel.

"Then why am I staring at your shield on my desk? Reynolds brought it to me."

Part of Grady wanted to be angry at Cassie for alerting Williams, but he knew her heart was good, at least for the most part. "I can't give the case to Thomasville. I don't care whose jurisdiction it is. They've already had it. They've done nothing about it and now I've got a mom and a daughter missing. I've gotta find them." Heat burned in Grady's gut.

"Unacceptable. You were given a direct order to pass the case off to Thomasville."

Grady gripped the wheel of his SUV tighter, pressing a little harder on the accelerator, feeling the engine vibrate under his foot. "It doesn't matter what you say, Lieutenant. I'm going to Thomasville."

"You are not! I am giving you a direct order to pass off this case to Thomasville and let them handle it."

Grady felt his heart clutch in his chest, heat flushing through his body. "We don't even know if Macy is in Thomasville, Lieutenant, and Kate Chandler *is* within our jurisdiction."

"I don't think I need to explain this to you, Detective. The original report was made in Thomasville. The daughter's missing status is likely correlated to the mother. Who knows? Maybe Macy Chandler left her family and Kate's going to join her. Any way you look at it, it's not our case. More specifically, it is not your case. Reynolds seems to understand that. What's your problem?"

Grady gritted his teeth. Through thin lips he said, "Lieutenant, I don't agree."

"It's not your job to agree, Detective!" Williams bellowed on the other end of the line. "It's your job to do as I say. I'm your commanding officer. Now, get back here immediately and work on the cases I've already assigned you, or I'm gonna end up keeping your badge permanently."

Grady hung up.

He turned up the radio, ignoring another call from Williams and then one from Cassie, the sound of heavy metal pumping through the SUV. The only thing more intense than the guitar riffs and the drumbeat was the tension in his body. He felt like every muscle was primed for a fight. His mind surged with questions, each thought devoted to trying to find Macy and Kate.

As he drove, he thought about the two women. Where were they? Were they together? Were they apart? If they were together, why hadn't Macy communicated with her family? Was the case really tied together, like Lieutenant Williams thought it was? He shook his head, focusing his gaze on the snowy road ahead of him, trying to shake the questions into a manageable order, the entire time seeing his mother's face looming in his mind. He'd never regretted killing his father. His only regret was watching his mother suffer for so long.

And now both Kate and Macy were suffering. That was unthinkable to him, something Grady simply couldn't process.

Seeing a green highway sign that read, "Thomasville Lake, 56 miles," he stepped on the accelerator, feeling the vibration of the engine underneath him. There was something about this case that was driving him. Something that he knew he wouldn't be able to let go of until he had answers.

commanding officer [illegible] wondering lately and work on the cases [illegible] already assigned him, or [illegible] permanent.

[illegible]

He turned up the radio, finding another [illegible] Williams and then [illegible] sound of [illegible] through the [illegible] the [illegible] and the [illegible] was the [illegible] in his body. He felt like every muscle had [illegible]. His mind [illegible] with questions, each thought [illegible] to find Mary and Kate.

As he drove he thought [illegible]. Were they [illegible]? Were they apart? If they were [illegible] he [illegible] with his family. [illegible] he [illegible] his head [illegible] and [illegible] his [illegible] mother's [illegible] never [illegible] his father. His [illegible].

[illegible] Kate and Mary were [illegible]. That was [illegible] simply [illegible].

[illegible] the [illegible] Lake [illegible], he [illegible] feeling the [illegible] of the [illegible] about this case that was [illegible] him [illegible] he knew he wouldn't [illegible] until he had answers.

39

Noah stood in the doorway of his sister Lisa's family room, watching Gabe and his cousin Elise battle each other in some videogame. The two kids were alternately laughing and then silently chewing their lips, trying to outmaneuver the other one, black plastic controllers in their fingers, the buttons and knobs clicking on and off as the pair made their video likenesses run along a path or climb a high mountain. It was good to see Gabe relax, Noah thought.

Noah looked down at the ground for a second. All of them had been running on autopilot since Macy left. It was hard to believe it had been four months already. A lump formed in his throat. Where was his precious wife? In his mind, he replayed scenes of Macy over and over again, her slightly crooked smile, the song that she would hum while making dinner, the way she curled her body up in the softest chair in the corner of their family room, a book spread across her lap, her eyes hardly leaving the page for hours.

She was gone, and now Kate was gone too.

It felt like a deep well of frustration and anger was bubbling up inside of Noah. He gripped his hands into fists, resentment building in his system. If Macy had stayed, they wouldn't be dealing with this. None of them would. Noah felt paralyzed. He'd done what he thought Macy wanted him to do while she was traveling. Just keep going. Keep the house running, keep his marketing business going, keep Kate and Gabe moving forward in their lives while she had a little adventure.

That's all it was supposed to be.

But somehow trouble had found Macy. The kidnapper had asked for a key, and for the life of him, he couldn't figure out what that was. Maybe it wasn't a physical key? Maybe it was a password — a set of numbers or letters that would open something. And why did the kidnapper think he had it?

Noah spun on his heel and walked down the hallway to the kitchen. He could smell a fresh pot of coffee perking. Lisa was sitting at the kitchen table with her laptop, typing away. She glanced up, looking at the kids first and then at Noah. "There's coffee," she pointed.

"Thanks."

Noah walked over to the coffee pot, seeing the tendrils of steam curling up from the edge, the aroma of a dark roast floating through the air. He reached into the cabinet and got out a cup, filling it halfway. He took a single sip, the liquid hot and bitter in his mouth.

He cleared his throat. "What are you working on?"

"Just a newsletter..."

Lisa had a job as a freelance content writer, which allowed her to work remotely. Her husband, Mark, made good money as an engineer, so Lisa stayed home, but had found herself bored as her kids got older, so she'd picked up a few clients, helping them tune up their website content, newsletters, and emails. She glanced at the kids. "They seem to be having fun." Her face softened. "I'm really glad you came. Seems like I haven't seen you in a long time."

What she didn't say is that she was sorry that now both Noah's wife and his daughter had disappeared.

When Noah had decided to marry Macy, it wasn't a universally popular decision in the Chandler family. Macy Dixon seemed like a handful, was what his father said at the time. His father had never changed his mind about that. Macy had come from a big family in Texas and ended up in Pennsylvania as a student at Bedford College. To Noah's family, she seemed wild — a little too quick to laugh, a little too quick to spend money, and a little too quick to go on her adventures and leave Noah behind.

But those were all the things that Noah loved about Macy. She was everything he wasn't. He loved the fact that she was a risk taker, bubbling over with joy, someone who squeezed the juice out of every single day she was alive. Noah knew himself. He was more sullen, more serious and focused, not to mention more traditional. And now that she'd been gone for four months, he found his personality sliding back down into the deep dark hole where she'd found him when they were students.

I need you back, he thought, his heart sinking.

Noah had just sat down at the kitchen table next to Lisa, resuming his observation of the kids when his phone rang. Noah's heart skipped a beat as he looked at the screen. It was an unknown number. Could it be...?

Shooting up from his seat, Noah grabbed the phone, answering as he walked to the other side of Lisa's house, closing himself in the extra bedroom she told Noah he and Gabe could use while they were there. "Hello?" he whispered.

"Hello, Noah," the tinny voice replied.

"What do you want? Where's my wife?"

"You know what I want. The key. Do you have it? Macy's feeling a little anxious about getting home. It would be nice for her to see her children again."

Children? The fact that the word was plural gave Noah pause. Maybe the kidnapper didn't have Kate? Noah was silent for a second, trying to straighten out his thoughts before answering. "What key are you talking about? I don't know anything about a key."

There was a gravelly chuckle on the other end of the line. "Oh, don't try to play me, Noah. Husbands and wives, they don't keep any secrets. They tell each other everything. Especially a girl like Macy. She's like an open book."

Heat built in Noah's cheeks. Whoever was talking sounded like they were way too familiar with Macy. "You keep your hands off my wife. You hear me?"

There was a pause on the other end of the line for a moment. "She's lovely, you know. I've really enjoyed getting to spend time with her. I'm sure she's lonely. I bet she would like to get back to her family. But if you don't have the key, I might just have to keep her for myself. I'd be more than happy to take care of her loneliness myself."

Noah sucked in a breath. "Listen, I would happily give you this key if I had it. But I have no idea what you're talking about. Maybe we can meet somewhere and —"

"And what?" The voice suddenly sounded angry. "I want the key! If you want to see your wife back in one piece, you have twenty-four hours. I'm tired of being patient. I'll contact you tomorrow and give you a place where we can meet. And if you don't, you can rest assured you'll never see your wife alive again. I'll be more than happy to send her back to you in pieces. That's a promise!"

The line went dead.

Noah dropped the phone on the bed as he slumped down onto the edge of it. A film of perspiration covered his forehead. He used the sleeve of his shirt to wipe it off. Twenty-four hours wasn't much, especially when he had no idea what the kidnappers wanted, aside from the mysterious key.

Noah stood up, grabbing his backpack, charging out to the kitchen where Lisa was still sitting in front of her laptop. He scooped up his own computer from the table. She looked at him, frowning. "Where are you going?"

He cleared his throat. "I gotta get home. There's some work stuff I need to handle," he lied. The whole family knew that Macy was on one of her adventures. No one on his side of the family knew about the kidnapping or the ransom demand for the key. Explaining it to them would have created a lot of drama. His parents would have flown up immediately from Florida amid a flurry of "I told you so's" and "You probably should never have married that girl."

Noah couldn't take that. He knew himself. It would break him.

Lisa shook her head. "Have you looked out the window in the last hour? We've got lake-effect snow coming in. At this point, nobody's going anywhere."

Noah glanced out the window. In his preoccupation of watching Gabe play with Elise and the call from the kidnapper, he'd never noticed that the weather had changed and not for the better. The City of Erie, where Lisa lived, wasn't just getting the snow that he'd experienced in Pittsburgh the day before. They were getting a downright blizzard. He pressed his lips together. The weather didn't matter. He had to go. He had to try to get Macy and Kate back and he had to be in Pittsburgh to do it. "Like I said. I gotta go."

Lisa shrugged, looking back at her computer, her face slack. "All right. Good luck. Let me know when you want to come and get Gabe."

Noah strode through the family room where Gabe was still occupied with his cousin, ruffling his hair as he walked by, leaning over and whispering, "I'll be back. Have a good time." Distracted by the video games, Gabe didn't bother to ask any questions.

Outside, the weather was exactly as Lisa had promised. A minute of blowing snow alternately swirling in tornado-like shapes would give way to a line of precipitation coming across the driveway in a single sheet, the wind driving it nearly horizontal. Noah struggled out to his car. From his footprints in the driveway, in only the last hour or two, four inches of new snow had already covered Lisa's driveway.

Noah got into the Mazda and started the engine, tossing his backpack on the passenger seat, flipping on headlights and the windshield wipers as well as the defroster. He would need every tool the SUV had to make it through the accumulating snow.

Pulling down the driveway, he realized he could hardly see. Apparently, snow blindness was real. He knew Erie was prone to lake-effect snow, but he'd never seen a storm like this one. Everything in front of him had turned to white, the snow coating everything on Lisa's street, from the roofs, to the mailboxes, to the road.

Noah had heard Lisa describe lake effect snow before, but he'd never experienced it in person. He frowned. It seemed too early to be getting this much snow. They weren't even to Thanksgiving yet. He gripped the wheel tighter. He understood the phenomenon. Cold air would cruise across Lake Erie, pick up moisture making the clouds heavy with water vapor from the large body of water before it froze over the winter. As the nearly pregnant clouds hit the shore, the land jutting up in the rolling hillsides of what was the Appalachian foothills of Eastern Ohio and western Pennsylvania, the clouds had no choice but to dump their cargo. That meant lake-effect snow. And lots of it. Lisa had told Noah about a story of cities in the snow belt that had actually needed to call out the National Guard to clear the streets and get the city operational again. Lake effect snow was no joke and now Noah knew why.

As his car slipped and skidded down the road, he kept his

eyes focused forward, his mind singularly pinned on the weather, his wife and his daughter. Where were they? He felt his heart skip a beat. His breathing was shallow as he guided the vehicle back onto the freeway, hoping that road conditions were better. He had nearly zero visibility. His stomach clenched into a tight knot. He pressed the accelerator again squinting at the snow-covered road in front of him. It was nearly white-out conditions.

Trying to merge onto the freeway, he heard a deep horn blast from behind him, coming from a semi-truck. He hadn't seen it in the blanket of precipitation. Alarmed by the oncoming semi, Noah jerked the wheel and slammed on the brakes, sending the SUV off the side of the road, bumping down an embankment. The semi kept going, the blare of its horn receding in the background. Noah sat breathlessly for a few minutes, trying to calm himself down. After a minute, he shifted the vehicle into reverse, trying to get himself off of the side of the road and back on the freeway toward home. All he heard were the tires spinning. He tried going forward. Same result. Frustrated, he slammed his fist into the steering wheel. He was stuck.

As much as he wanted to go home to find Macy and Kate, he wasn't going anywhere soon.

40

Kate Chandler had arrived in the tiny town of Thomasville in the middle of the night. Quickly realizing that her plan to go find her mother would be nearly impossible in the dark, she found a spot behind the Thomasville General Store where she parked her car next to an overfilled dumpster, dousing the lights. It was cold out, colder than she anticipated. She spent the hours waiting until daylight huddling in the driver's seat, shivering, turning on the heat for a few minutes every hour or so, wrapping herself in a towel she had in the back seat of her car from a beach trip over the summer. It smelled faintly like sand, suntan lotion, and mold, the memories of the warmer days long past. A few times, she had considered texting her dad to let him know where she was, but she didn't. All he would do would be to freak out and tell her to come home.

She had no intention of doing that. Not without her mother.

As the morning broke, Kate stirred from a light sleep. Blinking and rubbing her eyes, she wasn't sure if it was actually sleep at all. It felt more like a twilight rest, like she was half-asleep and half-awake, expecting some bored police officer to tap on her window and tell her to move along.

But it didn't happen.

A thin light crested up over Thomasville, the clouds still heavy in the sky, a swirl of tiny snowflakes dodging and darting through the air before finding a place to land. Kate started her car, turning on the heat full blast, trying to stave off the chill in her bones, and drove carefully out of the parking lot, her head on a swivel. Down the road about a mile, just as the heat was starting to course through the sedan, she spotted a café with its lights on.

She pulled in, leaving the heat on in the car for a moment, waiting for the chill of overnight to wear off. She stared at her backpack. From inside one of the pockets she fished out her wallet. She had a little bit of cash, her debit card, college ID, and an emergency credit card her dad had given her. Shoving her wallet into her pocket, Kate slipped out of the car, locking it as she walked away, making her way across the slippery parking lot, almost falling as she pulled the door open to the café.

Kate saw a sign by the door that indicated the Thomasville Coffee Company was a newer addition to the community. From the date on the framed sign displayed inside the doorway, containing the first dollar bill the company had ever earned, it appeared the business had only been around for two years. Kate glanced around her, feeling the warmth of the heat from the café soak into her clothes.

In front of her, placed against the right-hand wall of the store, was a long counter outfitted with an ornate brass and stainless-steel coffee maker, the kind that looked to be imported from Europe. Probably Italy, if Kate had to guess. The cafés near Bedford College had the same kind of set up. In addition to the coffee maker sputtering and throwing off steam, there was a glass bakery case filled with decoratively displayed pastries. Along the back wall were wooden bread racks filled with loaves of different types of bread and bagels.

Kate walked up to the counter, ordered herself an Americano with cream and sugar and a plain bagel with cream cheese. She was starved. As she went to check out, she saw a brochure stationed near the cash register. It was green on the front with the gold letters reading "Thomasville Lake — A Great Place to Visit!" Kate grabbed one and waited at the end of the counter for her coffee and her breakfast.

A moment later, a skinny dark haired young man with a full sleeve of tattoos on his right arm walked to the end of the counter where Kate was standing and handed her a mug and a small plate. Sticking the brochure under her elbow, Kate grabbed the mug and plate with a nod to the young man and walked to a table in the corner, choosing the seat where she could see the doorway.

Settling herself against the cushion, she wrapped her fingers around the mug, trying to get the final bit of chill out of her bones from spending overnight in her car. It wasn't supposed to be this cold this soon. It wasn't even Thanksgiving yet. She knew the likelihood of the snow sticking around was pretty small. Her father always said it was the shot across the bow, a reminder that more snow was coming and to get ready. If his theory was right, this blast should melt in a few days. Kate thought for a moment about her dad and then pushed the thoughts aside. She was sure he wouldn't be happy that she hadn't told him where she was. She'd left his texts unanswered as well, even powering down her phone as soon as she got to Thomasville. She didn't want anyone to know where she was. Her mother had reached out to her and her alone. Kate knew in her gut that it was her responsibility to find her mom. Her dad was too worried and the police were too uninterested. Macy's only hope was Kate.

As Kate lifted the hot cup of coffee to her lips, she frowned.

The weather wouldn't make it any easier for her to find her mom. Why couldn't she have sent the message a month ago, when the weather was still warm and Kate could have hunted for her in Thomasville without the weather being a factor?

Kate spread a thin layer of cream cheese on her bagel, broke a small piece off and stuck it in her mouth as she opened the map she'd found at the counter by the cash register. The interior of the paper was filled with a colorful geography of the area, bright blue ink indicating the shape of the lake, little stands of trees printed on the paper here and there, brown dots noting where the cabins were located. Kate took another sip of her coffee and chewed her lip. If the map she was staring at was accurate, there were even more cabins in the area then she remembered from when they'd been there in the spring. She felt her stomach tighten. It could take her weeks to find the right cabin. Her mother might be gone by then. Really gone.

"Can I get you a refill?" A voice interrupted her thoughts. The young man that had made her coffee stood in front of the table, holding a stainless-steel insulated coffee pot in his hand. Kate glanced up and read his name badge. Thomas. She raised her eyebrows.

"Sure." As he poured the coffee, she looked at him more closely. He had dark hair, almost the same color as hers, but unlike hers, which was long and soft, the young man's seemed to jut out in every direction from the top of his head. Studying it, Kate decided it wasn't intentional. It looked like his hair grew that way. He was thin and tall, probably almost six feet in height, but not quite. He had green eyes and a slight stubble growing across his chin. As she pulled her coffee cup back toward her, she glanced at him. "Is your name really Thomas?"

He glanced down at his name badge and nodded. "Yep. I get that question a lot. I am indeed Thomas from Thomasville."

Kate shook her head, a smile pulling at her cheek. "Is there anything to that? Like, are you an original Thomas?"

"I also get that question a lot," he grinned. "Unfortunately, the answer is no. The original Thomas family the township is named after had Thomas as their last name. From what I read, they were Quakers from England. Started a small church here on the outskirts of town. I think the building is still there." He cocked his head to the side. "Actually, I think you can read about it in that brochure you have." He glanced at her. "You new here? Visiting? I haven't seen you around before."

Kate hesitated. "Visiting. I was here with some friends in the spring. We rented a cabin. I think we want to do it again over Christmas break so they sent me here to scope out a good place to stay," she lied. She pointed to the map. "These are all cabins around the lake?"

Thomas nodded. "Yeah. There's a heck of a lot of them. The fun side is down here." He pointed to the wider section of the lake. "That's probably where you were earlier. There's a pizza place, paddleboard and canoe rentals, and waterskiing — stuff like that. If you're coming here at Christmas, that stuff will be closed. The lake will be frozen over."

Kate nodded. "What about this part of the lake?" She pointed to the narrower side of the lake at the far end.

"You know, I don't head down there very often." Thomas scowled. "I think there's a lot of permanent residents that live down there. They don't like the noise and the chaos from the summer crowd."

Kate frowned. "So you don't live in one of the cabins by the lake?"

"No, I live in town with a couple of buddies. We rent a house." Thomas glanced over his shoulder. There were two people in line waiting, one of them glaring in his direction. "Listen, I gotta get back to work. People get angry if they can't get their morning coffee." He pulled his cell phone out of his pocket checking the time. "There's a visitors center down the street. The lady that runs it is really nice. She could probably help you better. I think they open in about an hour if you want to hang out here until then. I'm sure she can help you figure out where you and your friends can stay at Christmas. You never know, maybe I'll see you then?"

As Thomas walked away, resuming his post behind the counter, Kate felt a little guilty for lying. Thomas seemed nice.

Looking up, she checked the time on the clock mounted on the wall. As Thomas said, the visitor's center would open in an hour. It might be exactly what she needed.

41

Grady had just driven across the Thomasville Township limits when his phone rang. He glanced down at the screen, pursing his lips. It was Noah Chandler. "Noah? What's going on?"

"The kidnapper called again. I can't get home. I'm stuck in a ditch on the side of the road. I was trying to, but I got stuck. A semi just about ran me off the road..."

Grady looked around him, listening. Noah was rambling. Grady saw the sign for Nelson's Hardware and pulled in, throwing his black SUV into park. He needed to concentrate on what Noah was saying. "Slow down. What's going on?"

Noah sucked in a sharp breath. "It's Macy. The kidnapper called again."

This time the words were coming out more slowly. "Okay, how long ago?"

"I don't know. Maybe twenty minutes, a half-hour ago? I don't know, I..." The words drifted off.

Grady leaned back in his seat, staring straight ahead of him as a few cars drove slowly past, making their way through the snow-covered roads on the main drag in Thomasville, Arch

Street. "It's okay, Noah. You have every right to be upset. I need you to slow down and tell me what that kidnapper said." There was no way Noah was going to talk if he was upset. Grady needed him calm and clear-headed.

"He said something about being tired of being patient."

They weren't going anywhere fast in this conversation if Noah was going to parse out information in minuscule amounts. If he wanted Grady's help, he'd need to spill all the details. "Did you record it, like you did the last one?"

"No. I didn't. I didn't think about it. I'm sorry."

"Don't worry about it. Just take a breath and try to tell me what happened." It actually wasn't all right. Having the recording would have made everything easier. There was nothing about this case that was easy, though.

Noah spent the next minute recounting the conversation he'd had with the kidnapper, the renewed demand for the key, and the questions Noah had about what they were asking for.

"He said he's going to give me twenty-four hours to get the key or he's gonna return Macy to us in pieces." The next words came out in a whisper, as if Noah could hardly speak. "Detective, I have no idea what he's talking about. I just want my wife back. My daughter too. I don't know what to do. You have to help us."

Grady leaned back in his seat. His fury at Lieutenant Williams had dissipated on the drive into Thomasville. He was feeling calm. Focused. With the pressure of the department off his back, he knew he only had one job, and that was to find Macy and Kate Chandler and return them to Noah and Gabe, to make their family whole again. In the back of his mind, he could see the reunion, he could see Noah closing the front door of their home and Grady pulling down the driveway, knowing that at least one family had been restored.

Even if it wasn't his...

Grady ran his hand through his hair and stared down at the

floor of the SUV noting there was a single gum wrapper crinkled in the corner. He pressed his lips together. He would get to that later. "Alright, Noah, this is what we're going to do. Get yourself someplace safe and stay put."

"I was trying to get back to Pittsburgh, but the roads are really bad. I'm stranded on the side of the highway. I'm staying with my sister in Erie."

Grady nodded. That made sense. He'd heard on the radio on the drive into Thomasville that the lakeshore areas of Pennsylvania were getting pummeled with snow. It wasn't as bad near Thomasville, that was for sure. For that, he was grateful.

"Good. Call for a tow and stay there with Gabe. I'm going to do some digging. If you don't hear from me, don't worry about it. Just call me if you hear from the kidnappers again, okay?"

"Yeah, that sounds okay. I can do that. What about the deadline? He said we only have twenty-four hours."

"I'll be back to you as soon as I have anything. I'm going to do everything I can to get your wife and your daughter back to you in one piece. We'll find both of them, no matter where they are."

"Thanks, Detective."

"You're welcome."

Grady ended the call and put the SUV back into gear, a film of perspiration on his palms. Time was ticking. He hoped he could fulfill his promise.

42

Detective Hunter Franco hadn't been sleeping, at least not since the shadows of Detectives Max Grady and Cassie Reynolds had crossed the threshold of the Thomasville Police Department. Although he thought that simply filing the information report on the disappearance of Macy Chandler would assuage his sometimes overly guilty conscience, he was wrong.

It didn't.

When something was bothering Hunter, he was fine during the day, keeping himself occupied with work or chores. Unfortunately, he couldn't say the same about the night when the questions he had surging in his mind surrounded him, pecking away at the inside of his mind like a flock of angry birds. Luckily, there was no one in his house on the outskirts of Thomasville to disturb with his late-night pacing other than his bloodhound, Romeo. Romeo didn't seem to mind, spending the time staring at Hunter as he paced and fidgeted, watching his owner for a few minutes and then resting his long face with sad round eyes and droopy ears down on his dog bed with a harumph.

It had been a day and a half since the detectives from Pittsburgh had descended upon Thomasville, carting with them the story of the disappearance of Macy Chandler. Their inquiries had left Hunter with more questions of his own.

And they weren't only about Macy.

Since Grady and Reynolds had visited, Hunter's boss, Andy Bennett, had for all intents and purposes, disappeared. Hunter had seen him come into the station, go directly to his private office in the back of the building and close the door. It didn't open for hours. Hunter had received precisely one email from Andy during that time, instructing him to look through cold case files that had never been settled in Thomasville to see if there was anything that could be done with them. Hunter knew it was nothing but busy work. The only actual case they had at the moment, given the fact that the busy summer season was over in Thomasville, was Macy Chandler. Based on the way Andy was acting, either he was ignoring the fact that Grady and Reynolds had made a personal visit to them, or he didn't care.

Hunter wasn't sure which one it was, although he had a sneaking suspicion it was the latter and not the former. As far as anyone in the office was concerned, Detective Andy Bennett was already retired. The reality of the situation meant one thing and one thing alone — whether intentionally or functionally, Hunter Franco was the only operational arm of the Thomasville detective bureau.

And he had a missing person on his hands.

Not able to get the story of Macy Chandler out of his mind, Hunter had started his investigation in the same spot that all good investigators did — on social media. He'd learned the trick during training when a formidable-looking man with a thick beard and a shaved head from the US Marshals led a fugitive tracking class at the Academy. It was one of those career option kinds of days where people from what seemed to be a million different law enforcement agencies came in and talked to the police academy students about what their career could look like. The man from the Marshals, whose name Hunter couldn't remember, had said one of their best tactics for tracking people they were looking for was on their social media feed. The man's voice echoed in Hunter's head. "You'd think they'd be smart enough not to post themselves, their friends, where they'd just gone to eat, or their girlfriend, but you'd be wrong. I can't tell you how many people I've caught because they've decided to post something on one feed or another."

Macy Chandler, while she didn't have a robust social media presence, at least had her picture posted, which Hunter added to his file when he got into the office that morning. The rest of his investigation into her online life had led to basically nothing. She hadn't posted anything in the last six months, a full two months prior to when she'd disappeared. Worse yet, she wasn't a regular poster or commenter at all, at least from what Hunter could decipher, though he was no social media expert.

Staring at the file that morning in the station after leaving Romeo at home, Hunter began to wonder if Macy Chandler was even in Thomasville. He shook his head, drumming the end of his pen on the notepad in front of him for a second. The information he had only skimmed the surface and what he did have was six months old. He stared up at the ceiling again for a second, thinking about the visit from Grady and Reynolds. They seemed so sure that Macy was in the area. Was that actually true?

Standing up from his desk, Hunter shrugged on his coat over a long-sleeved Thomasville Police Department Detective Bureau polo shirt he wore, zipping it up. He glanced out the window. It was still snowing outside. Luckily it was light, nothing that the state road crews couldn't handle with ease, at least for the moment. He grabbed his cell phone and wallet, stuck them in his pockets, and lifted a set of keys for one of the department's SUVs off the hook by the front door, giving Becky, who was making yet another pot of coffee, a wave.

She called after him. "You headed out?"

Hunter gave her a single nod. "Yeah. I have to follow-up on a couple of things. Old cases. Ones Andy wants me to try to clear."

"Okay," Becky said brightly. "You need any of those files from your desk to take with you?"

"No," Hunter said. "I've got it all in my mind," he lied. The last thing he needed to do was tell Becky that he was tracking down Macy Chandler. Knowing her, she'd move as quickly as her stubby legs could take her back to Andy's office to turn him in. What she didn't know wouldn't hurt her. "I'll see you later. I'll have my cell phone with me. Give me a call if anything pops up."

"Will do."

43

Outside, Hunter trotted to the SUV, slipping up the hood on his coat as he did. The sky was what he called fifty-fifty — half clouds and half sun. It matched his mood. At that moment, a peek of blue sky was visible overhead, long rays of gold sunshine poking out from between thick lines of angry clouds dumping swirls of snow down over Thomasville. Hunter jumped in the SUV, slamming the door, turning it on.

Using one of the department's vehicles was one of the perks of being an officer, even if he was only able to use it while he was on duty. He pulled his phone out of his pocket and pulled up the profile picture he'd found of Macy Chandler. She was blonde with bobbed hair and a big smile. The border of the picture he'd found of her had a distinctly Christmas theme, dated from the year before, ornaments and stars floating on a red background encircling her face and shoulders. He zoomed in on the image, furrowing his eyebrows. She was nice-looking, someone he would expect to be pleasant and kind.

Reading people's faces was something Hunter had become very good at. For any police officer, it was critical to be able to make a split-second judgment about someone. That gut feeling could be the difference between life and death and the ability to go home at the end of the day, and not in a body bag.

Hunter was sure at that moment that Macy Chandler would like to go home too.

Backing the SUV out of the parking spot next to the Thomasville Police Department, Hunter turned it out on the road, driving cautiously. From the white haze on the streets, he could tell that the roads had been salted, but that didn't mean that there weren't still patches of ice. The last thing he wanted to do was crash the SUV and then have to spend the day doing reports and giving statements to Andy Bennett. Avoiding his boss seemed like the best strategy for the moment, at least until the chief got back and life returned to normal.

Hunter sighed. The most frustrating thing about the Macy Chandler case was the lack of leads. But as he knew from his training, not training he'd gotten from Andy Bennett, but from a series of videos he'd watched the night before when he was unable to sleep, sometimes the only way to break a case open was to get out on the road and shake the trees.

Hunter chewed his lip. If he were new in town, there were a few places that he would go. He had to expect that Macy Chandler would have hit at least one or more of those spots. Maybe, with a little legwork and some luck, someone would recognize the picture he had of her. If no one did, then at least at the end of the day, he could tell Grady and Reynolds that he'd actually done something to help.

One of the most frequented stores in Thomasville was Nelson's Hardware. Nearly everyone who came into Thomasville ended up there eventually. Hunter drove down the road and pulled into the parking lot, jogging into the store, spending as little time in the cold as he could. Inside, he stamped his feet on the mat, getting the salty drips of melted precipitation off of them. He walked to the counter. Joe Nelson, the great-grandson of the original Nelsons that had started the hardware store, gave him a nod. "Hey, Hunter. You're here early. The department need some salt?"

"No, Joe. I'm working on a case." Hunter pulled his phone out of his pocket and scrolled to the picture of Macy Chandler he'd found. "Any chance you've seen this woman before? She likely would've stopped by here sometime in July."

Joe narrowed his eyes at the picture for a minute and then rubbed his chin. "July? Hunter, we are always so busy in July with Independence Day that I can hardly keep my head above water. Maybe? I don't know. I can't say that I for sure recognize her. She kinda looks like every other blonde lady that walks in the store. No disrespect meant, if you know what I mean."

"None taken." Hunter decided to press a little more. He wasn't going to give up that easily. "This woman, her name is Macy Chandler. She was coming in from out of town. She probably would have asked you questions that the out-of-towners ask like, you know, where to go to eat, where she could stay, where she could buy a certain item. Any of that ring a bell?" Hunter held up the picture to Joe again.

Joe's eyes settled on the screen for a second then looked back at Hunter. "No, I'm sorry to say I got nothing." He pointed up at a surveillance camera mounted on the wall near the ceiling. "I can give you the security footage we have though, but it only goes back for thirty days, at least what I have here. I can request it from the company that hosts everything if you want. They said they keep everything on the cloud for a year. You want me to do that?"

Hunter blinked. It didn't sound like Macy Chandler had been at the store, but then again sometimes digging a little deeper was the only way to get answers. He pulled his business card out of his pocket. "That'd be good, Joe, if you don't mind. You can have them email it to me at the address listed on the card. If they could pull June first on forward that would be helpful."

Joe raised his eyebrows. "That's a lot of video footage to watch, Hunter."

"Don't I know it," Hunter said, spinning on his heel and walking out of the store.

Jogging back to the SUV, Hunter made a mental note that Joe owed him surveillance footage as he drove down the street, hoping to have more luck at the Thomasville General Store.

44

Two hours later, Hunter had visited a half dozen or more sites across Thomasville, all places that he thought someone new to town might stop. He tried at the general store, the Thomasville Coffee Company, the visitor center, where Marybeth had assured him that someone as pretty as that she would never have forgotten, and the laundromat where old man Green admitted he had no idea who came in and out of his facility and had no surveillance cameras installed that might help with the search. Hunter finally tried the Silver Skillet, a favorite neighborhood breakfast place where the waitresses were too busy to answer his questions and the manager had gone home sick.

Frustrated at his lack of progress, Hunter sat in his vehicle for a few minutes, mentally going through the list of places he had available to him. He left the department's SUV parked in front of the Silver Skillet restaurant and stared down the street. Out of the corner of his eye he saw movement, a woman walking toward The Greenery, their local flower shop, which did an amazing amount of business in the spring, summer, and fall months as couples flocked to Thomasville to get married with the lake in the background. Although the last thing Hunter was in the mood to do was go talk to yet another person, he knew it was part of the job, a job he would likely have sooner than later if Andy Bennett's behavior was any indication.

Slipping out of the SUV, he slammed the door behind him and locked it, trotting across the street and pulling open the door to the flower shop on the heels of the woman who had just unlocked the door. She turned around, her eyes wide, looking startled. "I'm sorry. I'm not open quite yet. Could you maybe come back in a half hour or so and give me a chance to get set up?"

Hunter tugged at the side of his coat, showing his badge. "I'm Detective Hunter Franco from Thomasville PD. I'm sorry for barging in on you like this. I have a couple of questions."

The woman frowned and then took off her coat, hanging it on a hook behind the counter near the cash register. "I suppose so. What's this about?"

From inside his pocket, Hunter pulled out his cell phone, finding the picture of Macy Chandler again. "Is there any chance you've seen this woman before? She would have stopped by your store in July at some point. Her name is Macy Chandler."

The woman looked at it, cocking her head to the side, rubbing her chin with her fingers. "Can you make it bigger for me?"

Hunter handed the woman his phone. He watched as she zoomed in on the picture, staring at it. She looked up at him and handed it back. "Yes, I'm pretty sure I saw her. Is everything all right?"

Hunter's heart skipped a beat. "Do you have any idea when she might have stopped in your store? Remember anything she said?"

The woman paused for a second as if she was acknowledging the fact that Hunter had answered her question with one of his own, effectively displacing her request for more information. She pressed her lips together. "I think, if I remember correctly, she bought a big bunch of daisies." She walked over to the computer. "Let me have a look here."

Hunter waited, his chest tightening, his heart starting to beat a little faster. Finally, someone had admitted to seeing Macy Chandler in Thomasville. Maybe her husband, Noah, had been right all along. He shook his head, guilt washing over him. They should never have ignored Noah's first visit. Never.

Hunter glanced around him as he waited for the shop owner to search for information on her computer. The flower shop was filled with dried silk flower arrangements, the scent of fresh flowers from the refrigerated cases in the air. One corner of the shop seemed to be dedicated to bridal bouquets displayed on a table around a fake wedding cake that had been decorated with an elaborate assortment of silk flowers, showing off the prowess of the designers that worked in the shop. On the opposite wall was a veritable garden of green plants, everything from a wild-looking overgrown fern to the sharp leaves of the plant he only knew as "Mother-in-law's tongue."

The woman's voice interrupted Hunter's thoughts. "Here it is." She furrowed her eyebrows at Hunter. "Can I see that picture again?"

Hunter held out his phone. The woman behind the counter looked at it and then back at the computer. "Yes, yes. I'm pretty sure this is who this was. I remember it now. She came in early. Said she was traveling and had decided to spend a little time at the lake. She'd seen the daisies in the window and wanted a bouquet to take with her."

"Did she say where she was staying?" The question caught in Hunter's throat.

The woman shook her head. "Not that I remember. I guess I kind of assumed from the looks of her that she'd be staying at one of the cabins around the lake. Looked to be that type, you know. Free-spirited, like she came up to spend some time in nature or something. Not that there's anything wrong with that, mind you."

Hunter nodded. The lake attracted all types. "Of course not." Hunter chewed his lip, then continued. "Did she happen to say what she was doing in the area?"

The woman looked down at the ground for a minute, her lips pressed tightly together, little narrow wrinkles forming around her upper and bottom lip. Then she glanced up, her face brightening. "She said she was a writer. Was working on a set of poems she hoped to have published. The flowers reminded her something about her poetry. Said she wanted to look at them and enjoy them. Inspiration for her work, I guess."

Poetry. Hunter's heartbeat quickened. There couldn't be that many people who came up to the lake that wanted to work on a book of poetry. The story fit Macy Chandler perfectly. "Do you happen to have the date on that sales receipt of when she was here?"

The woman nodded. "Sure. It was July seventeenth. I can print you off a copy if you'd like."

"That would be great."

As Hunter waited for the woman to print off the receipt, he paced around the store, picking up a business card from the front desk in case he had follow-up questions. Knowing Macy had been in the area meant there was something to the story that Noah Chandler had not only told them, but had told Pittsburgh police detectives. Part of him wanted to run out to his SUV and quickly dial Detective Max Grady and let him know, but given the way their meeting had gone, Hunter decided against it. Better for Hunter to follow up and get something concrete before he decided to clue in the other officers. Grady looked like the kind of guy that had a big temper on him. The last thing he wanted to do was be in the sights of someone like that. It was bad enough he had to deal with Andy Bennett.

"Here you go," the woman said.

Hunter took the sheet of paper from her and held up the business card. "This you?"

The woman nodded. "Yeah. Nancy Clemens. I'm the owner."

"Nice to meet you, Nancy. Thanks for the help." Hunter turned on his heel and walked out of the store.

[illegible] he wanted [illegible] the [illegible] of [illegible] the [illegible] had enough [illegible] had to deal with [illegible] Bender.

"[illegible]" [illegible] said.

[illegible] the [illegible] paper from her and [illegible] the [illegible] "[illegible]"

[illegible] "Yeah [illegible]"

"N[illegible] Thanks for the [illegible]" [illegible] turned on [illegible] heel and walked out of the store.

45

Dario couldn't stop pacing. He'd sent Lola back to the city earlier than he normally did, a full day earlier, in fact. Lola seemed to be only too happy to leave. Things were coming to a head and he wanted her out of the way. It wasn't just because he wanted to protect her, although that was part of it. He wanted the space to be able to do what he needed to do without her sad eyes judging his every move.

From the moment he'd suggested Lola help him, Dario knew she wasn't fully on board. Not only was Macy Chandler her boss, but she was also friends with Macy. Dario had positioned it carefully, telling Lola that Macy would feel more comfortable if she was around people she knew. Sure, they were going to hold her, but it was one thing for Dario to hold Macy captive. If her friend Lola was there, it might make the experience a bit more palatable, if that was possible for a kidnapping.

He'd been right and wrong all at the same time.

He was right about the fact that having Lola around made things easier, not only for Macy, but for him. He'd been wrong about Lola though. He thought that no matter what, she'd side with him. They were family, after all. Her allegiance and loyalty should have been to him, but over the last few weeks, he'd seen it break, cracks in her normally quiet veneer starting to pop up. She'd been arguing with him about the way they were treating Macy and how they needed to let her go. Dario knew part of it was because Lola was afraid they'd get caught. They'd already talked about it. If they did and the police came asking, Lola was to tell them everything, to trade information for full immunity in the case. Dario was willing to take the hit if they got caught.

That was an if...

With any luck, it would never come to that. Macy or her family would give him the key, he'd set her loose and run like hell, first for Texas and then for the border as soon as he cleared out the safety deposit box. Dario ran his fingers through his dark hair, a scowl on his face. The anger had built in his system over weeks and months. He put everything on the line to get the key from Macy. He was sure she had it. How could she not? But then Lola had suggested that maybe the key never existed. Maybe it was just a fable that their family had spun over decades of family dinners. That single question had nearly put him over the edge. He'd quit his job and given up his life in order to pursue the key. And if there wasn't one, what then? He'd end up spending the rest of his life in jail for absolutely nothing.

Dario paused for a minute, listening. He could hear Macy moving around upstairs, pacing back and forth just like he was downstairs. She'd tolerated her captivity better than he expected. For the most part, she was patient and kind, only asking for a few limited things, other than desperately wanting to go home. She hadn't screamed or yelled or even uttered a vile word in his direction. She had more self-control in her little pinky than he did in his entire body.

That wasn't to say she wasn't upset. He'd caught her crying a few times when he'd walked in the room, after they'd allowed her to see their faces. The recognition had come instantly, although instead of pleading with him as he'd expected her to do when she realized it was Dario that had taken her, she'd become quiet, even cold. She'd turned away, freezing him out, as if her disappointment in the fact that he'd kidnapped her was more than she could bear. That phase had lasted for about two weeks, Macy simply turning away anytime Dario walked in the room. Now, she was simply civil. That was it. Nothing more.

He could see in her eyes that she thought it was a cold betrayal.

He gritted his teeth. While part of him wanted to feel bad that he'd hurt Macy, another part of him didn't care. He wanted the key and what it represented, what it would unlock for him. He would do anything to get it. Shaking his head, Dario interlaced his fingers behind his head as he continued pacing in the family room below where Macy was being held. Time was running out. He might have to resort to more persuasive methods if she didn't give him the key soon. As much as he didn't want to have to hurt Macy, she and her sniveling husband were leaving him no choice. They kept protesting that they didn't know anything about the key, but that was an impossible thought in Dario's mind.

Dario stopped moving for a moment, his jaw set. It felt as though someone had suddenly stiffened his back into a rod of steel. He was strong. The strength in his body was part of the legacy of being a Gilbert, a Gilberto from Spain. Strength, unity, and loyalty were their hallmarks through the generations. It was something Macy Dixon and her family didn't know anything about.

But he would teach her, no matter what it took...

46

Macy had been pacing back and forth in the small room in the upstairs of the cabin for the last twenty minutes, as best as she could tell with no clock on the wall and no way to tell the time. After a few weeks of being held hostage, she began trying to judge time by the way the shadows crept along the window ledge in the small room in the cabin. It was feeling more claustrophobic every single day.

Walking a straight line across one wall of the room, she hugged her arms to her body, hoping the movement would help keep her warm. The wind had started to blow again, the thin walls of the cabin no match for the lines of snow that kept whipping across Thomasville Lake. Macy stopped for a second squinting, staring out the window. Across the other side of the lake, she could see the tree branches bending in the wind and then stopping and straightening as the gust disappeared. As another gust charged across the lake, they would bend again, stop and straighten. She swallowed. That was what life was like, wasn't it? There would be a series of trials and tribulations where people would have to bend. Then the winds that brought the trouble in the first place would die down and things would straighten up. But the lesson was to bend and not to break, wasn't it? Macy turned away, chasing a lump of fear back down into her gut, starting to pace again when she heard heavy boots on the steps. Dario. She might bend, but she wouldn't break. Never.

A moment later, she heard the locks on the outside of the door click open. The door pushed into her space from the tiny sitting room outside. Dario stood, his shoulders back, his arms hanging at his side, his fists balled. Macy took a couple of steps back, sucking in a breath. There was something about the set of his jaw and the look on his face that instantly made her afraid.

"What do you want?" Macy asked, her eyes wide. Her voice came out as a whisper. She backed up towards the bed and sat down on the edge of it, her knees and feet pressed together.

"You know what I want," he growled.

Macy's heart skipped a beat. It took all of the self-control she had to not reach up and grab the pendant around her neck. Telling him she didn't have it was easier when she didn't know about the key, but now she did. Until the cord had broken around her neck, she'd had no idea what he'd been talking about. She looked at the floor, hoping he couldn't see the flush of redness in her cheeks. At least her necklace was hidden underneath the sweatshirt Lola had given her. "You keep asking for the same thing, Dario. I don't have what you want. What is this key anyway?" Macy pressed her lips together. Maybe he knew what the address in Fort Worth was and what it represented.

Dario started to pace in the room, glaring at her every few steps. Macy noticed his knuckles were white, his body tense and coiled, as if a deep well of anger had balled itself up inside of his body and he was trying to keep it under control. She held her breath, waiting for him to respond.

"You know, I keep wondering how it's possible you keep

telling me you have absolutely no idea what the key is." His voice was low and gravelly. "You Dixons, that's how you roll, isn't it? Lies and deception through every single generation. That's how you all managed to get ahead — by stealing from families like mine."

Macy shook her head slowly. Yes, now she knew about the key, but stealing? "Dario, I've known you for a long time. What are you talking about? Why don't you just spit it out and then you can let me go."

"Let you go?" he scoffed. "You've got to be kidding me. You are the one thing that is preventing me from getting what I want. You aren't going anywhere until I get it." He stopped, towering over her, his face twisted and angry. "Do you understand me?"

A shiver ran down Macy's spine. It was the first time he'd been that firm with her. It sounded like a threat, one that tied her gut into a knot.

Macy didn't say anything for a minute, waiting. She stared at the floor, her mouth dry. Everything in her wanted to leap off the bed and bolt for the door, but she knew Dario was bigger and faster than her. There was no doubt in her mind that he would grab her if she tried to make her escape. After that, with how angry he seemed, it didn't seem likely that she would get away with trying to escape without some sort of punishment. He hadn't been physical up until that point, but she could tell by the tension in his body that something had changed. What, she didn't know. Macy sat frozen on the edge of the bed, looking down at the floor as she heard Dario's boots start to stride back and forth. She didn't dare look up at him.

"You keep saying you don't know anything about the key, Macy. How is that possible? You and I, we grew up in the same area. And somehow, your family ends up making millions on the oil fields. And you know what my family was left with? Nothing. And now, your family, Dixon Oil, they are worth nearly a billion dollars. A billion. In my mind that's just unthinkable. And here I am, a Gilberto, a person who owned the land next to your family's until you stole it."

Macy looked up, her eyebrows furrowed. "Stole it? Dario, what are you talking about? That was two generations ago." The words came out of Macy's mouth as her stomach sunk. She was Macy Chandler now. Not Macy Dixon. No more. She'd left that life behind in Texas. She didn't want to be part of Dixon Oil. Sure, she was an heir to the Dixon fortune, but that was something no one knew about, not even Noah and the kids. She didn't want any part of that. After seeing how her grandfather treated some of the people that worked for him, that was enough.

Her memory flickered. She'd been out one night as a child, going for a ride with her grandfather, Gerald Dixon, sitting next to him in his pickup truck as they passed through the oil fields just after dark, checking to make sure that a pump he'd fixed earlier in the day was still working. Her grandmother had not wanted Macy to go, saying the fields were no place for a young lady, but her grandfather agreed to her request. She remembered the conversation, her grandfather saying, "Macy is a Dixon, Lynn. She has every right to see what's going to be rightfully hers in the future. She might as well start now. You can't protect her forever."

That night, as Macy had sat in the truck driving through the oil fields with her grandfather on a dusty, bumpy central Texas road after nightfall, her grandfather had stopped his truck, squinting into the distance. He threw it into park, grabbing a shotgun from the gun rack just behind them. Sliding out of the truck, he looked back at Macy. "Stay here. Don't leave the truck. I'll be right back."

Macy frowned, watching her grandfather stride away. As best she could remember, she hadn't been more than ten or twelve years old. She'd scooted up on the seat, resting her palms on the dash, getting as close to the windshield as she could without actually leaving the truck, staring into the darkness, curious about where he was going. She saw the silhouette of her grandfather stride off into the distance, the shotgun in his hands approaching two men on horseback who had stopped by the Dixon oil rig they were checking.

A second later, Macy heard yelling, saw the shotgun in her grandfather's hands raise and then a brilliant light as a series of blasts left the end of the gun. A moment later, Macy, her eyes wide and her mouth hanging open, stared as the figures fell off of their horses, the horses running away, terrified by the sudden noise of the shotgun blasts.

Without any change to his expression, Macy's grandpa turned and strode back to the truck, replacing the shotgun on the rack, the smell of burning gunpowder filling the truck. Macy sat back in her seat, looking at her grandfather, not saying anything. He reached over and put his hand on the back of her head. She remembered quivering under his touch. It was the same hand that had pulled the trigger and killed two people only a moment before. He looked at her in the darkness as he flicked the headlights of the truck on. "Macy, the oil business is brutal and dangerous. There are times we have to do stuff we'd prefer not to. We've been having trouble with people sabotaging our wells. Any time they're on our land, they are trespassing. I know what you saw was bad, and I'm sorry you had to see it, but what you need to know is they were on property that wasn't theirs. When I told them to leave, they wouldn't. So I did what I needed to do in order to protect you and to protect our business." Starting the truck, the engine rumbling, Gerald looked at Macy. "You can't tell anyone what you saw. Do you understand?"

Macy remembered looking down at her hands. They were shaking. She nodded yes.

From that moment on, she was no longer Macy Dixon. She was just Macy.

Years later, when she'd met Noah, she'd been vague about her family's history, always saying Dixon was a common name, which it was. Noah didn't seem all that interested in knowing much about her family anyway. He was far more interested in knowing about her. She liked that. And since they'd started dating when she was in college, there'd been no real reason to go back to Texas. Her dad had always stopped to see them while he was traveling. By the time she'd met Noah, Grandma and Grandpa Dixon weren't able to travel anymore. And Macy's parents, while they benefited from the Dixon Oil money, weren't involved in the management of it. After what Macy had seen, they knew better than to bring the company up in front of Macy or Noah. That gave Macy a cushion, one where she didn't need to talk about the oil business with Noah.

When her grandfather had passed away a few years before, Macy had gotten a letter delivered to her office at Bedford College via courier. She'd been surprised, having to sign her name that she'd received it. Opening it, it was a letter from her grandfather's attorney, Bill Garrett. She'd quickly read it and stuffed it in her purse. It said she was the heir to a cool one hundred million dollars. It would be kept in trust for her and managed by a professional team. There was no action she needed to take unless she needed funds.

She never had. Macy had stuffed the letter in the bottom of the small safe they kept at the house, under an envelope that had some emergency cash and their passports. After what she'd seen her grandfather do, she didn't want any part of the Dixon money. It was blood money. Nothing more. Nothing less. She knew there'd come a day when she had to deal with her legacy, but she never imagined that Dario Gilbert would be the one that forced her hand.

Then again, money did funny things to people...

47

After remembering the men that her grandfather had killed, Macy looked up from her perch on the edge of the bed. Dario was still pacing back and forth, the wooden floor creaking under his heavy boots. The sour smell of perspiration filled the air. He looked like one of the animals at the zoo Macy had taken Kate and Gabe to see when they were little, a wild creature trapped behind fences and glass who had no reason to be cordoned off that way. "Give me the key, Macy." His voice had a sharp edge. "You must have it. There isn't anyone else."

With everything she had, Macy fought the urge to reach up and grab ahold of the pendant around her neck. Although she'd turned her back on her fortune, it didn't necessarily mean that she'd be willing to hand something over to Dario, especially after the way he'd treated her. He'd kept her trapped for months. Four long months away from the work she loved, her husband, and her children. She'd withstood him up until that moment. She wasn't going to give up now.

"I don't know what kind of tales you Gilbert's have been

spinning, but I don't have this key you keep talking about. Noah and I, we only have keys for our cars, our house..."

"Stop it!" Dario howled, throwing his hands up in the air. He swung his arm toward her desk and grabbed a glass from the table, launching it against the wall. "I'm tired of your lies! You know exactly what key I am talking about. It's the key that opens the safety deposit box where the Dixon diamond is held."

Macy's mouth ran dry as the shattered glass covered the floor. The Dixon diamond? Was that actually real? She hadn't heard anything about that since she was a child. Even then, it sounded like a fairy tale, something spoken of in whispers and hushed tones.

Without giving her a chance to ask any questions, Dario started pacing in long strides across the room. "The Dixon diamond, Macy. You think we Gilbert's didn't know anything about it? The stories have passed down through generations in my family, how your grandfather stole land from my family, land that then he found a ton of oil on. My grandfather, he went to that land auction with the last few dollars he had. He'd worked for years to save up to buy his own land, so he didn't have to work for people like your grandfather, sweating in the hot Texas sun, digging wells, servicing them, making sure they were pumping out that black gold from the ground. And then, when he shows up to the auction, your grandfather, just out of spite, outbids mine by a measly one hundred dollars." Dario spun and stared at Macy. "And that's the reason that you have what you have and I have nothing."

"Dario, I never took any money from the Dixons."

Narrowing his eyes, Dario took two steps closer to her, close enough in the small room she could feel his body heat. He'd only been that close to her one other time and it had been years ago. "You may never have taken any of the money, Macy, but you have it. I have nothing. And the way that I look at it, the value of that nineteen-carat perfect diamond that's sitting in the safety deposit box in Fort Worth is exactly the same value of the land that your family stole from me. So, give me the key, Macy. If you give it to me, you can walk outta here right now."

The words hung in the air. Macy set her jaw, looking up at Dario, who was leaning over her, his dark skin flush with anger. "Dario, I don't know anything about the key," she said, the words coming out slowly.

The words hit Dario like Macy had just lit the wick to a bomb. Macy flinched as she watched him draw his hand back as though he was going to slap her. He stopped just before his arm whipped through the air. He shook his head, walking toward the other side of the room, mumbling to himself. "I can't. I can't..."

Macy stared after him, curious. "You can't what, Dario?"

The words hung in the air.

Dario spun around, his expression stony. "I can't slap the mother of my child."

A wave of nausea ran over Macy, her stomach clutching into a small, tight knot. She didn't say anything, her face reddening, staring at the ground. The only noise in the room was Dario's voice cutting through the air. "You think I don't know, Macy? Kate? Isn't that her name? Genetics are no liar, Macy. She looks like a Gilbert, doesn't she? That beautiful, long black hair. And the timing is just right, after that night..."

Macy lifted her eyes, looking at Dario, pressing her lips together. "Don't you ever say that you're her father. Noah is her father. Noah was the one that got me through the pregnancy. Noah was the one that rocked her to sleep and dried her tears all these years."

"Say what you want," Dario hissed. "But you know she's mine."

Macy spun away from Dario and the small bed, staring at a spot on the wall, feeling the hot sting of tears in her eyes, trying to force them back down. It had been one time. She and Noah had just had a fight about one of his past relationships. It had left Macy feeling off balance just as Noah had gone out of town. They'd only been married for a couple of years. Macy had gone to a bookstore while he was gone, bored, trying to get out of the house. She'd gone to a café after that, toting her books along with her, ordering a cup of coffee. Dario had walked by, asked her what she was reading, then joined her for coffee. They ended up down the street for a drink, comparing stories of being raised in Texas. A bottle of wine later, she found herself locked in the women's bathroom with him, his hands all over her body.

She hadn't seen him again, not until he decided to kidnap her.

Macy bit her lip and turned toward him, holding her head straight, her eyes level. "Kate belongs to Noah and I. She's a Chandler. Not a Dixon and not a Gilbert. And I don't know anything about a key." With that, Macy turned and faced the back wall of the cabin, feeling the cold wind blow through the thin cabin walls. She laid down on the bed, curled herself up, pulling one of the rough blankets Lola had gotten her up over her legs. She wouldn't give Dario the satisfaction of seeing her cry. She would shut down. Ignore him until he went away. In her mind, she started to count, keeping her mind focused on the numbers she pictured in her head. One, two, three...

At eleven, she heard the floor creak, the door close, the locks clicking closed behind her.

She was alone. Again.

48

Dario had never felt anything like the anger he felt at the moment he clicked the locks closed to Macy's room. She'd all but admitted that Kate was his. But as far as the key that opened the safety deposit box to the Dixon diamond, she hadn't budged.

Dario couldn't decide whether she was lying, like all of the Dixons did, or if she truly didn't know anything about it. In that case, it would have been his family that was the liar, spinning tales that had poisoned his mind and caused him to give up everything he knew on the hunt for a single treasure that had the power to change the trajectory of his life.

Dario swallowed, his life spinning around him. He could feel a black hole of anger growing inside of him, threatening to swallow him up. Adrenaline surged through his system as he set his jaw. The reality was someone was lying, but he didn't know who.

As he stormed down the stairs and got into his truck, leaving Macy by herself in the little, cold cabin with nothing to eat, he didn't know what to believe anymore.

Running into Macy at the café had been nothing but dumb luck. He'd been on his way through town, bidding on a construction job on the outskirts of Pittsburgh. There was a one-in-a-million chance he would bump into Macy at that bookstore. It was only when they got into the bottle of wine did they realize they'd both grown up in Texas. She hadn't given him her maiden name, but he knew who she was as soon as she told him her parents' first names. At that moment, it hadn't mattered to him. She was pretty and young, with a wild, lopsided grin on her face, sparkling eyes, and a laugh that seemed to run over every inch of his body.

And it had only taken that one time to tie them together.

As his search for the diamond intensified, he couldn't help but go back and do research on her. It was five years later that he discovered through the amazing powers of social media that she'd had a child. Interestingly, it hadn't been Macy that had clued him into the fact that he had a daughter, but Noah. Dario had scrolled back through years of Noah's posts, seeing Kate grow up right before his eyes. She had the same dark hair, the same wild look in her eyes that all the Gilberts did.

Dario hadn't thought anything of it, quickly playing it off, knowing that he wasn't in any position to challenge Macy for custody. He was a nomad, going from city to city, bidding on construction jobs, quickly putting together a crew and completing them and then moving on to the next city, only returning to Texas when the weather got too cold up north. He didn't want to be a father.

Ten years later, when he'd gone home, he'd realized Texas was filled with disappointment for him. Driving around the outskirts of Fort Worth there were signs all over the place. Nearly every rig he drove by read Dixon Oil.

And then when on her deathbed, his grandmother Anna Gilbert, had told him about the diamond and that it was his job to get it back to restore the Gilbert name, Dario had willingly accepted the challenge. He literally had nothing to lose.

Dario hadn't done anything about it for a few years, until his luck ran out in the construction industry. After losing a few jobs, nearly running out of money more than once, he barely made it back to Texas. Crashing with his sister and her family for a while, down on his luck, he felt like he'd lost his reason to live. One night, drinking a cheap bottle of whiskey on his sister's back porch, he remembered the story about the diamond.

That's when he started formulating a plan to get it back.

What he didn't count on was the story ending up with Macy. After two years of research and hunting down leads, asking nearly everyone he knew in Fort Worth about the diamond, only about half of the people seemed to believe it was true. Of those people, no one seemed to know where it had gone, until one night the Christmas before, a cousin of his had mentioned that the Dixons had one granddaughter that they favored above all others, but that she'd been a disappointment to them. She'd turned her back on the family, even though they'd given her something very valuable. At first, Dario was sure that one of the grandkids had simply gotten an inheritance that was larger than the others, but when pressed, his cousin had said, "No. The way I hear it, the one granddaughter has the key. I guess that diamond is supposed to be worth about fifty million — the same amount that land would've been worth today, if her grandfather hadn't stolen it from us."

That night was the night that Dario had started formulating his plan to get Macy Dixon-Chandler and get the key back for the Gilberts, once and for all.

Driving the truck on the narrow road down Thomasville Lake after confronting Macy again, Dario pounded his fist on the steering wheel. Two years of research and two more in planning and nothing had gone to plan.

He set his jaw. Pulling onto the I-79 freeway toward Pittsburgh, he knew it was time to change things in his favor. No one would stop him. Not until he got what he wanted… the diamond.

49

Chris Talley was frustrated. He'd spent the day trying to get a hold of his girlfriend, Kate Chandler, after being released from the irritatingly inquisitive minds of Detectives Grady and Reynolds at the Pittsburgh police department. He'd gone home, taken a shower, trying to rinse the combination of the airport smell and the odor from the police station off of his body. He'd sent Kate a text, letting her know he was back in town, wanting to see if she wanted to get together later.

She'd never responded.

Thinking she was going through another one of her pouting episodes where she was mad at him for some mysterious reason, he waited a few hours, figuring her father had overreacted about her disappearance. That couldn't be true, could it? Kate wasn't missing. She was just playing possum, angry about something that had happened and ignoring everyone. They'd been together long enough for him to know that eventually she would respond. She would yell and throw her hands in the air for five or ten minutes, her black eyes flashing, after which they would end up in bed together, the tangle of the sheets seeming to solve all of their problems.

But checking his phone as he closed out his email for the day, Chris realized that he still hadn't heard from her. He'd worked later than he'd expected and had lost track of the time. Concerned, he picked up his phone, his eyebrows furrowed. He tried dialing her, but her phone went immediately to voicemail, as if she'd shut it off. Chris looked around his apartment. There was nothing going on and he was too edgy to sit by himself. He'd spent a week in Los Angeles and the time change was catching up with him, the three-hour difference making him feel like it was still five o'clock in the afternoon, not eight o'clock at night. If that was any indication, he'd be awake well later than usual.

Shaking his head, Chris picked up his car keys and his cell phone, shoving them in his pocket, pulling on a coat over the sweatshirt and jeans he was wearing. With all the travel, his company had given him the day off from hospital and doctor visits, peddling the newest drugs, smiling and cajoling the medical staff to let him get a minute with their doctor. Looking around, he realized he was tired of sitting in his apartment. He needed to get out, to get some fresh air. It was time to make a surprise visit to Bedford College.

Swinging by Kate's dorm, sure she was holed up in her room, Chris followed a young freshman girl in, who giggled and twittered seeing his good looks, quickly letting him in the dorm when he mentioned that he was Kate's boyfriend. "Oh, she's so lucky," the girl cooed, holding the door open for him. Chris took the steps in twos and stood in front of Kate's door, knocking. Maybe she'd fallen asleep and hadn't realized what time it was. Hopefully, she'd be excited to see him.

A minute went by, then another. No answer. A mousy-looking young woman with glasses and brown hair passed him, a hat pulled down low over her ears, her backpack slung over her shoulders. "If you're looking for Kate, she hasn't been here all day. At least I haven't seen her." She shrugged.

Chris nodded but didn't say anything, waiting for another minute, frustration filling him. When Kate didn't answer, he turned and went back down the steps, jogging out to his car, nearly slipping on a patch of ice, at which point he muttered a flurry of curse words. Getting in, he turned on the heat at full blast. Maybe Kate was at home with her dad for the evening? They had spotty reception in the neighborhood during storms. Maybe Kate was in a dead spot or the snow had limited her service.

The drive to Kate's parents' house from Bedford College only took about twenty-five minutes. It was a manageable commute for Macy when she wasn't out on one of her adventures. Squinting as he drove, Chris remembered the detectives mentioned that Macy hadn't been home in a while. He scowled as he drove. Kate had told him when Macy left, but he'd forgotten about it. They usually hung out at school or at his apartment. The detectives had mentioned four months. Had it really been that long? Part of Chris felt bad for not knowing the answer to the question, but it wasn't like he and Kate were married, after all. It was her family. Her problem. Not his. He had enough issues to deal with.

The drive to the Chandler residence took fifteen minutes longer than it normally did. The snow was still coming down, heavy fat flakes flying almost horizontally across Chris's headlights as he drove, making it nearly impossible to see. The road was even worse in the Chandler's neighborhood, where apparently the plow trucks hadn't visited recently. There was a good three inches of heavy snow on the road, not enough to be impassable but definitely enough to slow down his progress.

As Chris pulled up out front and parked his car on the street, he glanced at the Chandler's driveway. Kate's car wasn't there. Maybe she'd parked in the garage. Their house had a four-car garage, only two of which were in current use since Gabe wasn't old enough to drive and Macy had taken her car to God knows where. Knowing her dad, he'd probably told Kate to park inside so she wouldn't have to scrape her car later. There weren't any other cars on the street, save for an old pickup truck parked a couple houses down on the side of the road. Chris thought he'd seen a figure inside as he passed, but he didn't really pay attention. He sat in the car for a minute, staring at his phone, texting Kate that he was sitting outside. He waited for an answer, when a shadow passed by the driver's side window.

"Are you Chris?" the man asked as Chris rolled down the window...

50

Dario's fury had driven him the entire way to Pittsburgh. He'd been sitting in his truck for the last hour, contemplating confronting Noah about the key or making the next ransom demand call from right outside of Macy's house when a silver sedan had pulled up in front of the property.

Dario knew time was running out. He had to up the ante. Macy was freezing him out, pretending not to know about the Dixon diamond, but there had to be a way to get the information he wanted. He chewed the inside of his lip. It was nearly impossible for him to believe that Noah Chandler didn't know about Macy's fortune or about the key. Dario checked the time on his phone. It'd been about twelve hours since he called and warned Noah that he only had twenty-four hours. But given what he'd been through with Macy, he wasn't sure he could wait any longer. As far as he could tell, there were only a few choices in front of him. He could wait until the next morning and make the final ransom demand. If it wasn't satisfied then he would have to do something about Macy, something that would prove how serious he was. He didn't want to hurt her, but she wasn't giving him any choice.

Or, he could charge into Noah's house, and take action that night.

Sitting by himself, he'd decided to go up and pound on the door, but then quickly realized no one was home after standing in the freezing cold for a few minutes. Maybe Noah was at a late meeting or picking up Gabe. Dario had trudged back to his truck and waited until he saw a lone sedan pulled up in front. It was a silver BMW, the cheapest version on the market, but a BMW nonetheless. He saw the interior light flick on. It was a young man with blond hair, as far as Dario could tell from where he sat down the street. Dario watched for a moment, the muscles in his chest tightening. The young man would look at his cell phone and then stare at the house, as if he was waiting for someone. Dario pulled out his cell phone and did a quick search trying to figure out who was sitting and waiting.

From the back of the young man's head, he was too young to be a friend of Macy's or Noah's, and definitely too old to be a friend of Gabe's. Dario narrowed his eyes. He quickly searched Kate's social media and found a picture of her with her boyfriend. Yes, her boyfriend was blond. A sudden surge of anger pumped its way through his system. That was his daughter. Who was this man waiting for Kate? He had no right to be dating her, not without Dario's approval.

From the glove compartment of the truck, Dario pulled out a pistol, quickly shoving it in the back of his waistband, underneath his jacket. He got out of the truck and strode through the snow toward the silver sedan. Dario pulled his coat a little tighter around him, adjusting the gun at the small of his back, feeling the cool metal soak into his skin.

He walked quietly up to the vehicle, the dark covering the majority of his movements, the young man inside, so enthralled by what was going on in his cell phone, Dario was relatively sure he didn't notice anyone was near his car until his shadow passed by. Dario used a single knuckle to rap on the window. The young man jumped, making a face and then rolled the window down.

Dario already didn't like the looks of him.

"Are you Chris?"

"What do you want?" the young man asked.

"That's not a nice way to greet your girlfriend's father," Dario said, his voice dark and low. Rage filled him as he reached into the car with both hands. Kate's entire life had gone by without him in it. He'd been frozen out, just like Macy had frozen him out about the key. No longer able to contain his anger, he grabbed the young man's collar and hauled him towards the window. Letting go with one hand, Dario reached inside, unlocking the door and opening it, yanking the young man out, his body falling into the snow.

"Father?" the young man mumbled, jumping up after hitting the pavement. "I don't know you. My name's Chris Talley. I date Kate Chandler. She lives in that house over there. Her dad is Noah. Not you."

Not you...

The words cut Dario to the core, his stomach tightening. It was as if every time he tried to engage with the Chandler family, he got boxed out. No was their favorite word. "Not you" was the refrain of every interaction he'd had with them, even with Macy, and she was his captive.

His gut churned with anger. He grabbed Chris by the coat collar again, shoving his back against the side of his BMW. "I'm Kate's dad."

A flash of confusion ran across Chris Talley's face in the dim light. "Listen, I don't know what you want, man. But I don't have any cash on me. And I don't know who you think you are, but I date a girl whose name is Kate." Chris shifted underneath Dario's hands, shrugging away from his grip.

"You should get out of here. I don't want to have to mess you up."

Dario narrowed his eyes at the threat. He and Chris were nearly the same size. When Dario had shoved him, Dario noticed that amount of muscle on the young man, but looking at him, Dario bet that Chris Talley, or whatever his name was, got his muscle from some expensive gym membership, not from hard work, which is where Dario had gotten his. Dario had been in his fair share of street fights before. Everything in him told him that Chris Talley had never had to lift a finger against anyone. "I'm gonna ask you this question one time. Where are the Chandlers?" Dario needed to get to Noah, and soon. Maybe he could use the kid's relationship with Kate to get to Noah. Maybe.

"I don't know," Chris said, brushing the snow off his coat, a grimace on his face. "I'm not their keeper. I'm only looking for my girlfriend. As for the rest of them, I have no idea. Why don't you go up to the house and find out, whoever you are."

Dario shook his head and grabbed for the young man again, getting a hold of his coat collar. The boy was being disrespectful. "You know, you need to learn a lesson in speaking to people." Dario narrowed his eyes. "Tell me where the Chandlers are. Now."

"I told you, dude, I have no idea. Now get your hands off me."

Chris wrestled his body away from Dario for a moment, Dario feeling his hand slip off of the young man's coat collar. Dario had a flash of Chris Talley enjoying the spoils of the Dixon fortune. Maybe Kate had gotten her hands on the diamond and had bought this young man the fancy car. Maybe Kate was the one he needed to find, not Macy. Dario narrowed his eyes. The Chandlers needed to be taught a lesson. Dario nodded towards the vehicle. "You're right. Get in your car and drive away." No one would stop him from getting what he wanted. Not Macy, not Kate, and certainly not her mouthy boyfriend.

Chris gave Dario a side eye and twisted away from his grip, getting back in the car. A second later, Dario heard the car start. He lifted the back of his coat, whipping out the pistol, quickly putting two shots in Chris's chest just as he put the car in gear. His body slumped to the side, the car rolling away, hitting the fence at the other end of the street. Dario stood and watched for a moment, tossing the gun into the snow, then turned on his heel, got into the pickup truck and drove away.

Dario glared down the road as he drove, his jaw set, his eyes cold. The message was sent. None of the Chandlers would be safe until Dario had the key. Now what would Macy and her family do? If they hadn't figured it out already, time was running out, and so was Dario's patience.

so [illegible] Kate, and certainly not her [illegible] boyfriend.

[illegible] away [illegible] in the car. A second [illegible] heard [illegible] start. He lifted the back of his coat, slipping out the pistol [illegible] Charles [illegible] to put the car in gear. His body slumped to the side, the car rolling away, hitting the [illegible] at the end of the street. [illegible] stood and watched [illegible] into the snow, then turned on his heel [illegible] the pickup [illegible] drove away.

[illegible] down the road as he drove [illegible] cold. The [illegible] Monroe [illegible] Chandlers would [illegible] attention. [illegible] had the key [illegible] Nate [illegible] family [illegible] had [illegible] was running out [illegible] McQuaid [illegible].

51

Grady had just checked himself into a tiny bed-and-breakfast on the outskirts of Thomasville, auspiciously called the Thomasville B&B, grateful to get out of the cold when his phone rang.

"Where are you?" Cassie asked.

"I think you know exactly where I am. What's going on?"

"It's Chris Talley, the guy we interviewed this morning. Patrol just found him dead down the street from the Chandler house. Two shots to the chest."

Grady shook his head, his mouth drooping open. "What? What are you talking about?"

"You heard what I said." Cassie paused, her voice low. "I don't know what to say. Maybe you were right. Maybe we should've kept him overnight for questioning."

There was no point in crying over spilled milk. What was done, was done. Grady had seen more than his fair share of dead bodies during his career. Chris was another to add to the list. He chewed his lip. What it pointed to was that whoever had Macy was upping the ante. The kidnapper was now going after the family. "Did they find the weapon?"

"Yeah. Tossed in the snow. No prints though. The salt truck had come around. Between the salt and the slush, it disintegrated any prints that were on the grip. Not that there were any there anyways. For all we know, it's so cold the killer probably had on a pair of gloves." Cassie paused for a moment. "There is something else though that you should know."

"What's that?"

"The gun was registered to Noah Chandler."

A chill ran down Grady's spine. He knew as well as anyone that just because a gun was registered to someone didn't mean that was the person that pulled the trigger. But given the fact that Noah Chandler was right smack dab in the middle of his wife's disappearance and professed to know nothing about where she was, it seemed to be a bit of a stretch. "I don't think there's any way Noah Chandler pulled the trigger, Cassie."

"Listen, I know you don't want to believe that the husband's involved, but..."

Grady started to pace in the small room he was staying in at the Thomasville B&B. "It's not that. I talked to Noah this afternoon. He's stuck in Erie. He took Gabe up there to keep him safe. They're staying with his sister. I bet if you ping his cell phone you'll see he's still there."

There was silence on the other end of the line for a moment. Grady could hear rustling in the background. "Yeah, you're right. He's there. How long is the ride from Pittsburgh to Erie?"

Grady shrugged. "Last time I did it, it took me a couple hours. In this weather, probably longer."

"Doesn't look like the time works out then. The body is still warm."

Grady stopped moving, narrowing his eyes. Cassie didn't say anything for a moment. He wondered if she felt guilty about letting Chris Talley go. She was the kind that would. "Are you there?"

"Yeah. I'm here."

Grady swallowed, staring out the window from his room at the B&B into the darkness. A knot formed in his gut. He should have been there to back up Reynolds on the call. But then again, he'd turned in his shield. Grady set his jaw. He was on his own and he knew it. "Why are you calling me? I mean, I appreciate the heads up, but..."

"Because we're partners."

"Not anymore."

"I wouldn't be so sure about that."

52

Grady spent the next few minutes talking to Cassie, trying to hold back his anger at the fact that they'd released Chris Talley in the first place. Sure, the guy might've been uncomfortable having to wait in the interrogation room or in some holding cell at Pittsburgh Bureau of Police all day, but at least he would've been alive. But Grady bit his lip. That was water under the bridge. There was nothing they could do about it now. Hindsight was twenty-twenty. They had no way of knowing Chris would be a target only a few hours later. "You don't think the daughter is behind it, do you?"

Cassie sucked in a breath. "I have no idea. Like I said, we didn't get any fingerprints off the gun. And if Noah is in Erie, someone got his gun and used it. Who that is, I have no idea." There was a pause at the other end of the line. "Listen, the coroner's office just got here. I gotta go deal with them. Stay in touch, okay, Grady?"

"I'll do my best."

Grady said the words although he didn't particularly believe them. There had been a reason he'd walked away from the department. Cassie wasn't one of them, but she might end up being a casualty in the war he was fighting against Lieutenant Williams and all the regulations foisted on him by the Pittsburgh Bureau of Police. With all of their rules, he could barely do his job. That's why his shield was, at that very minute, sitting on Williams' desk and not on Grady's belt.

As he ended the call, Grady looked around the room, it was neat and clean, decorated with pictures of Thomasville Lake in the summer, a single queen-size bed in the middle of the room draped with a floral bedspread, the smell of deodorizer hanging in the air, two brass lamps in the room, one on each of the nightstands.

Grady walked to the sliding glass door at the one end of the room, using a single finger to pull the filmy white curtain aside. With the weather and the corresponding lack of visitors to Thomasville, the woman at the desk had upgraded his room to a lake view with a balcony, not that he'd be using it. He needed a place to sleep and shower and that was it. Other than that, he was on the hunt for Macy and Kate, the missing mother and daughter. As much as he didn't like it, there wasn't much he could do in the darkness, not until at least daybreak when he could see what was in front of him. The thought left a pit in his stomach. "Just one more night, Macy. I'm gonna find you," Grady whispered into the darkness.

Off in the distance, he saw a wash of inky blackness. He decided that must be the lake. It was obscured by the storm blowing through. As much as the balcony might have offered great views of the lake where families or couples could have their morning coffee in good weather, it was currently covered by at least six inches of snow. Turning away from the window, Grady sat down on the edge of the bed, with a sigh, thinking about what Cassie had said, the image of Chris Talley's face floating in his mind.

He pushed it aside. Chris Talley was dead. Two shots to the

chest by a gun from the Chandler household. There was nothing to be done for him, at least not now.

Interlacing his fingers in his lap, Grady realized that couldn't be a coincidence. It had to be a message. Things were getting serious, and fast.

Questions loomed in his mind. They still didn't have a suspect and now there was a murder attached to the two missing women. Kidnapping was one thing. Murder was entirely different. Chris Talley was Kate Chandler's boyfriend. It was possible her disappearance and his murder had nothing to do with the disappearance of Macy. Possible, but not likely. While it was entirely possible that Macy's disappearance, Kate's disappearance, and Chris Talley's murder were tied together, it was equally as possible that they weren't. Maybe Kate and Chris had gotten into some sort of fight and she had decided to kill him with one of her father's guns. She had that look about her with her flashing dark eyes. Or maybe somehow Noah Chandler had come back, leaving his phone and Gabe in Erie as his alibi, driving back through the snow and taking out the boyfriend.

But why? Noah hadn't said anything to Grady or Reynolds about Chris Talley. Nothing negative or positive — only that he was Kate's boyfriend.

Grady sat on the edge of the bed, chewing the inside of his lip. From years as a detective, Grady knew that even the kindest, most mild-mannered people were capable of heinous crimes when pushed. Desperate men did desperate things. That said, Noah didn't strike Grady as a criminal mastermind. And that still didn't explain where Macy was or the kidnappers' request for a key. Grady got up and started to pace, his fingers pressed into his forehead. This case had more twists and turns than he knew what to do with.

A second later, his phone rang. There was no number, the incoming call just marked with "Unknown." Grady frowned at the phone, a chill running down his spine. Not many people knew how to reach him, especially those with unknown numbers.

"Grady."

"Detective, we haven't had a chance to meet yet, but I thought maybe we should talk," a tinny voice replied.

Grady recognized the voice immediately. It was the same voice from the ransom demand call that Noah Chandler had played for him and Cassie.

Grady's thoughts clattered in his mind, lining up like cars on a railroad track, consequences and options filing along behind them as the kidnapper drew in a breath. Grady pressed his lips together, listening. Now, if he could just choose the right words. The kidnapper was smart, he'd played the long game. There was no reason to play dumb. "Okay. I assume you're calling about Macy Chandler."

"Not exactly."

Not exactly? What could the kidnapper want that didn't have to do with Macy? They were three seconds into the call and Grady's curiosity quickly turned to impatience. "What do you want?"

"I wanted to know if you saw my most recent handiwork. Seems there's been a tragic accident in front of the Chandler house."

Grady's heart tightened in his chest. The kidnapper was all but admitting to killing Chris. "You mean the murder of Chris Talley?" Grady didn't have a problem blurting it out. He was tired of playing games.

There was a chuckle on the other end of the line as if the kidnapper was delighted that Grady knew. "Oh, I see the Pittsburgh Bureau of Police is on top of their game tonight."

Grady narrowed his eyes. He had the urge to tell the kidnapper that he was no longer with the police department, but he didn't want to confuse the issue. If the kidnapper felt that Grady no longer had the power to deliver what he wanted, then the kidnapper might very well stop talking to Grady. And that's what Grady needed at that moment — for the kidnapper to talk, and talk a lot. "Yeah, very clever to kill the boyfriend with one of Noah's guns."

"Poetic justice, if you ask me. The gun was one Noah got for Macy. She had it in her car. Too bad I left it there for you. I was planning on using it on her."

Grady stiffened. "Yeah, I heard you started the clock ticking. How much time is left?"

"Less than you'd like, Detective, unless you can get me what I want."

53

A thin veneer of sweat had found its way to Grady's forehead. He had to keep the kidnapper talking. He quickly pressed the record button on his phone and then asked, "Why are you calling me? What do you want?"

"I have had only one simple request throughout this entire exercise, and yet no one seems willing to give it to me. I don't want to get into details. It's not for me to tell, but I will tell you a great debt is owed to me and my family. It can be paid with the key. I will trade Macy's life for it."

"I've heard this story already. Not sure why you're telling it to me. I don't have any keys you'd want and I don't have any power to make the Chandlers give you the key, whatever it is. But key or no key, what I can tell you is that if you don't release Macy, you are going to be spending your life in prison. I can promise you that."

The kidnapper chuckled. "Don't make promises you can't keep."

"What does that mean?" Grady felt the heat rise to his cheeks.

"I called the department. They said you're on a leave of

absence. Something about personal issues. Sounds like something big is going on there, huh? Since you don't have a job, you might want to go visit your family but, oh, that's right, the only family you have left is your institutionalized brother and your chain-smoking mother. That's because you killed your father, isn't that right, Detective? Amazing what you can find out on the Internet."

Grady gritted his teeth. Everything in him wanted to start bellowing at the kidnapper, whoever he was, on the other end of the line. Grady's personal life was none of the kidnapper's business. How he had found out, Grady wasn't sure. The kidnapper was taunting him. "I'll ask you again, what do you want?" Grady growled.

The tinny voice chuckled on the other end of the line. "Did I get under your skin a little, Detective? The truth hurts. Poor Macy, she's had to deal with some unfortunate truth about her daughter today. Maybe you don't know either? Have you taken a hard look at Kate Chandler? I don't mean a look into her background. I mean, have you looked at her? Isn't it curious that she doesn't have the same features as the rest of the family. I wonder if there is something to that..."

Grady narrowed his eyes. The kidnapper was clearly trying to communicate something. He hadn't mentioned anything about Kate being missing. Did the kidnapper not know? Grady bit his lip, thinking for a second. He didn't want to respond too soon, but the kidnapper had made a pretty pointed comment about Kate's appearance. Grady racked his brain, replaying the images he had of Kate in his mind. Yes, she did look different than the rest of the family, but genes skipped generations. If the kidnapper hadn't said anything at all, Grady might not have thought about it. But yes, Kate had darker hair and tanner skin than either of her parents. He decided to play dumb. "Can't say I have. Is there something you want to tell me?"

There was silence on the other end of the line for a

moment. For a second, Grady thought the kidnapper had hung up. "The key to understanding this case, Detective Grady, is family and loyalty. Once someone gives me the key, you'll find Macy Chandler to be safe and alive. But my patience is running out, and so is the clock. There are ten hours left. After that, I can't guarantee Macy's safe return, at least not in one piece." There was a pause. "Tick tock, tick tock, Detective Grady. I'll be in touch in the morning."

54

Kate had spent the entire day looking for her mother, but had come up short. She'd gone to the visitor center as Thomas had suggested, but the woman drew a blank even when she saw a picture of Kate's mother. "Honey, I'm sorry to say that there are tens of thousands of people that come through Thomasville every summer. If you expect me to remember a single one, I just couldn't. I can barely remember what I had for breakfast."

With that, Kate left.

She spent the rest of the day driving around the lake as best as she could in the snowy weather, looking for her mom's car parked out front at one of the cabins. She knew it was a long shot. It was more likely that the kidnapper had hidden it somewhere or had gotten rid of it, but it was the only thing that Kate could think of to try to find her mother. Kate scoured the north and south shores of the lake, plus the west end, where the town was. As she'd gotten closer to the east end of the lake, where the permanent residents were, the roads had gotten noticeably worse. The last thing she wanted to do was get her car stuck in a snow drift and have to spend the night in her car again.

Discouraged, Kate headed back to town. She sat in her car as it started to get dark, waiting. She'd stopped by the coffee company, finding Thomas again. He'd recommended a small bed-and-breakfast on the outskirts of town. Kate had driven there, put her car in park and stared at the credit card her father had given her for emergencies. This was an emergency, wasn't it? Her mother had been kidnapped and Kate needed to go and find her. If her dad knew the circumstances, she was sure that he would agree. Shutting off her car, Kate strode into the bed-and-breakfast. At the desk, a woman with dark hair tied into a ponytail, her pale face devoid of any makeup, greeted her. "Can I help you?"

"I need a room for the night."

"You're in luck. With this weather, no one's here, save for one other guy that just checked in." She fished a set of keys from behind the desk, ran Kate's emergency credit card and handed it back to her. The woman pointed. "Up the steps and at the end of the hall. I gave you a room with a private bathroom. There's a balcony, but then again, in this snow, I don't think you're going to want to sit out there anyway."

"Probably not. Thanks."

55

After the kidnapper called Grady, Grady spent the next thirty minutes pacing back and forth in his room processing what he'd heard. He pulled a notepad out of his bag and started jotting things down. They started as random thoughts, but began to form into a pattern as he wrote more things out.

If there was one thing the kidnapper was right about, it was that they were running out of time. Grady looked out into the darkness again, frustration washing over him. With the snow, there was no way he'd be able to do anything until first light, and that's exactly when the clock on Macy's life would end. Maybe, just maybe, Grady could get the kidnapper to extend the deadline if he called again. It had been four months. What was a few more hours?

Grady shook his head, feelings of despair running through him. He felt cornered, as if he had nowhere to turn. The kidnapper had renewed his demand for a key. But as far as Grady could tell, there was nothing he could do about that. No one in the family seemed to know what the key was. He knew he certainly didn't.

A moment later, his phone rang. Cassie. He ignored it. She didn't need to know the kidnapper had called. If the kidnapper had found his number, then it was getting far too dangerous. The last thing he wanted to do was put Cassie in harm's way. He just couldn't bring himself to do it. Flashes of the night he'd killed his father loomed in his mind. It was one thing to be in a fight, something else to see others get hurt. No. No one else needed to be in danger. Just him.

Grady strode over to the window, staring outside again. He was missing something, something big. He felt like the kidnapper had given him a full set of clues, but he was still in the dark. Literally. Was there any way for him to find Kate and her mom? Were they together? Clearly, the kidnapper had made a point of saying that Kate looked different than the rest of the family. What was he saying? Why was that important? And what was the comment about the key to the issue being family and loyalty? Clearly, the kidnapper thought something had been stolen from him — something big — and Macy was responsible, or she had the power to fix it.

There were more questions than answers, and he knew he wouldn't find them staying in the bed-and-breakfast for one more minute.

Grady took one more look around the room he was staying in and one more look out the window. He shook his head, pressing his lips together. It didn't matter how bad the weather was. He needed to find Macy Chandler, and find her before time ran out.

56

Kate tossed her backpack on the bed in the room she'd gotten at the bed-and-breakfast, used the bathroom, washed her hands and came back out, staring at the empty room. It was quaint in a way. She sniffed the air. It smelled clean, like laundry that had just been done. Sheets, maybe. She walked to the window that led out onto the balcony and stared out into the darkness, quickly turning away. She knew in her gut her mom was close by. But where?

Kate plopped down on the edge of the bed and kicked off her shoes, crossing her legs underneath her. She stared at the picture hung in the corner of the room. It was of a boat floating placidly on Thomasville Lake, a few fishing lines extended off the back of it, the silhouettes of two fishermen outlined in the sunset. It looked so peaceful.

Kate turned away. To other people Thomasville might be a peaceful place to visit. It wasn't to Kate.

She sat on the bed for a minute, gathering her thoughts and then fished the note she'd gotten from her mom out of her pocket. Unfolding it again, she stared at the handwriting. She'd gotten enough notes and birthday cards from her mom that she knew without a doubt the looped, scrolled handwriting was her mother's. It was nothing like her own writing, which was all sharp edges and points. But then again, she and her mom weren't much alike. Her mom was into the deeper meaning of words, the beauty of nature, constantly absorbed by her feelings and what she was experiencing. Kate sometimes felt like she was from another planet. She was analytical, decisive, and orderly.

Maybe that's exactly why Macy had sent the note to her.

For a minute, Kate imagined if her dad had gotten the note, Noah would've probably freaked out, called the detectives, thrown his hands up in the air, wiped his forehead and started pacing, worrying the entire time the detectives were trying to figure it out instead of taking action on his own. But Kate wasn't that way.

And her mother knew it.

Kate shook her head slightly, sitting on the edge of the bed, rubbing her arms with her hands. She had hours and hours in front of her before the sun came up. She couldn't simply sit in the hotel room, sleeping in the comfortable bed with the soft pillows and getting a good night's sleep waiting to find her mom until first light. A pit formed in her stomach as she imagined her mom, cold, huddling terrified in the corner of a room or tied to a chair, bound and gagged, barely able to breathe. Thinking about it made Kate want to throw up. If she ever got her hands on who had done this she would...

There was no time to think about revenge now. Kate studied the note again, reading the words slowly, mouthing each one of them without making a noise. Her eye caught on the reference to the snow globe. Kate dug around in her backpack and pulled it out, staring at it. She gave it a gentle shake and then looked inside of it again. Even with the fake snowflakes flying around, she could see the little blue lake in the center of it, the cabin, and then the sign. She stopped, her mouth hanging open.

The sign.

Something in Kate's mind clicked. She'd seen a sign exactly like the one in the snow globe at some point during her travels around the lake. She blinked, staring up at the ceiling, trying to remember. As she did, doubt filled her mind. Was her mom actually being that specific? Or was she just pointing Kate to the fact that she was at Thomasville Lake?

Kate scooted back on the bed, flattening the note on the fabric, staring at it again, tracing her finger over the words. She knew her mom had a memory for details. Her students were always amazed at how she could decipher the most minute change in meaning in a poem, simply by the placement of a comma. It would be like her mom to remember something like a tiny sign.

But where was it?

Kate hopped off the bed and started pacing, one arm crossed in front of her chest, the other one resting on the side of her face. She'd driven for what felt like miles around the western edge of the lake, crisscrossing the narrow roads. She paused for a second and reached for her backpack, pulling out the map she'd gotten that morning at the Thomasville Coffee Company, unfolding it and placing it next to the note. Maybe if she looked at them together she'd remember?

She bent over the map, tracing her finger over the twisty roads, trying to retrace her steps from that day. If she remembered correctly, it had been around mid-day when she'd seen the sign. But where was she?

Kate paused for a second, closed her eyes and held her breath, trying to force herself to remember what had been around the sign when she'd seen it. Opening her eyes, she looked at the map. She remembered the view from the spot where she had seen the sign was near the southern side of the lake, near where the paddleboard rental was. Kate frowned, staring at the map. Placing her finger on the spot where the paddleboard rental was she tapped her finger on the paper. The sign was in that area. Was that where her mom was?

There was only one way to find out.

57

Against what Kate was sure would be anyone's better judgment, she pulled her coat back on, tugging a knit cap from the pocket, pulling it down over her dark hair and slipped her feet back into her tennis shoes. Shaking her head, she realized she needed boots, but with the quick winter onslaught, they were still at her dad's house. Grabbing her bag, she picked up her keys and walked out of the room, closing the door quietly behind her. Using the back entrance, she slipped outside and into her car, turning it on.

The headlights from her sedan cut through a new layer of fluffy white snow on the ground. A chill ran through Kate's bones. She shivered, reaching for the knob for the heat and turning it up as far as it would go. Part of her felt guilty. What if her mom was cold at that moment? Kate swallowed, realizing her throat was dry. She needed to be stronger. Even though things hadn't always gone smoothly between the two of them, her mom was counting on her. She had to do something, or she'd never be able to live with herself. Maybe if she did, if she was able to find her mom, things would be different. Kate could only hope.

Putting her car into gear, Kate eased the vehicle out of the parking lot for the bed-and-breakfast and back onto Arch Street, heading down the slope that led to Thomasville Lake. Her car slid a couple of times, but Kate gripped the wheel tighter, slowing down a bit until she got to the bottom. She squinted in the darkness, trying to make out the road between the fat flakes of snow that were blocking her vision.

Once at the bottom, she turned her car toward the paddle-board company. If she remembered correctly, like many things in Thomasville, it included the town's name. As she got closer, she saw the sign. She'd been right. It was called Thomasville Paddle. She shook her head. If she was able to get her mom out of Thomasville in one piece, it was a name that would never cross her lips again. She was sure of that.

Edging her way along the shoreline, Kate followed the road until it narrowed and darkened, the streetlights that graced the sides of the visitor prone areas far behind her. Kate gripped the wheel tighter, feeling the car slip and skid on the dark roads. Whatever the road crews had been able to do in town, they hadn't matched it beyond where the paddle boarding facility was. Kate stared into the darkness looking for the sign.

As the road narrowed in front of her, Kate began to see the woods loom thicker and larger, the dark silhouettes of trees jutting up to the sky, the evergreens thick, needle-covered branches covered in piles of fluffy white snow. The trees that had lost their leaves for the season had snow stuck to their empty branches and their trunks, clumps of snow blowing off as the wind passed near them, leaving the already dark and treacherous road even more so with every inch Kate drove. Kate gritted her teeth, gripping the wheel even tighter. She was crazy to be out in the storm and in the darkness trying to find her mom, but part of her knew she didn't have a choice. It was now or never. It was as if she felt like she had an invisible clock ticking in the back of her head. And it was running out...

Kate leaned forward, still gripping the wheel, staring into the darkness. She passed a mailbox on the right-hand side, the post crooked, the red mailbox looking like it was hanging on for dear life. Another quarter mile ahead, there was another driveway that jutted off to the side with another old mailbox. Kate shook her head, squinting into the darkness. She knew the sign was there somewhere. Where was it?

After another seven minutes of driving, Kate noticed the road narrowed even more. She'd gone this way earlier, passing through the wider portion of the edge of the lake into the slimmer section that Thomas had described to her that morning. She drove down the road a little farther, a knot in her stomach, inching her car forward, hoping the wheels would stay on the slick roadway. The sign still hadn't appeared. Where could it be? Off to the right up ahead, she saw a cabin looming in the distance, the lights on. As soon as she passed, she was surrounded by inky darkness again, the road rising up in front of her, her tires skidding on the untreated surface. Kate pressed on the accelerator a little harder, knowing that if she didn't get some momentum going, she'd never get up the hill. Holding her breath and gripping the wheel until her knuckles were white, Kate leaned forward, urging the fishtailing sedan up the slippery road.

At the top she saw what she was looking for.

Off to the right, there was a small wooden sign that sat only about two feet above the ground, well less than that with the snow mounding up. Made of dark wood with a matching square wooden base, it had been cut out of a plank, the letters etched into it with a router and then painted black. She'd seen signs made like that at the county fair, where a word or name someone wanted to have on the sign was etched into the wood, the entire surface painted black and then the sign sanded to reveal the black letters. It read, "Thomasville Lake." Nothing more, nothing less.

It looked just like the one in the snow globe.

Kate pressed the brakes, stopping her car in the middle of the road, the breath catching in her throat. Kate stared at the woods surrounding her. Was her mom nearby? In one of the cabins? Was she still alive?

Easing off the brake, Kate pressed the accelerator again, her heart beating a little faster. There was no way she would have pointed Kate in this direction if this wasn't where she was.

Or where she had been.

The thought struck Kate like a lightning bolt out of a clear blue sky. She'd been so focused on finding the sign it never occurred to her that if her mom had been held captive for the last few months, there was no telling where she was now. All of her searching could lead to nothing. Her mom's note could represent the beginning of the search, not the end of it.

Kate set her jaw and stared into the darkness. No, there had to be a reason her mom told her to come to Thomasville Lake. There had to be. Her mom had to be here somewhere. She felt her chest clutch, her eyes damp with tears. It'd been a long time since she cried over anything and she wasn't about to start at that moment.

Her mom was there. She had to be.

Pushing the raw fear away from her and down into her chest, Kate inched her vehicle forward, following the road as best she could.

For the next mile or so, there was nothing to see except for the dark silhouettes of snow-covered trees, undergrowth and shrubs covered in a fresh coating of powdery white snow. There were no mailboxes, no cutouts for driveways and no signs of life.

Nothing.

Kate was thinking about out how to turn her vehicle around in the road when she saw a dim glow. Curious, she leaned forward, her heart skipping a beat. It was a cabin. There were only two lights on, one in an upstairs room and one downstairs. But it was too far off the road for Kate to see anything other than the outline of the cabin amid the dim glow of the lights.

Pulling off the side of the road as far as she dared, Kate doused her headlights and watched the house for a second, turning on her phone in case she needed the flashlight. Frustrated that she couldn't see more, she decided to get out. Closing the door of her car quietly behind her, Kate pocketed the keys and stood still for a moment.

The blanket of new snow across the Thomasville Lake area muffled the noise of everything around her. There were no animal or bird noises, not even the ones that were normally out at night. The only thing Kate could hear was a slight whisper of the wind through the trees. As she stood there, she could feel the cold soaking up through the bottom of her shoes. She needed to make a decision. Either she was going to go investigate or she was going to get in her car and turn around and head back to town.

Pulling her hood up over her head, Kate zipped up her coat and started walking quietly toward the cabin. A knot tied up her gut as the cold ate through her clothes. She sucked in a sharp breath, the exhale making a cloud of condensation as she breathed.

She glanced up at the cabin on the hillside. Finding her mom was only the first step. What she would do after that, she had no idea.

only two lights on: one in an upstairs room and one downstairs, but it was too far off the road for Kate to see anything other than the outline of the cabin and the flickering glow of the candles.

Pulling off the side of the road as far as she dared, Kate doused her headlights and watched the house for a second, [illegible] on her phone to use the weak little flashlight [illegible] dared, but she couldn't see [illegible] she [illegible] to get out. Closing the door of her car quietly behind her, Kate pocketed the keys and stood still for a moment.

The blanket of new snow across the Adirondacks [illegible] muffled the [illegible] of everything around her. [illegible] animal or bird noise, [illegible] that were usually out at night [illegible] Kate could hear was the [illegible] of the wind through the trees. As she stood there, she could feel the cold soaking up through the bottom of her shoes. She needed to make a decision. Either she was going to investigate or she was going to get in her car and turn around and head back to town.

Pulling her hood up over her head, Kate zipped up her coat and started walking [illegible] toward the cabin. [illegible] her [illegible] the [illegible] She [illegible] the cabin, making a cloud of condensation as she breathed.

She [illegible] of the cabin on the hillside. Knowing [illegible] only the first step. What she would do after that, she had no [illegible]

58

The cabin itself was built into the side of the hill above a twisted driveway that snaked past dozens of thick-trunked trees. Kate slipped twice going up the incline, the second time dropping to her knees and quickly scrambling up, worried that someone would see her, the snow cold against her bare fingers. But luckily, the night was so dark, the moon obscured by the heavy snow clouds and with her black coat on, she was nothing more than a ghost.

Or at least that's what she hoped for.

It took her another ten minutes to make her way up the steep, curved driveway. The cabin hadn't seemed that far up the hillside when she'd first spotted it, but seeing the glow of the lights in the woods was nothing like the distance it represented.

Out of breath from the steep ascent, Kate stopped for a moment as she got close to the cabin, squatting down behind the heavy trunk of a tree. She could feel the cold of the bark soak into her fingers, the rough texture against her skin. The last thing she wanted to do was be spotted, so she sat hidden behind the tree for a moment, watching, waiting for any sign of life.

It was another two minutes before she saw anything. Kate was barely able to breathe as she watched the house. A dark-haired man appeared at the window in the lower level. Kate narrowed her eyes, digging her fingers into the rough, frozen bark of the tree she was hiding behind. She looked at the truck that was parked near the cabin. She frowned. It didn't have any snow on it at all, as if it had been recently driven. If her mom was in that house, would he have left her there?

Kate waited for another second, focusing her eyes on the small window on the second floor of the cabin.

Kate cocked her head to the side, squinting into the darkness. Overall the cabin was a strange structure, one that her eyes were having trouble deciphering in the darkness. From what she could see, it looked like the upper and lower levels were built into the hillside with two separate entrances. It wasn't a cabin in the traditional sense of the word, like something she'd seen in a log home magazine or online. It looked more like two rickey wooden boxes that had been glued together against the curve of the hillside. Strange, she thought. Just as the thought passed through her mind, she saw the flicker of a shadow near the upstairs window and then a person appeared. There was a blanket wrapped around her shoulders, the sheen of blonde hair against the light.

Kate's breath caught in her throat. It was her mom. She was sure of it. Pulling her phone out of her pocket, Kate lifted her phone to take a picture. She needed evidence that her mom was there. Evidence she could show to someone who could help her.

At the last second, as her finger touched the screen to take the picture, she saw a little icon in the corner that looked like a lightning bolt. But it was too late. She'd already pressed the button. The flash went off. Against the darkness it had to look like an actual lightning bolt to the people inside. Kate held her breath. She saw the woman upstairs look at the window and press her hand on the glass, as if she was reaching toward whoever was looking for her.

The man downstairs didn't have the same attitude. She saw him stop, stare out the window, his shoulders broad and strong, the angle of his jaw set. He disappeared for a moment away from the window. Kate was frozen into place, her heart thundering in her chest, the edges of her breath ragged, fear nipping at her.

A few seconds later, the side door to the lower level of the cabin opened up, the man silhouetted in the light behind him. There was something in his hands.

A shotgun.

A surge of adrenaline flooded her body. She had to get away. Scrambling up from behind the tree, Kate ran as fast as she could down the hill, slipping and sliding, falling on her side with a thud as she rounded the curve, descending toward her car. She thought she could hear footsteps, yells from the man behind her. As she charged toward her car, she heard the crack of a shotgun blast leaving the barrel. Ducking near the closest tree, she heard the pellets land in the bark of another tree next to her, the rain of wood chips covering her. She shrieked, covering her head with her arms and kept running.

Kate didn't have time to think. She had to get back to her car and get away before the man and his shotgun found her. Standing up from the spot where she'd fallen, avoiding the punishment of the shotgun pellets, she ran as fast as she could down the slope of the driveway, at one point falling and hitting the ground hard, feeling her wrist crack underneath her. Pain shot through her body, but there was so much adrenaline pumping in her system, she kept moving. Two more times she slipped and skidded down the driveway before getting to her car.

As she made it to the road, there was another boom from the shotgun, branches overhead exploding just above the hood of her jacket, raining down snow and shattered pieces of wood from the tree on top of her again. The man was a good shot and he wasn't giving up, even though Kate was off his property.

Kate screamed, her voice echoing off the hillside. She ran down the road, slipping and falling again, this time cracking her head on a rock covered by snow as she fell. Pain shot throughout her face and her neck. Struggling to her feet, she got up and kept running just as another shotgun blast passed close to her. She could feel the air move near the side of her head. Whoever was chasing her, whoever was holding her mom hostage, wasn't trying to scare her off.

He was trying to kill her.

59

Another echo from the shotgun ricocheted off the hillside as Kate darted for her car. Terror running through every inch of her body, Kate pushed away the pain and got in, quickly turning on the engine. She didn't dare turn on the headlights. That would only make her an easier target. Throwing it into gear without putting her seatbelt on, she turned the car around on the narrow road and took off in the direction that she'd come, hearing a final boom from the shotgun as she drove. About a mile down the road, she finally dared to put her headlights on. The man had a truck. Kate glanced in the rearview mirror. He was certainly going to chase after her, wasn't he?

Pain surged throughout her wrist and her head. Kate reached up with her good hand to feel a trickle of warm, sticky blood running down the side of her face. She must've hit her head on the rock coming down the driveway. Her only hope was to get back to town and get help, not only for herself, but for her mom. She drove with a single hand gripping the wheel, cradling her broken wrist in her lap.

There was a sharp curve in the road up ahead. Kate blinked,

her mind foggy all of a sudden, the edges of her vision starting to swim, black dots peppering the inside of her eyes. She realized she must have fallen harder than she thought she did. Sucking in a deep breath, she pressed on the brake, trying to slow her car down, but it was too late.

On the slick road just south of Thomasville Lake a little over a mile from where she'd found her mother, Kate's little car slid on a patch of ice, careening off the side of the road, landing in the darkness with a thud, Kate's unseatbelted body banging around inside of the car like a pebble inside of a tin can.

The car tilted precariously down the steep embankment of the road, Kate's body wedged against the seat. The front bumper of the car was caved in by the trunk of a tree that had dumped its load of snow down on the car as it got hit, covering the windshield. Another tree trunk held the car from falling down the remainder of the hillside.

Groggy from the accident and from hitting her head, Kate doused the lights on her car and shut off the engine.

She needed help. She whimpered into the darkness. She was alone. In the storm, no one would be able to find her. The man would be coming, she was sure of it.

Sucking in a deep breath, Kate tried to calm herself. Her heart was pounding in her chest. She'd found her mom but if she didn't get help, Kate would die with the knowledge before morning probably of hypothermia. She fought the urge to pass out from the pain of her wrist and her head. She dug around in her pocket and found her phone.

Kate glanced over her shoulder, trying to see if headlights were coming near her. The man at the house had probably seen her drive away. It could be only a few minutes she had until he would come to kill her. And given the shotgun shells he'd welcomed her with, she was sure it wouldn't take long before he'd shoot her and probably her mother too.

She couldn't let that happen. Kate dug through her pockets.

One of the detectives that had shown up at her dad's house had given her a business card. Using the dome light in her car, she quickly typed it into her phone, switching the light off again.

Kate held her breath, hoping there was enough signal for her to make a call.

"Detective Reynolds." A woman's voice answered the phone.

"Cassie? This is Kate Chandler."

"Kate? Where are you? Are you okay?"

"No I'm not. I need help. I'm injured," she stammered. "A man, he shot at me. But I found my mom."

Kate spent the next minute describing to Detective Reynolds what had happened. Detective Reynolds listened patiently, only interrupting and asking questions when she needed to.

Kate blinked, trying to clear her thoughts, her words coming out in a tumble. "I'm gonna send you my location. I need help. I'm scared! That man, I think he's going to come and kill me. I can't get away. I'm stuck in my car. I'm down on the side of the road. What do I do?" All of the emotion Kate had been holding inside came out at once. She started to shake, every inch of her body quivering with fear and cold.

Cassie answered quietly, but firmly, "I'm sending help, Kate. Stay where you are. We're on the way."

One of the detectives that had shown up at her dad's house had [illegible] questions [illegible] her about [illegible].

Kate held her breath [illegible].

"Detective Reynolds," a woman's voice answered [illegible].

"[illegible] Kate Chandler."

"Kate? Where are you? Are you okay?"

"No, I'm not. I need help. I'm hurt," she stammered. "A man [illegible] at me. But I [illegible]."

Kate spent the next minute describing everything [illegible] what had happened. Detective Reynolds [illegible] only interrupting and asking questions [illegible].

Kate blinked, fighting back tears [illegible] though [illegible] I'm going and [illegible] I think I'm going [illegible] behind the door. Whatever [illegible] Kate had been holding [illegible]. She started to shake, every inch of her body [illegible] with heat and cold.

[illegible] answered quickly [illegible]. "I'm sending help, Kate. [illegible]. We're on the way."

60

Grady had been staring out the window of his B&B room when he saw his phone light up. Cassie again. He ignored the first ring, grunted, and then by the third decided to pick up.

"I'm glad you picked up," Cassie said.

Grady furrowed his eyebrows. "What's going on?"

"Kate Chandler called me. I'm on my way to your location. You're in Thomasville, right?"

"That's right. Is she here?" Grady's heart skipped a beat. Kate Chandler was in Thomasville?

Grady could hear scuffling from her end of the line, as if Cassie was doing something. After a minute, he realized she was driving. "She is. Listen, we have a situation. She found her mom, but whoever's holding her chased Kate away from the house. She's injured. Her car's off the side of the road. The guy went after her with a shotgun. She's scared senseless, Grady. I'm still a little ways out. Can you get to her and stay with her till I can get there?"

Grady narrowed his eyes. Cassie wanted his help? After he'd quit the department? "You want me to call Thomasville

PD? They have jurisdiction, remember." He was sorry the minute the words came out of his mouth.

"Not funny, Grady. There's a reason I called you and not them. She needs help *now*." There was a distinct edge to Cassie's voice.

Grady gave a single nod. He balanced the phone between his ear and his shoulder as he picked up his coat, starting to shrug his arms into it. "I'm on my way. Just tell me where I'm going. Find somewhere safe to stay when you get here. This guy is dangerous. I don't have time to go into it, but he just called me."

"Noted. Kate sent me a text with her exact location. Sending it to you now. I'll meet you there as soon as I can."

A moment later, after grabbing his gun, Grady was out of the hotel room, running down the steps, jumping into his SUV and starting it up. His phone pinged. Cassie had sent the coordinates. He tapped on the screen, waiting for the directions to connect. The storm had made everything run slow, even the triangulation of the satellites floating above his head thousands of miles away. But a moment later, the directions came up on the screen. He narrowed his eyes looking at it. It was going to take him a little bit to get to Kate. He whispered under his breath, "Hang on, Kate. I'm coming."

As the words passed over his lips, a flash of memory flickered through his head. It was of his mom the night Grady killed his father, his mom collapsed in the corner of the bedroom, her arms up over her head, protecting her face. His mom, at that moment, had been in fear for her life.

Now Kate was in the same situation.

His face stony and his stomach tight, Grady shifted the SUV into four-wheel-drive and headed out of the parking lot, driving as fast as he dared to on the snow-covered roads, down Arch Street, descending toward the lake and then picking up the road where the cabins were located. His thoughts raced.

How Kate had found her mother, he had no idea. But that wasn't the most important part of the situation. He needed to get to Kate, to protect her from whoever was going after her. It had to be the kidnapper or an accomplice. If she'd already been shot at, there was no telling what the kidnapper would do to her if he found her before Grady did. A chill ran through his body.

Grady couldn't let that happen.

[illegible] there and found her mother. She had no idea. But it was [illegible] the only important part of the situation. He needed [illegible] to protect her from whoever was using [illegible] her [illegible] account. If she'd already been [illegible], there was no telling what the kidnappers would do to [illegible] found her before we did. A [illegible] ran through his body.

Grady couldn't let that happen.

61

Driving the narrow roads around Thomasville Lake had been treacherous enough during the daylight, but at night time it was twice as bad. It was clear that the Pennsylvania State Road Department hadn't put any time into clearing the roads around the cabins that day, other than possibly giving them a cursory push earlier, but since then inches of snow had piled on top of the work they'd done, making it almost impossible to see where the road began and ended. A couple of times, Grady felt the SUV bump on the side of the road, the faint lines completely obscured by the piles of snow accumulating on the surface. He jerked the wheel just in time to keep all four tires on the paved surface. The last thing he needed to do was get the SUV stuck miles from where Kate was stranded.

Nearing the spot where Cassie had sent him, Grady slowed down, his heart thundering in his chest, narrowing his eyes in the darkness. Where was Kate and where was the man with the shotgun? It was nearly impossible, with the heavy coat of snow, to tell what was road and what wasn't. Everything had been blanketed in a coat of white. In the darkness, his headlights seemed to bounce off of every single surface, none of them intelligible one from the other. About a half a mile from where the GPS was taking him, it suddenly blanked out, blinking in warning, "No Signal."

Grady pounded his fist on the dashboard. "Not now!" he bellowed.

He had no choice about what to do next. He'd have to keep going with or without help from the technology. Checking the odometer on his SUV, he pressed the button for the trip meter. At least he'd know when he was close. Grady glanced up at the road. Not having an exact location for Kate would make his job even harder. If she was off on the side of the road, it wasn't likely that he would see her car, at least not until he was on top of it.

Losing the GPS signal was wasting valuable time. Grady glanced at the screen. Still nothing. He eased the car forward, watching both sides of the road. Cassie had said that Kate was stranded on an embankment. That at least limited what side he should be looking on, he realized, seeing the rise of the hillside to his right. She had to be on the left, the side that led down to the lake. Grady leaned forward over the steering wheel, trying to see, hearing the heat blowing across his face. The only other sound was his breath catching in his throat, the whoosh of blood and adrenaline in his body.

Seven minutes later, after passing over roads that were nearly completely snowbound, Grady slowed down. He had to be close. He knew it. The GPS was still blinking helplessly on the screen, but the trip meter was at a half a mile. How the cops in Thomasville did it, he wasn't sure.

Oh yeah, that was right. They didn't bother, so they didn't have problems with their GPS. Andy Bennett and his crew were probably fast asleep in their cozy beds, not worried one iota about Macy Chandler or her daughter. Grady gripped the steering wheel tighter. He couldn't get caught up in Thomasville's incompetence.

Grady stared into the darkness, seeing what looked to be a set of shallow tire tracks crossing the road up ahead of him already partially hidden by the snow. He narrowed his eyes. Tracks like that indicated a vehicle, not an ATV. If it was Kate, then her car should be off to the side.

Grady's eyes scanned the side of the road. He saw a tree and then the glint of something that looked like metal reflecting the light bouncing off from his headlights. Grady slowed, peering to his left. As he got closer, he could see it. It was a car, off the side of the road, just like Cassie had explained.

Grady threw his SUV into park and jumped out, leaving his car door open, the headlights blazing across the road, reaching for his gun. He slid down the snow-covered embankment, his heart pounding in his chest. His fingers were almost instantly numb from the cold. Going to the driver's side, he tried to open the door, seeing Kate's wild eyes inside. He held up a hand. "Kate, I'm Detective Grady. We met yesterday. Cassie called me. I'm here to help you. Hold on!"

The words seemed to visibly calm the startled young woman, whose eyes were darting around the car, her movements sudden and jerking as she motioned to him. From inside, he could see a trickle of blood running down the side of her face as she rattled the driver's side door. It wouldn't open. Grady stopped, looking at the car. The front end had rammed into a tree as it slid down the embankment, twisting the frame. It was going to make it difficult to get her out of the car. Grady climbed through the snow on the other side of the tree, approaching the passenger side. The passenger side door was jammed shut too. Grady went to the rear passenger door, pulling on the handle. Nothing would open. He made his way back toward the front passenger door, where he could see Kate. He cupped his hands around his mouth, hoping she'd be able to hear him better. “Cover your face! The doors are jammed. I have to break the glass!”

Kate’s mouth hung open for a second, her eyes wide, then she gave a single nod, pulling her coat up around her face and ducking her head. Grady lifted his gun, holding it by the barrel and not the grip. He aimed the grip at the window and with a single swing, hit the corner of the glass, the window shattering into a million small pieces. Holstering his gun, he put his head inside. “Are you okay?”

Kate whimpered for a second and then looked at him. “I guess so. My wrist. I think it’s broken. But, my mom...” She didn’t finish her sentence.

Grady lowered his voice, speaking calmly to Kate, his training kicking in. It looked like she was in shock. “Let’s get you taken care of first. We can get your wrist fixed. Can you crawl towards me?”

“I-I think so...” Kate stuttered.

“Okay. Just take your time. There’s no hurry.” That wasn’t actually true, but rushing Kate wouldn’t help.

As Kate started to move, she paused. “What about the man with a shotgun? Is he coming? He tried to kill me!”

Grady blinked for a moment and then stared at the young woman. “Kate, I need you to listen to me. I’m here to help you and protect you. Follow my voice and come towards me. We need to get you out of this car. That’s the first thing we need to do. We’ll take this one step at a time.” Grady needed her to move, and move quickly. If the man holding Macy Chandler was coming after them, as Kate suspected, the two of them were sitting ducks on the side of the road near the wrecked car. Grady needed to get her out of there and get her someplace safe.

Kate blinked again, as if the words were just now registering. Slowly, she moved her arm and pushed off the seat, crawling over the console and onto the passenger side. As she reached her hand out the window, Grady extended his arms forward, catching her under the armpits, dragging her toward him, backing up through the snow. She pushed off with her legs, and cleared the window, Grady dropping her down outside the wreckage. He looked at her, wrapping his arm around her shoulders and under her side, half lifting her up. "Okay. That's good. Now, we need to climb up. I gotta get you to my SUV, okay? You'll be safe there."

Kate nodded, not saying anything. Grady could tell by the way she was moving she was injured, probably worse than she assumed, but after dealing with crime victims for years he knew the adrenaline flowing through her system had numbed the pain, at least for the moment. It was a basic biological response, one of the benefits of the fight or flight tendencies every human being had wired into them before birth. It was her survival mechanism.

That was exactly what they were trying to do at that moment. Survive.

62

After struggling up the slippery hillside, Grady and Kate finally made it out onto the road, Grady wrapping his arm underneath Kate again, half dragging and half carrying her to the passenger side of his vehicle. He opened the door, the headlights still blazing, the heat pouring out from inside. "Climb in," he said, helping Kate inside and shutting the door.

Grady went back around the other side of the vehicle, jumped in and slammed his door closed. He threw his vehicle into drive, spun it around on the slippery road and headed back towards town. Kate looked at him, her eyes wild. "Where are we going? My mom is the other way!" She held up her phone, a picture of a woman in a window visible.

Grady shook his head. "I can't have you out there with me, Kate. I gotta concentrate on getting your mom back. I can't do that with you. I gotta get you someplace safe. Tell me everything you saw. Everything. Don't miss a detail."

Grady focused on the road, listening as Kate recounted the details of what happened — the note she got in her mailbox the night before, how she'd snuck off campus and slept in her car, the search she made during the daylight until she realized that the sign for Thomasville Lake was more than just a general location, that it had been meant to point her directly to her mom.

Grady glanced at Kate as he drove. She was pale in the darkness, almost as white as the snow surrounding them. A sob caught in her throat. "And then I saw her, Grady. She was in the window. She put her palm up to the glass like she knew I was there. You have to get her."

"You said the man at the house came out with a shotgun?"

Kate nodded, wiping her nose with the edge of her sleeve. "Yeah. My dad took me deer hunting one time when I was a kid. It was definitely a shotgun. The man chased me right off the property. I'm not sure he saw it was me, though. It was dark and I had my hood up."

Grady's phone rang. Cassie. "Where are you?"

"Pulling into town. Did you get Kate?"

Grady glanced at the young woman, who was balled up in the front seat of his SUV. Looking at her, she looked so broken and fragile, she could have been two years old as easily as she was twenty-one. "Yeah, I've got her. She's pretty banged up. Meet us at the bed-and-breakfast on Arch Street."

"Got it. See you in a minute."

Grady was silent for the rest of the trip, carefully navigating the SUV on the slick roads, back up the hill into Thomasville. Everything was closed, the town completely dark and shut down for the night, no other cars or pedestrians out, only the glow from some of the storefronts visible in the darkness. For a moment, Grady had a flash of what Thomasville must be like in the summertime, college students walking up and down the streets, laughing and joking, young couples in love, their arms intertwined around each other, holding hands, families with youngsters running up and down the sidewalks carrying bags of taffy or billowy clouds of cotton candy.

But not tonight. On that night, everything in Thomasville was black.

A few minutes later, Grady pulled into the bed-and-breakfast. He parked alongside Cassie's SUV. She hopped out, opening the passenger side door. Kate sighed. "Thank you," she said quietly.

Grady ran around the front of the vehicle, helping Cassie get Kate out. They walked together, the snow continuing to blow around them, the three of them making their way to the back door of the bed-and-breakfast, guiding Kate inside. Grady felt the heat from inside soak into his clothes, taking the chill out of his bones. He'd been so focused on rescuing Kate, he hadn't even felt the bone-freezing cold. The two of them walked on either side of Kate, helping her to the elevator, then taking her to the second floor. "I have a room here," Kate said.

Grady cocked his head to the side, a smile tugging at his cheek. "So do I."

Cassie raised her eyebrows, her strawberry blonde hair tied low in a ponytail behind the back of her neck, her body bundled in a thick gray coat, a hat jammed down over her ears. "Well, fancy that. Kate, let's go to your room."

From out of her pocket, Kate fished a plastic keycard. As she got to the door, Cassie took the card and held it to the sensor, the light blinking green, the door unlocking for them. The two of them helped Kate get into the room, get her coat off and get her settled on the bed. Cassie returned a minute later with a glass of water, pulling the blankets up and wrapping them over Kate. Using a washcloth, Cassie dabbed at the cut on the side of Kate's head and examined her wrist. She glanced back at Grady, "She's got a pretty good lump. Looks like her wrist is sprained too. I'll get some ice for it."

Grady nodded, waving Cassie away from Kate's bedside. They stood by the door. "Concussion?"

"Probably." Cassie looked at Grady. "She said she found her mom. Did she tell you that?"

Grady nodded. "Yeah. She showed me the picture while we were driving. You think you can handle her here in case the guy chasing her shows up?"

"Yeah." Cassie walked back toward Kate, sitting on the edge of the bed.

Kate had been resting her head against the pillows, her eyes closed. They fluttered open for a moment. "You aren't leaving me, are you?" she asked, her eyes wide, the fingers of her good hand gripping Cassie's forearm. "What about my mom?"

Cassie glanced at Grady and then back at Kate. "Sweetie, I'm going to stay here with you. Detective Grady is going to go and see if he can find your mom. How does that sound?"

As Kate nodded, Grady was a little surprised that Cassie didn't insist on going with him, but he was grateful. Kate needed protection. He couldn't be two places at one time and someone had to go after Macy before it was too late.

Grady zipped up his jacket and walked toward the hotel room door, Cassie trailing him. He turned around to look at Cassie. "You'll be okay here with her? Does she need to go to the hospital?"

"Probably. But the closest hospital is a half hour from here in good weather. Longer tonight. I think she's stable enough. I can stay with her until you get this thing with the mom resolved. You gotta have some backup and I might end up being the closest. You think you can handle this by yourself?"

Grady shrugged, the knot in his gut growing, surprised he wasn't getting a lecture from Cassie about going rogue. "We'll see, won't we."

63

Detective Hunter Franco had been sound asleep in his bed, the head of his bloodhound, Romeo, draped over his feet when his phone rang. He'd finally fallen asleep after not sleeping the night before, worried about Macy Chandler. He blinked, rolling over and dislodging Romeo's head, which earned him a grunt. He wondered if he was dreaming, until his phone sounded again. Reaching in the darkness of his bedroom at his house on the edge of Thomasville, Hunter felt for his phone. "Franco," he managed to mumble.

"Detective? Sorry to wake you. This is Watkins."

Neil Watkins was the night shift desk officer for Thomasville PD. "What's going on, Neil?" Hunter rubbed his forehead and sat up. Romeo sniffed unhappily, stood up on the bed, circled twice and then flopped down, sending tremors through the mattress as his large body found a new spot to rest now that Hunter had moved his feet.

"We had a report of shots fired on the southern rim of the lake. No specific area. Some of the locals called it in. It's somewhere near 3782 Evergreen Ridge Drive. The caller was pretty freaked out. Was pretty sure there were three or four good size shotgun blasts."

"Why are you calling me? Don't you have somebody on the road?"

"I do, Detective, but the problem is Miller is at the hospital taking a report. He followed the ambo. Heart attack."

"All right. Send me the address. I'll head out and see what I can find."

Even though Hunter Franco was a detective, being one of the newer guys on the Thomasville Police Department meant that he was on call at night if the guy that was on duty was already busy. Hunter grumbled as he got out of bed. If this call had happened only a few weeks earlier, they would've still been on their summer visitors schedule, three different officers on the road at all times, especially at night, when they were needed to deal with people who'd had too much to drink, their idea of fun usually turning into some sort of a brawl at one of the local bars.

Frowning, Hunter pulled on a pair of jeans from the dirty clothes basket next to his closet and grabbed a sweatshirt from the hook near the door of his bedroom. He wandered into the adjoining bathroom, relieved himself and quickly brushed his teeth, splashing a little water on his face, trying to wake up. As he walked out to the bedroom, he grabbed his cell phone, checking the time. It was just after two o'clock in the morning. He shook his head. The shots were probably from somebody who'd spotted a bear and was trying to scare it off. Black bears were all over Pennsylvania. They sometimes even made it over the border into the eastern portions of Ohio, but for the most part, they liked the wooded hills and valleys that made up the Appalachian Mountains, which meant they were more confined to Pennsylvania and New York than anywhere else. Walking to the door, he sighed, grabbing his gun and holster and pulling on a thick coat over his sweatshirt. With any luck, he'd take a quick drive, discover there was no problem and be back to bed within the hour.

With any luck...

Walking out to the garage, Hunter got in his charcoal gray Jeep, started it up, and flipped on the headlights, pulling out of his driveway.

After winding his way through a few of the side streets, Hunter found his way onto Arch Street. Everything looked abandoned, little snow drifts formed next to some of the shop doors, ones that would require quick shoveling out in the morning. He'd checked the forecast before he went to bed. They were supposed to have a break in the snow, but not for the next twenty-four hours. After that, the temperatures were supposed to climb back up through the fifties, maybe even touch sixty, which would make all this snow quickly melt, turning everything back into mud. That was November in Pennsylvania.

Hunter shifted the Jeep into four-wheel-drive as he descended down Arch Street toward the lake and then turned right. Evergreen Ridge Drive was on the south side of Thomasville Lake and ran from just beyond where the paddleboard company was located all the way to the far east end. If he remembered correctly, it became North Evergreen Ridge Drive as the street circled the way around the lake at the far east end. Hopefully, he wouldn't have to drive that far.

His Jeep slipping and sliding its way down the road, Hunter made a mental note to reach out to the road superintendent in the morning. Sure, the early heavy snowfall was unexpected for Thomasville, but the way the roads were at that moment, Hunter wasn't sure anything without four-wheel-drive could make it through the snow, including fire trucks or ambulances. It looked like Thomasville PD wasn't the only municipal function of the township that needed to up their game. The road department did too.

It took Hunter another half hour of driving ploddingly slow on Evergreen Ridge Drive before he spotted the address that had reported the shotgun blast. The cabin was dark, likely the people that reported the issue already warm and fast asleep in their beds again, the threat, in their minds, passed. Hunter stopped the Jeep and glanced left and right. He didn't see anything, at least nothing worth reporting.

Now at the far end of the lake, Hunter turned his vehicle around, heading back toward town. After driving for about ten minutes, he saw the reflection of what looked like the rear lights and bumper of a car off the side of the road. Frowning, he slowed, pulling up next to it. From the glove compartment of the Jeep, he pulled out a flashlight, rolled down the window and shone it down the hillside. It was a car, a small sedan. From where he was sitting, he couldn't see the license plate.

Shaking his head, Hunter got out of the Jeep, zipping up his coat and trudging down the steep embankment. He tapped on the driver's side window, brushing off the snow that had accumulated on it, wondering if someone was huddled inside. He looked and didn't see anyone, though he saw what looked to be a drip of blood on the dashboard. Confused, he searched the rest of the car using the flashlight and saw the passenger side window was busted out. Hunter climbed around the back of the vehicle, going behind the tree it had smashed into, memorizing the license plate number. He walked down the hillside, shining the light in front of him.

As he got to the window, he looked for the glass to be glistening on the ground, waiting for the shards to crunch under his boots. They didn't. Cocking his head to the side, he looked in the interior of the vehicle. The broken glass from the window was inside, not outside. Clearly someone had smashed it from the other side. Shining his flashlight on the ground, Hunter stopped where he was. There looked to be two sets of footprints in the snow, one larger, probably belonging to a man wearing boots, and one smaller, probably belonging to a woman. Hunter frowned. What had happened out here? He looked up at the hillside and wondered if the car wreck had anything to do with the shotgun blasts that had been reported. Where were the people that were in the car?

Climbing back up the embankment, Hunter got back in his Jeep and dialed Wilkins back at the station. "What did you find?"

"Nothing on the shotgun blast, but I did find an abandoned vehicle skidded off the side of the road." Hunter gave him the closest address. "Can you send a tow truck out?"

"It'll have to wait until the morning. Roads are too bad. If I send it out now, you'll end up with the tow truck and the car off the side of the road."

Hunter shook his head. "Yeah, I can see that. We gotta get the road crews out here now. Unless you've got four-wheel-drive, this road is not good. It's going to be awful if we have an emergency." Hunter scanned the area in front of him, staring out the windshield of his Jeep. "Before I hang up with you, I grabbed the license plate number. Can you run it for me?"

"Sure. Give it to me."

Hunter read off the combination of letters and numbers. "It's a Pennsylvania plate. Late-model blue sedan. Four-door."

"Hold on for a sec. System is running slow."

"Sure." Hunter waited while Wilkins ran the license plate number. Something about the situation didn't seem right. Who would be driving on the road at this late of an hour in this bad of conditions? It was nearly a whiteout. And why were there two sets of footprints leaving the vehicle, the glass smashed inward? Hunter shrugged to himself as he waited for Wilkins. It could be something as simple as a good Samaritan helping the driver out of the vehicle. Maybe the blood meant the driver was injured and they were already on their way to the hospital. If that was the case, Hunter would do the report later, but something in his gut told him there was more to the story.

Wilkins cleared his throat. "The car comes back to a Kate Chandler out of Pittsburgh."

A chill ran down Hunter's spine. "Kate Chandler? Did I hear you right?"

"Yep. That's what it says."

"You've got to be kidding me."

64

Once Grady was satisfied that Cassie and Kate were safely locked away in the bed-and-breakfast on Arch Street, he stepped out into the hallway of the B&B. Cassie would tend to Kate's injuries, the two of them holed up safe and warm. Grady closed the door firmly behind him with the promise that he would get them information as soon as he had it. "Be careful," Cassie whispered before he left.

"I will."

As much as it would have made sense for him to call Detective Andy Bennett to let him know he was in the area, technically, Grady had quit his job. If he needed backup, it would have to be Cassie, but for all intents and purposes he was on his own. Alone.

Out in the parking lot, the weather had let up a little bit, the long bands of precipitation giving way to a light dusting of snow coming out of the air, the snowflakes making their way in lazy zigzag patterns from the sky to the ground, seemingly having all the time in the world to make their journey.

But unlike the snow that could come and go as it pleased, Grady knew Macy didn't have that same luxury. Based on what the kidnapper had told him, in just a few hours, the deadline would approach. His shoulders tightened. What would happen to Macy after that, he had no idea.

The good news was, if Kate Chandler had been correct, they now knew where Macy was being held. Although Grady could've waited until the morning, he knew time was ticking. Kidnappers were known to make rash last-second decisions, moving their victims from place to place in the last few hours before a meet, paranoid their demands wouldn't get met, often killing the person they'd been holding at the same time the exchange was supposed to take place. Grady couldn't live with that. He couldn't take that risk with Macy's life and live with himself.

Out on the road, Grady shifted his SUV into four-wheel-drive and carefully maneuvered down the hill on Arch Street back towards the lake. He turned onto Evergreen Ridge Drive and headed toward the same spot where he'd found Kate's vehicle. According to Kate, the cabin where Macy was being held was maybe another mile up the road. She'd been so freaked out at the time, she had a hard time remembering exactly how far it was. But, despite the fact that she'd been shot at and injured, Kate gave him a pretty good description of what the cabin looked like. He knew it was on the right side of the road, built snug up against the hillside, a light on in the upstairs and the downstairs, at least at the moment she spotted her mother.

Now the question was, could he find it and get to Macy in time to save her?

Anxiety nipped at Grady's gut as he drove. It felt like a flock of stampeding elephants had taken up residence in his gut. He was well and truly alone, about as far off the reservation as he'd been since the day he'd shot his dad. Ever since then, he'd grudgingly taken orders from people like Williams, who only wanted to play the game. Sure, there were times Grady had done his own thing, but he'd never gone too far out in left field.

Until now.

As he drove, the darkness hovering over Thomasville Lake seemed to only get darker. The wind, which had been nearly still when he'd left Cassie and Kate at the bed-and-breakfast a few minutes before, had strengthened, the weaving and bobbing of the trees picking up in cadence as he drove. Tornadoes of snow crossed in front of the beams of his headlights, the wind pushing the snow around into little dunes on the side of the road. Any sane person would be holed up until at least morning, waiting until the plow trucks could clear the dangerous hilly roads around the lake, but he didn't have that kind of time.

Neither did Macy.

Twenty excruciating minutes later, Grady found himself back at the site where he'd rescued Kate Chandler from her car. He glanced at it briefly as he drove by, continuing to head down the road. There was another fresh set of tire tracks, but no other vehicle in sight. From what he could tell, they looked to be outbound tracks on the right side of the road, not tracks as if the car was headed back in toward Thomasville, which would've been on the opposite side. Probably just a homeowner trying to get back to their cabin in the bad weather, Grady figured.

Anticipation prickled at the back of his neck as soon as he passed Kate's car. He was close. He could feel it in his gut.

Up ahead, he saw the first glint of light from the cabin. He narrowed his eyes, leaning forward in the SUV, trying to make out what was in front of him. With less snow coming out of the sky, it was making visibility a smidge better. But the darkness hovering over Thomasville was significant, a thick black blanket, the night almost completely devoid of any light at all.

Grady slowed his vehicle, dousing the headlights and stopping in the middle of the road. He stared toward the cabin. It was exactly as Kate had described it — two levels, built into the hillside, each floor with a separate exterior entrance. There was a truck parked out front, a light on upstairs as well as downstairs. Grady couldn't see any figures or shadows moving inside, but someone was responsible for the lights being on. His stomach did a flip-flop. He was likely staring at the location where Macy Chandler had been held lately for the last two months. What condition would he find her in? Would she be weak? Unable to walk or run? Would they have to bring an ambulance down the treacherous snow-filled roads to get her the help she needed? Grady's mind raced like a herd of wild horses.

The snow had picked up again, sheets of white flakes covering his vehicle. He stared out the windshield. "The only way around is through," he muttered under his breath while unclipping his seatbelt. It was time to bring Macy home... if he wasn't too late.

65

Hunter's heart skipped a beat as he drove down Evergreen Ridge Drive. He couldn't go much faster than about fifteen miles an hour, the snow blowing and whipping around his vehicle. The visibility had decreased again, after a brief respite, the headlights from his Jeep cutting through the darkness, snow suddenly pummeling the southern edge of the lake.

Hunter grabbed the wheel a little tighter, realizing he wasn't breathing very deeply. His chest hurt from the tension flooding him. If Kate Chandler's car had been found off the side of the road in Thomasville, that could mean only one thing — that she believed her mom was nearby. There was no other explanation as to why Kate Chandler's car would be off the side of the road in his jurisdiction. The weather certainly wasn't good enough for any type of house party and the roads were nearly impassable. No, there'd have to be something of value for her to look for.

And for Kate, he'd imagine it would be her mother.

The questions loomed large in Hunter's mind. He swallowed a lump in his throat. He was a detective, but barely. And he'd only been a cop for the last three years. He felt a tightness mount the back of his neck and shoulders. Was he really prepared to try to take action? Where would he even start? There were dozens, if not hundreds of cabins along the shores of Thomasville Lake. If Kate Chandler had found her mother, she was certainly nowhere to be seen.

Hunter replayed the scene from Kate's abandoned car in his mind. His memory kept sticking on the fact that the shattered glass window on the passenger side had glass on the inside of the car, not the outside. It wasn't physically possible for the passenger to break the glass and make it go in that direction. It had to have been someone on the outside. From the footsteps he'd found in the snow near the abandoned car, it was clear it was a male. As best he could tell, Hunter pieced together in his mind that Kate had been driving along the road, likely looking for her mom when her car slid off the embankment. Someone, a male, must have come along to rescue her.

Hunter shuddered. Rescue wasn't the only option. It was possible Kate had been kidnapped too.

Hunter scanned the road on either side, considering his options. For the most part the cabins on the southern edge of Thomasville Lake were all on the opposite side of the road from the lake itself, the terrain steep between the narrow roadway and the edge of the water. Some of the cabins at the far end of the lake were on the lake side of the road, but as for the others, the homeowners usually built trails they could use to either walk or drive an ATV down to their docks, sparing their legs the steep hike back uphill after a long day spent in the sun, floating on rubber tires or hanging out at their docks drinking with friends and family, recounting old times.

At least for the section of road Hunter was on, that limited the cabins to the right-hand side of the road. He peered off in the darkness, trying to see any sign of life, anything that would indicate it was a cabin he should stop at to try to find Kate. It was completely unreasonable to think that he could stop at every cabin in the middle of the night, pound on the door and do a manual search for Macy Chandler and her daughter. Based on what he'd seen at Kate's car, there was no indication where she'd been, only that she was driving back towards town.

Frustration gripped Hunter's chest. He should be home, curled up in bed with Romeo warming his feet, but here he was out in the middle of the snowstorm, trying to find a missing woman and her daughter with no leads and no help.

He shook his head. It would take nothing short of a miracle for him to find Macy or Kate, if there was anything left to find.

66

Macy couldn't stop shaking. She'd walked to the window at the instant the flash of a camera went off from somewhere outside. It was definitely aimed in her direction. Even though she was curled up on the bed, thinking about Dario's increasing rage as she refused to give him the key, she could still feel the cool of the pane of glass as she put her hand up, reaching out for help.

Someone had found her.

Or had they?

The four shotgun blasts that Dario had chased the person with camera off with had left a pit in Macy's stomach. She'd seen the silhouette of a person running away, but had no idea where Dario was. Had he killed them, chased them down and finished them, paranoid that his plan wouldn't work? Were they injured, bleeding somewhere in the snow?

Macy shivered. There were many good things about being a professor of literature, but one of the bad things was that she knew her imagination could run wild after living in the world of fiction for so long. She gripped her hands into little balls, trying to control her emotions, feeling the hot sting of tears form. She wiped them away before they could fall.

Macy sat completely still, listening. She'd heard the door to the downstairs level open and close and the shotgun blasts, but hadn't heard anything more, not in the last twenty minutes or so. Racking her brain, she tried to figure out how long it had been since she heard any movement down below. Panic filled her chest. What if Dario had left? She was still locked in the room with no way to get out. No one knew she was there, except for the person that had taken the picture. And if that person was dead...

Macy squeezed her eyes together, holding her breath. She couldn't lose hope.

Not yet.

Reaching out, Macy wrapped her fingers around the pendant that was under the thin sweatshirt Lola had given her. Dario was desperate for the key, but after everything he had put her through, there was no way Macy was going to give it up. She wanted to see what was at the end of the story, what was at the end of the address engraved on the back of it. It had to be something valuable, otherwise Dario wouldn't have been willing to give up his whole life to hold her hostage. Macy listened again, hoping that maybe Lola would show up. She'd seemed to be the voice of reason over the last few months, the one who'd managed to keep Dario from careening off the rails. But something inside of Macy knew that the shotgun blasts were evidence of his mental state. He was coming unglued and Lola was nowhere to be found to help.

In her mind, Macy wondered if Dario's story was that unlike many of the characters that she taught on through the years. Circumstances could throw a curveball at someone. How they responded was the real story. Some life circumstance or another had flicked a switch inside of Dario, causing him to take extreme action. Macy shook her head. In a way, part of her felt sorry for him. If he got caught, he would be the one who would become the captive. He'd spend years in jail paying for what he'd done to Macy.

And if she had the courage, she'd still have the key, her freedom, and the opportunity to see what the key unlocked if she was brave enough.

Macy got up, starting to pace, watching the window as she walked by. Where had the person who'd taken the picture gone? Were they coming to look for her, or for some other reason?

A shudder ran through her body. If they weren't coming to look for her, then they might assume she was a woman upstairs in the house, never knowing about the locked door that was keeping her captive. She felt her courage wane, her heart sinking, like the last glimpse of sunlight at the end of the day.

Macy spent the next few minutes pacing, trying to keep warm, trying to keep her thoughts under control, the patience she'd had with her situation over the last few months evaporating in front of her eyes. She was losing her grip. She could feel the fear surrounding her like a pack of hungry wolves. She'd been able to stave them off until that moment, but she didn't know how much strength she had left.

It was hard to tell how much time had gone by with no clock in the room. It could have been a few minutes or an hour, but eventually, Macy heard the door downstairs slam. She could tell by the heavy footfalls below her it was Dario. He'd returned. And there was no telling what kind of mood he was in.

She heard him coming up the steps, the stomping of his boots on the stairs sending waves of fear into her. Sitting on the edge of the bed, she wrapped the blanket tight around her shoulders, trying to hide the way her body was shaking. She couldn't let him see her break. She'd been strong for so long. She wasn't going to give up now.

Dario walked in the room, carrying a black shotgun with him. He glared at her, narrowing his eyes. "You heard the gun go off, didn't you?" he asked, the edge in his voice almost sounding like he was trying to bait her.

Macy sucked in a sharp breath, raising her eyes from where she sat to meet his gaze. She was terrified, but she couldn't let him see that. "I did."

"Someone was poking around the property."

"So?" A wave of nausea crashed over Macy, but she fought to keep her face calm and still. She wouldn't give Dario the satisfaction of knowing that he was getting to her, not now.

Macy watched as Dario set his jaw, the flicker of muscles running across the side of his face. "I think our time together is running out."

Macy pressed her lips together. "Well, that's a relief. I was about to run out of paper in my journal." She let the words roll off her tongue with a cutting level of sarcasm.

Dario's cheeks flushed. "I'm going to ask you this one more time. If you give me the answer I want, I'll put you in the truck right now, drive you to the center of town and drop you off. If you don't, then there are going to be consequences, consequences you may not like."

Macy swallowed. She knew what was coming. He'd kept his hands off her up to that point, but the look on his face said that time had passed. Did she have the courage to stand her ground?

"Where's the key?"

Macy flung the blanket off her shoulders taking two steps towards Dario. She lifted her chin, staring at him. It was the most eye contact she'd made with him since he'd taken her hostage. "I don't know what you're talking about. And even if I did, even if I had this mysterious key that you keep asking me about, I wouldn't give it to you, not after what you have put me and my family through."

Dario took a step closer to her, but didn't touch her. He was close enough that she could feel the heat of his body. "What I have put you through? What about what you've put my family through? All of you Dixons are the same. You steal and you don't care."

Macy cocked her head to the side, feeling stronger than she had in a long time. "That was generations ago, Dario. You can keep sharpening your ax about what you think may or may not have happened, but the reality is I am not responsible for any of it. What I have or don't have has nothing to do with me or you. It's just the breaks."

Dario leaned forward close enough that she could smell a sour odor coming from him. For a second, Macy thought he was going to lunge for her. She tasted bile in the back of her throat. If he did, there was nowhere to run to. She had nowhere to hide. She was with Dario and she was all alone.

Macy held her breath, waiting.

67

Grady sat in his SUV at the bottom of the road, staring up the driveway at the ramshackle cabin with the lights on, exactly as the picture Kate had showed him. He'd seen the figure of a man appear in the window upstairs, a small blonde woman standing in front of him. They looked like they were arguing. Grady narrowed his eyes. By their body language, it seemed that the woman knew her kidnapper, which didn't make sense.

But then again, it'd been more than four months.

Grady's mind began to race. There were more cases of friendly abductions than anyone ever wanted to talk about. Did Macy know the person who had held her? Had she gone willingly? Was it an affair that had gone wrong, or maybe she was tired of being a mom and a wife and wanted to walk away from her life?

Grady shook his head, cocking it to the side. That didn't make sense. If that was the case, why was there a ransom demand? Why had someone forged Macy's medical leave papers at the college?

Grady sucked in a deep breath. There would be time to ask

questions later. For now, he needed to follow the only lead he had, that Kate Chandler had seen her mother in the window of that house. Whether she was there willingly or unwillingly was another issue.

Sitting in the car, Grady zipped up his jacket. It was time to think tactically. As far as he could tell, the house had two entrances — one on the upper level and one on the lower level. From where he was sitting, he could see a truck parked in the driveway. That was likely the kidnapper's vehicle. Where Macy's car was, Grady had no idea. Grady glanced down at his cell phone, a fleeting thought about calling Thomasville PD passing through his mind. Based on the way they'd behaved, he decided to let it go. He'd be better off on his own, as he usually was. There was no one to question him. No one to slow him down.

Grady lifted up the hem of his coat and pulled his gun out of his holster, checking to make sure it was fully loaded. He tugged at the barrel and saw the glimmer of a brass round already in the chamber. Opening the glove compartment, he pulled out two more magazines that were filled and ready to go, shoving them in his pocket. He had no idea what he would find, except for the fact that whoever was in that house was armed. The shotgun blasts Kate told him about proved that.

Narrowing his eyes, Grady chewed his lip for a second. "There's no time like the present," he muttered to himself, sliding out of the SUV.

The first thing he noticed was the cold wind cutting through his clothing. It had picked up, the snow coming down steadily from above him, drifting down from the heavy clouds. He took a few steps in the snow, staying low. In that respect, he reasoned, the weather was doing him a favor, obscuring his movement. He'd have to move quickly and carefully in order to avoid a deadly confrontation with the kidnapper. Macy's life was on the line.

Grady kept his gun holstered as he hiked his way up the driveway, sticking to the side away from the house. His legs burned as he climbed the incline. He checked in front of him as carefully as he could. The man inside had a shotgun. What else did he have planned for trespassers? The only good news was Grady knew Kate had made it close to the house without bumping into any booby traps or tripwires.

But that didn't mean Grady would be that lucky.

About halfway up the driveway just before it turned toward the house, Grady stopped, ducking behind a tree, pulling his gun from the holster, the grip momentarily warm against his frozen fingers. The man was still upstairs in the room with the woman. He could see the silhouette of the man's back through the single window, a dim light cutting out his form. For a second, Grady thought he saw a peek of blonde hair, but then it disappeared again. Grady watched for a minute, the man looking more and more agitated by the way his hand was moving. But it was only one. Why wasn't his other hand moving? Was he holding Macy at gunpoint? Was he choking her, like his father had done to his mother?

Grady set his jaw. The man had to be stopped. He waited for a moment and then decided to angle for the lower door. His heart was beating fast, but steadily. He kept his eyes trained on the door, now and again glancing upward to see if the man was still upstairs. His best bet was to make entry through the lower door and then make his way up the steps, if he could find them. The cabin didn't look to be that big. They shouldn't be that hard to find. There weren't that many places to hide, or at least Grady hoped that was the case. As Grady got closer to the cabin, he could smell wood smoke, as if there was a fire burning somewhere inside.

Gritting his teeth and keeping his head down, Grady hunched over, running toward the back bumper of the man's truck and ducking down behind it, just as Grady saw the man inside turn toward the window, as if he'd heard something. There was no way he had. Grady had been completely silent, the thick snow muffling his footsteps. Grady could feel the cold and the damp soaking in through his pant legs, his hands already cold and frozen, still wrapped around the grip of his gun. He held it low in front of him. The guy had been reported to have a shotgun. Grady needed to be prepared.

Grady waited for a second, holding his breath. When he did let it out, he could see a puff of condensation coming out of his mouth against the glowing light that came from the inside of the cabin. It was dead cold. He ducked around the bumper of the truck and made his way toward the front of it, still staying low, using the truck as cover. Since he was alone, his best defense was to surprise the kidnapper.

Stopping at the front tire of the truck, Grady knelt down again, taking a couple deep breaths and staring at the door. The cabin itself was probably not more than about fifteen feet from where he knelt. There was a white screen door with peeling paint on it that shrouded an interior door, wood with a single glass window. The landing in front of the door looked like it had been swept off, the planks of wood visible against the snow.

Grady glanced upstairs and didn't see movement. He was at a bad angle, unable to see what was going on upstairs. He shook his head, pressing his lips together and then stood up just enough so he could move. Staying low, he jogged towards the side door, keeping his gun in front of him, pointing at the ground. He stood up as he got close to the door, stepping on the wood. As he did, he heard the wood give a loud creak.

If no one knew he was there before, they knew now.

"Here goes nothing," he whispered in the darkness.

68

Macy flinched. Dario looked like he was about to lunge for her when he suddenly stopped, looking toward the open door of the room. He glanced at her, the muscles of his face twisted and angry, his eyes wild. At that moment, Macy was afraid of what Dario could do to her. "Stay here," he growled. "We are not done."

Macy watched as he strode out of the room. Following, she made her way to the door, peering out. It was the first time she'd been unattended in months, even her bathroom trips supervised, either Dario or Lola lurking outside the bathroom door. Dario had disappeared. Macy made her way out into the sitting room outside the bedroom door, glancing down the stairwell. Dario was halfway down, looking out of a small window that wasn't any bigger than a porthole, staring into the darkness.

Macy felt the breath catch in her throat, her heart pounding in her chest. This was her chance, her opportunity. She couldn't let it pass. Turning on her heel, she raced for the opposite side of the house, toward a back door that led away from the cabin, dropping the blanket she was using to keep warm as she ran.

She only had seconds to get away. She knew Dario would be faster than her. Angling for the door on the opposite side of the house from where he was, she ran to it, quickly fumbling with the lock, her hands shaking. After what felt like a full minute, she got the door open running outside with only her thin sweatshirt protecting her from the cold.

The fresh air hit her like a ton of bricks, the cold making her lungs burn. She had no idea where she was. She stopped for a second, hearing the door slam behind her, her eyes wide. Fear prickled at her skin. Certainly Dario had heard the door slam. He would know she was on the move.

The breath catching in her throat, Macy started running down the hillside, slipping on the snow. As she made it to the first floor, she heard the door upstairs slam. "Get back here!" Dario bellowed. Terror raced through Macy's body. Whether he had the shotgun with him or not, she didn't know. If he did, she was a sitting duck. The only hope she had was the fact that she still hadn't answered his question about where the key was.

Macy screamed and ran down the hillside as quickly as she could, but she was no match for Dario's size and speed. As she rounded the front of the house, trying to get to the driveway, she heard his heavy breathing behind her. She felt the back of her shirt gather, choking her as he yanked her backward. One of his meaty hands clawed at her shirt and got a grip of it, stopping her in her tracks. She fell to her knees, screaming.

From out of nowhere, she heard another male voice. "Stop! Police! Let her go!"

Terrified, Macy held her hands up above her head. "Help!" she screamed.

A second later, she glanced up, seeing another man coming toward them, but Dario didn't give her a chance to escape. He pulled on her shirt and dragged her down the hillside yelling behind him. "Stay away or I'll kill her! I swear I'll do it!"

Fear grabbed Macy. She couldn't breathe. Dario still had a

hold of her shirt and a fat clump of her hair with it. She could only feel the pain of her hair ripping out of her scalp with every step. "Dario, please," she whimpered.

"I told you there'd be consequences if you didn't give me what I wanted. Now you'll see."

69

The whole scene played out faster than Grady could have ever anticipated. As soon as the wood threshold creaked, he heard silence from the inside of the house, then the thudding of heavy boots on the steps. "Are you kidding me?" he whispered under his breath, staying near the door. He thought he saw the shadow of someone approaching when all of a sudden he heard another door bang open and close above him on the other side of the house, the heavy boots going the opposite direction.

Narrowing his eyes, Grady made his way to the front of the house, and turned the corner, crossing the distance of the small cabin as he saw Macy Chandler being held by her hair. She was whimpering and crying. He could see the twisted expression on her face. It wasn't any different than his mother's had been all those years before. Rage flooded his system. "Stop! Police! Let her go!" Grady wasn't with the police anymore, but the kidnapper didn't know that.

The black-haired man holding Macy Chandler glared at him, said something to her Grady couldn't understand and then started dragging her down the rough, snowy hillside by the back of her shirt and her hair, using her as a human shield. Grady raised his gun, trying to get a shot off on the man, but it was impossible in the darkness and snow.

Grady ran after them, slipping and sliding down the hillside, but the few seconds the man had gotten on Grady and his apparent familiarity with the terrain put Grady at a distinct disadvantage. Where the man was dragging Macy Chandler as fast as he could move, Grady had to check and stop to see where he was to avoid tripping in the snow.

In the darkness, everything was black-and-white, the black, inky waters of the lake, the black trunks of the trees on the sides where they weren't covered in bright white snow and the heavy black clouds overhead. Everything else was white, the snow making a blanket over everything that Grady ran past.

Grady trailed the kidnapper and Macy, barely gaining on them. He yelled out, "Let her go! This isn't going any further!"

The man dragging Macy Chandler was about twenty-five feet ahead of him. Grady could hear her whimpering and crying from where he was, but it wasn't slowing the man down. She'd pretty much given up fighting. Her body was limp, her feet stumbling along as best she could in the snow over the rough ground. Grady tracked them, keeping his gun raised, running as fast as he could to keep up with them in the heavy snow.

Before Grady knew it, they'd made it the entire way down the hillside, the man dragging Macy toward him out onto the dock. Macy fell, her body limp, like a sack of potatoes onto the ground. The man dragged her to standing again, using her body to cover his own. "You're going to let me get outta here with her, or I'll kill her right now," he yelled to Grady, pointing the shotgun at Grady.

Grady raised his gun up, his heart pounding in his chest. He dove behind a tree trunk. Glancing toward the man, Grady realized he didn't have a clear shot. The way the man was holding Macy, her body would've taken the blow, not her kidnapper's. He couldn't risk it.

Seeing Grady was stopped, the kidnapper smiled, a small, thin grin pulling at the corners of his lips as he realized Grady didn't have a shot. His smile turned into a sneer as he dragged Macy backward on the dock, angling for a boat that was bobbing up and down next to it, dumping her thin body inside, her form disappearing. In the background, Grady could hear the lapping of the water on the shore. The storm had dumped a ton of snow, but not enough to freeze the lake, at least not yet.

Grady heard a thump and another cry as the man dragged Macy on board the boat and started it up, holding the shotgun up with one hand trained on Macy as he unfurled the lines.

Grady's heart thudded in his chest. He was going to lose them if he didn't do something fast. He ran up on the dock, slipping on the icy surface, dropping to a single knee. He stood up as the boat started to pull away from the dock. Grady charged, trying to grab the edge of it, thinking he could jump on while the kidnapper was turned away, steering into the wind. Grady's fingers had a grip on the side of the boat, but with ice and snow coating it, they slipped. As the man pulled away, he looked at Macy, grabbed her and did the unthinkable.

He threw her in the water.

Grady's heart sank. He ran to the edge of the dock looking out into the darkness. He couldn't see where she was. Did Macy even know how to swim? He ran back down to the shoreline yelling, "Macy! Macy! Over here!"

Just then, Grady heard another voice call out behind him, the shadow of a man passing him, racing for the edge of the water. "Grady! Go get him. I've got her!"

Grady stood stunned as he saw Detective Hunter Franco rip off his coat and dive into the cold black water.

Grunting, Grady started running up the hill, hoping that

wasn't the last time he saw both Detective Hunter Franco and Macy Chandler alive.

70

Grady's lungs were burning by the time he ran up the hill and got into his SUV, but he didn't have any time to wait. He jumped in, revved the engine and threw it into gear. Tromping on the accelerator, he drove as fast as he could down the trail, watching the small boat the kidnapper was on disappear across the black waters. Grady leaned forward, staring into the darkness, snow flying out behind his SUV like he was racing a dune buggy on sand. There were only so many places the kidnapper could go. The lake was land-locked. The kidnapper would have to get off the boat eventually. When he did, Grady would be waiting.

As Grady stepped on the accelerator, the snow flew up in front of him, blinding him. He pressed on, going faster and faster, not caring if he ended up on the side of the road. He had to stop the kidnapper.

As Grady rounded the corner, he saw the boat out in the center of the lake. It was angling for a dock on the far side. Questions pummeled through Grady's head. Did the kidnapper have another vehicle there? How was he planning on getting away? Grady reached for the gun on his side. It was still there.

He returned his hand to the steering wheel, gripping it harder, feeling his ragged breath in his chest, the tension surging through his back. He'd only have one chance to catch the man. If the kidnapper got into the woods, he'd be as good as gone.

As Grady rounded the far end of the lake, luckily the road conditions were better than they were on the south side, heavy stands of pine trees protecting the roadway from the bulk of the winter storm that was raging overhead. Grady kept one eye on the road and one eye on the lake as he saw the kidnapper angle the boat for the dock. He didn't have much time to catch up to him. If Grady didn't get to the man at the dock, the odds of him being able to chase the man down once he was off the boat were small. He'd likely lose him in the darkness, the man having the advantage of knowing the geography, where Grady didn't.

Fury grabbed the inside of Grady as he drove. He gripped the steering wheel tighter. Each moment he felt more and more angry seeing the way that the man had treated Macy Chandler. He could hear the yells of his father in his memory, the guttural moans of his brother Ben, the high, whimpering thin cries from his mother night after night.

From what he could see, Macy Chandler's kidnapper was no different. People like that man needed to be stopped. Permanently.

Grady made it around the far end of the lake and turned the corner toward the dock where the kidnapper was angling as he saw the boat slow. He pushed the SUV a little harder, feeling the tires slip and skid and then get traction. Slamming on the brakes on the hillside above the dock, the SUV skidding to a stop, he felt the brakes lock at the last second. Grady threw the SUV into park and ran down the hill, pulling his gun as he went. He could see the man at the dock, bending over, tying up the boat. Grady slipped and slid down the hill, losing his balance, a sharp pain running through his left ankle. Ignoring it, Grady got up, the breath heavy in his chest, running for the dock. He got there as the man stepped off the boat, his arms poised at right angles, ready to run, the shotgun still in the man's right hand. Grady shouted at the top of his lungs, his voice raspy. "Police! Don't move!"

Grady saw the man flinch, the shotgun rising up.

Grady didn't give the man an opportunity to take a shot. He lifted the pistol up to his face, lined up the sights, and let off two shots, bam bam, in quick succession, the explosion of the rounds leaving the chamber echoing across the lake.

Grady kept moving forward, keeping his gun up in front of his face and trained on the man as he watched the man drop to his knees, the shotgun clattering to his side in the snow. As the man fell, his body tipped over the edge of the dock into the water with a splash. Grady jumped up onto the dock, holding the gun in front of him looking for the man, but the body was gone.

It was over.

71

Two hours later, Grady, Cassie, Kate, Hunter, and Macy were huddled together at a small table in the warm breakfast room of the B&B. Grady had called Cassie on his way back from the lake, and found out that Hunter managed to get Macy out of the water before she got hypothermia. Hunter had called his desk sergeant, Neil Wilkins, when he retrieved Macy. Wilkins, stunned by the turn of events, gladly obliged by making a few phone calls to figure out where Kate Chandler and Grady had been staying, although in Thomasville, there weren't that many options.

Although Grady hadn't gotten the opportunity to see the initial moments of the mother-daughter reunion, from what Cassie told him, it had been emotional. Macy, soaked to the bone, thin and worn out from over two months as a hostage, grabbed ahold of her injured daughter, the two of them wrapping their arms around each other as though nothing would ever be able to pry them apart. The bed-and-breakfast owner, hearing the commotion downstairs, had quickly risen to the occasion, perked several pots of coffee, brought a carafe of hot chamomile tea to calm everyone's nerves, along with a selection of pastries and sandwiches that had been designated for the next day.

By the time Grady walked in, the majority of the crying had ceased, Macy and Kate sitting next to each other holding hands, the bed-and-breakfast owner bringing blankets and clean clothes from their lost and found for Macy and Hunter, to replace their wet ones.

Cassie intercepted Grady as he limped through the door. "Are you okay?" she asked, resting her hand on his arm. He glanced at her. He could see the worry and concern tugging at the edges of her face.

"I'm okay. Slipped and fell. I think it's sprained."

Cassie tugged on his arm and pulled him away from the table where Kate and Macy were nursing their mugs of hot drinks. She waved Hunter Franco over to them. "Hunter filled us in a little. What happened to the kidnapper?"

"You'll find him somewhere at the bottom of the lake on the far side with two slugs in his chest. Not sure he got the boat tied up. Last I saw it was floating off somewhere."

Grady watched as Hunter's face paled even more. "I'll call it in. They probably won't send a dive team out until the morning. They'll have to get one from the county that has dry suits so the guys don't freeze to death."

Grady nodded. "It doesn't matter. He's not going anywhere."

As Hunter walked away, holding the cell phone up to his ear, Cassie looked back at Grady. "Listen, Macy filled in some of the details for us while we were waiting for you. Turns out she knew the guy who was holding her. His name was Dario Gilbert. They grew up in the same area together. He had an accomplice, his cousin. Her name was Lola. You remember the name? She was the secretary from the college."

Grady turned and stared at Cassie. "You are kidding me. This was a set up the whole time?"

Cassie nodded. "Seems that way. I already called Williams.

He's already sent a team to arrest her. Based on what Macy said, it seems that the Dixon and Gilbert families have a long running feud. Dixon is her maiden name. I guess Macy's worth about a hundred million, heir to the Dixon Oil fortune." Cassie glanced over at the table where Macy and Kate were holding hands. A smirk formed on Cassie's face. "You want to know the craziest part of the whole thing?"

Grady furrowed his eyebrows together, looking at Kate and Macy. "What's that?"

"Her family had no idea."

Grady whipped his head around, staring at Cassie. "No idea? How does somebody go around worth a hundred million and no one knows?"

Cassie shrugged. "I guess Macy saw her grandfather kill two people when she was little. Somebody was trespassing on their oilfields in Texas. She never forgot it. Kind of turned her back on the whole family. And that's not the end of it."

Grady raised his eyebrows. "There's more?"

"You could say that. You know how Kate looks very different from the rest of her family?"

Grady nodded.

"Well, the kidnapper, Dario Gilbert, was actually Kate's father. I guess she and Noah were going through a rough patch. Had a fight or something. She bumped into Dario, had a quick hook up and never saw him again."

"You're kidding me?"

"I wish I was."

Grady shook his head. "That explains why they seemed like they knew each other. She say anything about the key?"

Cassie shook her head. "Nope. Said she doesn't know anything about it."

Grady narrowed his eyes. "You believe her?"

"I have no idea."

EPILOGUE

A week later, as Detective Max Grady was sitting at the Oakview Center working on a new puzzle with his older brother Ben, his phone chirped. It was Cassie. "Saw these two pieces of news. Thought you might want to know. Let me know when you're ready to come back."

Grady leaned back in his chair, looking at his brother, whose tongue was half sticking out of his mouth. He was concentrating on fitting two puzzle pieces together, ones that had no business being joined. Maybe that was the situation with Grady and police work. He'd have to see. Williams had already left him two phone messages to give him a call, but Grady hadn't bothered.

At least not yet.

Scrolling through his phone, he saw the links that Cassie had sent. The first one read, "Long Time Thomasville Police Detective Andy Bennett Retires." Grady clicked on the link, seeing the picture of Detective Andy Bennett standing in front of a cake at the Thomasville Police Department. The caption read, "Long time police detective Andy Bennett retires after 35 years of service. He's seen here shaking hands with Chief of Police Martin Savage." Grady squinted at the picture. In the background, he saw Hunter Franco smiling, a knowing look in his eye. The kid had grown up quick. In one evening, he'd gone from being a rookie detective to a veteran. He'd managed to save Macy's life and get her back to safety. That was probably more than Andy Bennett could say about his whole career. A warm glow of satisfaction floated in Grady's chest.

Grady went back to the text, clicking on the next link, shifting in his chair. His ankle ached. It was a news article from two days before, with a byline out of Fort Worth, Texas. "Long Time Missing Diamond Recovered. Valued at Over $50 Million." The subtitle read, "Anonymous donation made to Pittsburgh college." As Grady scanned the article, he saw that a Fort Worth jeweler had been asked to value a large, nineteen-carat rare pink diamond, the likes he'd never seen before. He was quoted in the article, "I feel privileged to have gotten to hold it in my hands. I've never seen anything like it. I don't expect I ever will again." The article went on to say that the diamond had been lost generations before, placed in a safety deposit box and forgotten about by the owners. The owner, an unnamed woman, had finally claimed it, quickly selling it to a Saudi Arabian Prince for the price of fifty million. That same anonymous woman had made a twenty-five-million-dollar donation to the scholarship fund at Bedford College.

Grady smiled. Despite everything she'd been through, Macy Dixon-Chandler had the last laugh.

The cold betrayal had turned into cold, hard cash.

A bitter, cold killer exacts his revenge in book two of the Detective Max Grady series, One Cold Heart.
Click here to check it out now!

If you'd like to join my mailing list and be the first to get updates on new books and exclusive sales, giveaways and releases, click here!

I'll send you a prequel to the next series FREE!

A NOTE FROM THE AUTHOR...

Thanks so much for taking the time to read *Four Cold Months*. I hope you've been able to enjoy a little escape from your everyday life while joining Grady on his newest adventure.

If you have a moment, would you leave a review? They mean the world to authors like me!

If you'd like to join my mailing list and be the first to get updates on new books and exclusive sales, giveaways and releases, click here! I'll send you a prequel to the next series FREE!

Enjoy, and thanks for reading,
KJ

A NOTE FROM THE AUTHOR

Thanks so much for taking the time to read [illegible]. I hope [illegible] a little escape from your everyday life while [illegible].

If you have a moment, would you leave a review? They mean the world to authors like me.

If you'd like to join my mailing list and be the first to get updates on new books and exclusive sales, giveaways, and releases, click here [illegible] a special [illegible] the [illegible] series [illegible]

Enjoy, and thanks for reading,

[illegible]

MORE FROM KJ KALIS

Ready for another adventure? Check out these series!

Investigative journalist, Kat Beckman, faces the secrets of her past and tries to protect her family despite debilitating PTSD.
Visit the series page here!

Disgraced Chicago PD Detective, Emily Tizzano, searches for a new life by solving cold cases no one in law enforcement will touch.
Visit the series page here!

Intelligence analyst, Jess Montgomery, risks everything she has — including her own life — to save her family.
Visit the series page here!

Made in United States
North Haven, CT
04 July 2024

54394024R00196